Orb

Istobarra

First edition

Copyright © 2014 Stephen Christiansen

Cover design by Randy Smith of The Cryptic Attic

www.thecrypticattic.com

Orbbelgguren Series

Book 1: Istobarra Commencement
Book 2: Istobarra Rising
Book 3: Maldev
Book 4: Transitions
Book 5: Qu'ellar Kre'jilen
Book 6: Qu'ellar Elggat
Book 7: Qu'ellar B'nossta
Book 8: Eclavarda
Book 9: Child of the Shard
Book 10: The Troll Wars
Book 11: The Rising Dead
Book 12: Temple of Tears
Book 13: The God Wars
Book 14: Senet
Book 15: Children of the Spider
Book 16: The Forbidden City
Book 17: Resolution

This book is dedicated to my daughter, Ruth Christiansen.

Ruth's imagination continues to surprise me and to inspire me to push the boundaries of fantasy. Her laughter and encouragements give the strength that is needed to carry on through the rough spots in writing and in life. She has often helped me with names, creatures, and characters. Ruth is truly a blessing and a joy in my life.

Characters:

G'eldlara Torrret – Matron Mother of house Torrret, first house of the city of Anarchia.
Xesst Torrret – Third daughter of house Torrret

Orbb'Rah Torvirr – Matron Mother of house Torvirr, first house of the city of Malzebowan

Elg'caress Barrindar – Matron Mother of house Barrindar, second house of the city of Malzebowan

Ilharess Olis'inth – Matron Mother of house Olis'inth
Dalharil Olis'inth – Oldest daughter of house Olis'inth
Drada Olis'inth – Second daughter of house Olis'inth
Medri Jabbress Olis'inth – Third daughter of house Olis'inth
M'elzar Olis'inth – house mage of house Olis'inth
Sarol Jabbuk – Weapon's master to house Olis'inth

Baebaste Melervs – a daughter of house Melervs
Nathnilee Zaurret – a daughter of house Zaurret
Naliara D'Silva – Oldest daughter of house D'Silva
Krenala D'Silva – Youngest daughter of house D'Silva

Lael Dalninil N'shtyl – eighth daughter of house N'shtyl

Yaszyne Phorudossa – Matron Mother of house Phorudossa
Dilayne Phorudossa – a daughter of house Phorudossa
Tanth Phorudossa – House Mage of House Phorudossa
Rhylaxle – agent in House Phorudossa

Irraste Do'tlar – Matron Mother of house Do'tlar
Yasrae Do'tlar – House leader of house Do'tlar
T'rissvyr Do'tlar – Weapon master of house Do'tlar
Alton Rinna Do'tlar – House Mage of house Do'tlar
Valenci – An Id Scourger

Agrong – a Deep dwarf smith
Xindarl Beldroin – apothecary
Valas Velkyn – Leader of the House of acquisitions from the city of Malzebowan
Rrosa Veldruk – dock master
Maldev – a houseless dark elf
Gorag – an orc

Map of Malzebowan

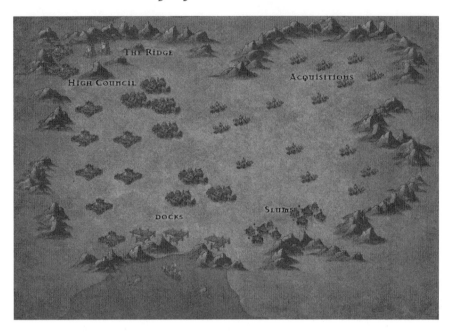

Book: House Olis'inth

Chapter: Ilharess

"*M*edri!" Matron Mother Ilharess Olis'inth shouted yet again, echoing off her throne room. "Medri Jabbress Olis'inth! If I have to repeat myself one more time I'll have your flesh flogged off your body!" Her dark elf skin turned hue with anger, her deep red eyes were wide and her whole body shook with a fury equal to that of a predator on a feeding frenzy. "I'll have you dipped in acid, boiled in oil, dismembered, ripped apart, and fed to the slaves!" Her voice echoed down the adjoining hallway and could be heard two rooms down.

Ilharess was well past her prime years in life and, not only was her body showing her age, but she had felt its onset some time ago in her joints. Her once beautiful long white hair was now almost gray, and in her frenzied stated of anger, was out of place and unkempt. Her facial wrinkles revealed the hard times of her life as Matron Mother. The silver spider silk dress she had on, although would have been revealing and flattering to others half her age, was now hanging on her like rags. At one time it would have been in fashion, but that was several years ago. Now it was a constant reminder of the status of her house, outdated, forgotten, and threadbare. She did have her snake whip on her side, a two headed snake whip. It, too, was showing its age. The snakes were slower than they ever had been and were more of a symbol of status than an effective weapon. In her mind she was still accurate and deadly with it, but there were too many times that she started to doubt this to be true, and she knew that this could prove to be her ultimate downfall, not her decline in age, but her decline in confidence.

Like most Matron Mothers, Ilharess' throne room was octagonal and was the third largest room in the whole of the fortress structure, with the chapel room being the largest and her reception room, a type of second throne room to meet for public affairs being the second largest. This was her private throne room, an inner sanctum where she only spoke to those closest to her, or at least those she wanted to think they were closest to her. To her right, the wall gave way to a stone balcony, some fifty or so feet up from the cave floor. It wasn't the highest platform in the city, nor did it have the best view, these were reserved for the ruling council houses, but it was still hers. Flanking just outside the exit to the balcony was two of her trusted female guards who were supported by several arcane wards set about the balcony. Ilharess trusted their scimitars, their adamantine chain mail, and their hand held crossbows with quails tipped with poison, and even their abilities to wield them. But she was just as paranoid as any other dark elf, and so the arcane magic was also set in place. One could never be too secure.

All about the room there were motifs of spiders, demons, webbing, and torture scenes that would make most intelligent species' blood run dry. A spider the size of a house feasting on a surface elf was on one wall, two demons pulling another surface elf apart were on another. There were shelves about the room with unlit black candles, skulls, and even a few metal fragments rumored to be part of their Goddess's, the Spider queen's, last metallic structure from the Abyss (though most believed that a deep dwarf had a few pieces of scrap left over from some common and worthless project and made off with a fortune and a good story). Her throne was black ebony, though the ebony was wearing off in places and at closer inspection one could see the stone throne under the black outer casing. Beside her throne was a small table with crystal decanters filled with various liquors and a few glasses, and beside them was a small bag full of coins. A set of huge wooden double doors were on her left wall, closed as they had been for the last half hour, flanked on the outside with two more trusted female guards also adorned with chain mail, scimitars and crossbows with poison tipped quails.

"And if you are fortunate it will be in that order! Get yourself into this chamber immediately!"

Ilharess was in such a tirade that she hadn't noticed the fact that the daughter that had caused her such wrath and anger had already entered the room and was leaning causally against the open door. Like most dark elves, Medri was slender; black skinned, and had long white hair. She had on her black leather corset and matching leather pants and boots. A hand crossbow was at her right hip, a bone dagger on her left, and a piwafwi clasped with a house insignia broach over her shoulders and draping almost down to the floor. She was not dressed as revealing as most though. She believed in her abilities, her spells, and her wits over her sexual prowess, which she believed were only used as a compensation for those who had nothing else to use. Since she was the third daughter to a house of very low standing, she neither had time nor opportunity, nor social acceptance to utilize such prowess. It wasn't that she hadn't been blessed with enough attributes to pull it off; she was just too low on the social ladder to be noticed. Her red eyes were examining her mother in pleasure since she enjoyed watching her mother's fits of rage, especially if she were the cause of them.

Ilharess looked up and finally caught sight of her daughter. "You kept me waiting ... again!" Ilharess screamed at the top of her lungs as she crossed the floor between the throne she had been sitting on and the open door in only a few strides. The outburst was such that the two female guards outside the throne room were shaken to such a degree that they thought their own lives were endangered, instead of Medri's. Ilharess's hand shot out and grabbed Medri by the throat and lifted her off the ground and then slammed her against the wall. Her face came within an inch of her daughter's so Medri could see the full fury she had felt. "I told you what would happen the next time you kept me waiting and now I shall..."

"We both know you're not going to kill me", Medri gasped, trying to gain air into her lungs through her mother's grip while her feet dangled freely off the ground. Her mother's grip tightened to show that she was indeed going finally end her daughter's life and nothing was going to stop her. "If you send Dalharil, then Drada will take her opportunity to attack you. And if you send Drada, then the reverse will be true. Either way there will be a second attempt at the throne as soon as the one sent has returned. This house will lose at least two if not three priestesses." Her words came in gasps, struggling between attempts at breathing. But despite her consciousness fading, she hadn't struggled under her mother's grip.

Ilharess threw Medri half way across the room and watched as her daughter landed with harshness on the cold, hard floor. Ilharess knew that her daughter was right. Both Dalharil and Drada have been eying the throne for quite some time now. Each of them would take the opportunity to attack Ilharess while the other was away. A daughter returning from the mission would use her achievement as a catalyst to show she was more worthy to lead than her own mother and would also launch her own assault. She wasn't afraid of such attacks, it was the way of the dark elves, and had no doubt that she would prevail, but it would leave her without at least one if not both of her priestesses. This would leave her house vulnerable to war from competing houses. So there it was. Medri was the only one she could send on this mission. She still wanted to beat her within an inch of her life, but the mission was tomorrow and there wasn't enough time to indulge in such matters and have Medri healed to full health before the mission started. There was just too much time, effort, money, and magic invested to have it all fall apart on emotional indulgences.

"I control the undead and I am the house mage, so yes Mother, I do know where I stand and I do know how to play the Senet board", Medri said regaining her breath.

"Shut up! Get out of my sight! Get yourself ready for the mission and pray to the Goddess you are successful!" Ilharess turned away from her fallen daughter and slammed a fist into the wall.

A couple items fell from their shelves from the force. Medri was right. Medri was a necromancer, a controller of the undead, and with the house mage currently assassinated; she had become the house mage. Ilharess could not afford to lose another member so soon.

'Why! Why?' She thought to herself, 'Why do I let her get to me like this?' But she knew the answer before the thought finished crossing her mind. Now she had become so furious, so emotional, that she had forgotten why she had summoned her daughter in the first place.

Medri pulled herself off the hard cold floor, smiled, bowed and left the throne room. Her smirk was hidden from her mother, as she knew that if her mother had seen it, she would have been pushed over the edge and the mission be damned.

Once her daughter was gone, Ilharess turned toward the balcony. As she approached it, she dismissed the two guards. "Go! Get! Get out of here and go guard elsewhere, anywhere just out of my sight." Both guards left in such a hurry, each believing that their Matron Mother would at last and finally loose so much of her temper as to throw them both off the balcony just to see which one would land in a broken heap on the cavern floor first.

Ilharess put her hands on the railing that surrounded the balcony, and breathed deep. She took in the sights of the underworld city outlined with faerie fire. She could just barely make out the high tier, the ledge that housed all eight of the ruling council houses along with The Temple, The Mages Guild, and The Fighters Guild. The only other guild of major importance was off to her right, also just barely visible, and that was the merchant guild, or the houseless rogue guild, whichever one was so inclined to call it.

Her house was falling apart, and she knew it, it was just a matter of time. Her consort had proven ill-chosen and had not supplied her with enough children, with only three daughters and one son. His disappointing performance had cost him his life as a sacrifice to her Goddess, the spider queen, although against advisement of both of her priestess daughters. It was rare that they both agreed on anything, but they knew the will of their Goddess and giving a sacrifice that was unworthy wasn't much of a sacrifice at all but more of a full blown sacrilege. The sacrifice not only removed the potential of any more children from him, it had removed the potential of any more children from any male. It had cost her any other potential consorts to look her way. None would even be in the same room for fear that any one of them would also be a similar regret to their Matron Mother and thus receive a similar fate. She could charm any one of them, but she knew that would not be productive, she was simply out of time.

She had already seen a foreshadowing about the ruling of her house and knew her reign was near an end. She also knew that her house would not fall because of another house, or because of inner fighting. Her own life was also coming to an end and the prophecy told her that it would not be at the hand of any of her daughters. She gripped the railing hard. Her time was coming soon.

'I can take care of her for you'; a voice came, though not to her ears, but to her mind. She knew who it was without even turning around. The voice in her head was alien and although she had heard it many times she still found its presence unnerving and slightly sickening.

"The train leaves tomorrow," she said aloud. She knew her visitor could read her mind and all she had to do was to think her thoughts and they would be heard, but she wanted to let him know that she was in control of the conversation. This was still her house, even if it were for only a short time. "Your payment for getting us in a winning bid is on the table." There was a moment of silence and then she heard the bag being picked up.

'Shall I dispense of the female for the usual fee?' The alien thought entered her mind. She wished it would stop doing that.

"She is on a mission. Once her mission is a success, then, yes, you may kill her."

If the intruder had smiled, she never knew. She never turned around, but knew her company was happy with her decision just as she knew it had left the same way it had come, into thin air.

She sighed again. What she needed was something to take her mind off of this brooding decline of emotion that she was sinking into. She made her way to one of the side tables that held several decanters of hard liquor. She chose a light brown pungent smelling liquid and poured herself a glass full. Without putting the decanter down, she drank the crystal glass down in one shot, poured herself another, and drank it down as well. The mushroom wine went to her head quickly. Putting the glass and bottle down, she smiled; letting the liquid take its effect. Then she came to a resolve and made her way to the dungeons. She wasn't going to have this evening wasted. There were several in the dungeon that required her attention and she was now in the right frame of mind to give it. With a little imagination and a bit of magic, she could make one of them look like Medri and she could relive her fantasy over and over again.

Chapter: The Mission

Medri made her way out of the throne room, past the two exterior guards that were still trembling from the ranting of their Matron Mother, and back down the hall she had come from. The hall echoed with the sound of her boots clicking against the stone floor and her piwfia flowed behind her giving the appearance of majesty. She passed a few male guards along the way, all of which stepped aside and gave Medri a slight bow. She may not be the Matron Mother, nor did she have any ambition to achieve such a goal, but she was still one of the highest-ranking individuals in the house. And since she was also a female, she was to be given the highest respect or these guards would find themselves joining the ranks of the undead guards she had control over on the top of the structure walls. As she meandered through the stalactite structure to her room below, she let her mind drift back to the starting of the mission she was about to embark on tomorrow morning.

House D'Silva, just one house lower than her own, had been making raids and attacks on their storehouses, businesses, and slaves. They had already lost two of their businesses and at least a dozen slaves to such raids. It had taken some time and bribing to find out which house was responsible. Of course a tortured orc slave from House D'Silva had confirmed it all as well (it later became one of her undead guards). After the information was revealed, the reason why had been obvious, House D'Silva was making their move; they were getting ready for war. A trap was set for the next D'Silva raiding party, and the then current house mage, M'elzar Olis'inth was sent to ensure the trap had succeeded. A false merchant party was created and made its way through the underworld with the hope that a raiding party from house D'Silva would make its move. The raiding party did attack a few days into the journey and was fended off. Although the Olis'inth's false merchant party had been successfully defended, one of his own guards, an infiltrator from House D'Silva assassinated M'elzar. It had become obvious that the whole raiding party was just a front to the blade that took out M'elzar, reducing their house by one less member.

This was all some time ago. Medri had become the new house mage due to her arcane ability and Ilharess had decided to have another child, hopefully an expendable male. Unfortunately the position of house consort was cursed to be short lived, and shorter still if he wasn't productive. A lover to the House Matron meets his demise in a painful and torturous fashion if he doesn't help the Matron Mother to produce the offspring she wanted. The consort wasn't productive. Somewhere, in the Matron's private chambers perhaps, Medri was sure the consort's beating heart was still in the jar it was placed in just after the sacrifice.

Although Medri was sure that any male would find the initial coupling with a House Matron to be a blissful experience beyond anything he could dream of, the price was very high. She often wondered why any male would take such a position; perhaps some magic charming was part of the whole process. Yes, she was now sure of it since no sane male would do so by choice. No wonder most males in the household shunned the Matron whenever she was about, any interest would be a fate of death. So, until some male lost his wits, or at least his will to whatever charming spell the Matron would toss out, Medri was the house mage.

About a year ago the city had moved. Just like that, up and moved. Anarchia, the name of her city, was known as the City of Chaos. It was believed that if the inhabitants of Anarchia had no idea what was going on than neither can its enemies. Every so often, without any schedule or warning, the ruling council would decide to move the whole city. Each individual would pack up, a new place would be found, and a new city would be created. It was maddening for anyone trying to make some sort of life, but it was believed to be a respectful honoring and offering to the Goddess of Chaos.

It was after the most recent move that their scouts had found out that they were fairly close to another dark elf city. Trade routes had to be formed, caravans had to be sent, political envoys were to be arranged, spies had to be deployed and a dozen other similar processes needed to be put into place with this new city. Every household that had a piece of any of these actions would do very well for themselves. A call went out for envoys from various houses, but it was limited, so only those who paid top coin would be promised a slot. The coins would be paid to the ruling council houses that had already secured positions in the caravan for free. It was well known that the ruling council and their houses were using this to bleed the smaller, less significant houses, dry.

When it was found out that a priestess from House D'Silva had secured a position in the first of the caravans, Matron Mother Ilharess Olis'inth saw her opportunity to extract her revenge. She would also secure a position and have the priestess find some fatal accident along the way. Ilharess had to choose which daughter to send for the assassination of the D'Silva priestess and after some thought; she came to the conclusion that it had to be Medri. Dalharil, her first daughter, and Drada, her second, would plan their assassination attempts at Ilharess herself if the other were away. It was best to keep the two daughters together to keep each other in check. Medri would have to carry out the mission, and with her necromantic abilities, she would be able to bring back an animated undead of the D'Silva priestess as a new undead guard for their walls, as a trophy of their kill.

Medri had gone down several flights of stairs and at one point had to duck under webbing that a fairly large spider had created. The spider was several feet in diameter and was welcomed in any structure dedicated to the Spider Queen; however Medri found them to be more of a nuisance. They seemed to be everywhere and were constantly in the way of where she wanted to be. Her undead, which didn't have the understanding of the political and religious structures or implications, would more than once disrupt these webs and therefore wind up being destroyed. It took so much time and effort to create these undead and she wished Matron Mother Ilharess would find some way to move the spiders to a different location. Of course such a thought was blasphemous.

Medri had made her way back to her room. She reached into her pocket and pulled out a bone key, inserted it into the keyhole, turned it, spoke a few arcane words and opened the door. Opening the door she saw it was as she had left it. There was a fine bed with purple spider silk sheets and a down feather pillow from the surface world. The pillow was expensive, but she found it was well worth it. There was a personal chest at the foot of the bed, locked of course, and trapped. A side table was next to the bed where she often had a candle burning, though not currently burning, and a dresser on one side of the wall. Another wall had several pegs to hang her gear. Finally there was a worktable where she did most of her personal necromantic studies. It was full of tubes, beakers, and flasks of powders, jars of dead creatures, a few books, and a skull with its eyes still intact in its sockets, which seemed to watch and follow her every move. These weren't the extent of her items, just the project she was currently working on. The rest of the items were in the house library or house laboratory where anyone could have access to them. A skeleton stood motionless in one of the corners.

She sighed. If her house were higher ranking, or if it were richer, then her room would be bigger, more luxurious. But there were others in her household that had it far worse. The slaves, for example, were fortunate if they even had a place on the floor to sleep where most of them used as a place to relieve themselves. The thought was revolting and she decided to put it out of her mind. She may have had a small room, but at least it was all hers. This thought brought her mind back to where she was. She stopped and looked in the corner by her bed. There, in the deepest of shadows was a huddled mass, sitting with its back to the corner and a ragged piece of burlap over itself, one she recognized as her personal goblin slave.

With a flick of her wrist an orb of soft purple fire came to rest slightly above the desk, barely lighting room. She sat in the chair that was next to the desk and rolled her head trying to relieve some of the tension that was resting on her shoulders. She picked up a bone comb from the desk and started to move it through her waist long hair, taking out the few tangles. She really didn't need to have her hair combed, but she found it comforting, a way to ease the day. She still had things to do before she left tomorrow and she wanted to make sure she was at her best.

"Get up", she said, breaking the silence.

She heard a rustling in the corner, and knew without turning, that it had to be the goblin standing to the best of its ability. It was a goblin after all, a slave, a lesser race, and an expendable being that could be put to death for any reason, even for the sheer pleasure of those around it. And death would be the least of its worries; at least there would be no more pain. No, it wasn't death if feared, but the torture chambers below where death would not come. The fear of being such a disappointment to any dark elf and being sent to the chambers had always kept the poor goblin continually shaken and it often found it difficult to do the best of commands, including merely standing.

"We have things in the market place to pick up tonight before we leave tomorrow and I want to be packed before then." She said without turning. She gave a slight look over her shoulder as she continued to comb her hair. With a flick of her wrist and slight mutter she had caused a slight click from her locked chest. "I want several outfits placed in my backpack and I'll hand pick the rest."

'We?' the goblin thought. 'Did she say we?' He understood the first "we" since he did often follow her to the market place to help carry items back, but it was the second "we" he was confused about. Was he now expected to go with her on the journey through the underworld?

"Yes Mistress", he said and slightly bowed. He moved forward and fetched her backpack from one of the pegs on the wall and started carefully, with as much caution as possible, to load her backpack with some outfits she would enjoy. He had a good idea what she would like; he had been her slave for quite some time.

It was a few minutes into the packing that the silence had been broken. Her door had been burst open, and there stood Drada Olis'inth, the second daughter to House Olis'inth. Her cold bitter eyes took in the scene. She was taller than her sister, but lacked the physical beauty that Medri had. She was scrawnier, resembling more of a night hag than the stunning dark elf she believed she was. She had on her priestess vestments over her fine dark elf chain mail, as she often did. Drada was a priestess of the Spider Queen and she was damn sure everyone knew it. Her mace hung at her right side by her single headed snake whip and a hand cross bow on her left side. Her white hair was in as much shambles as her mother's, representing the chaos of their city, their social order and their religious structure.

"I came to wish you well on your journey tomorrow, to give you the Goddess's blessing. And… what in the abyss is that thing doing with your garments?"

Slowly turning to face her older sister, Medri said dryly "He's packing them."

"If he was my slave, and he touched anything of mine, I would personally enjoy disemboweling him, among other things."

"Well, for starters, you didn't come here to give me the Goddess's blessing, you don't like me well enough and if you had your way and an opportunity, you would have a dagger at my back. Instead you came to give your disappointment that you aren't going on the mission yourself for your own personal glory. Or perhaps it is to give further disappointment that Dalharil wasn't going, and that you could try to kill our Matron Mother in her absence. Second, how I treat my personal slave is none of your business. You may be my older sister, but you aren't my Matron Mother ... ". And now, Medri thought, to move yet another Senet piece. "... at least not yet."

Drada let the last bit of the conversation entertain her mind for a moment. 'Yes', she thought, 'that is the core of the conversation', and a smile came across her lips. Her snake whip responded to her emotion, as it usually did, and slid to her hand as if caressing it.

"Speaking of which", Drada replied, "I find that our beloved Matron Mother has left you with such a small pittance, truly sad really. You are wasting your time, energy, and talents down here. If I were the next Matron Mother, then things would be different. I'm sure you would find yourself moved to a higher position, a larger room, and perhaps even first daughter."

Medri smiled. The offer wasn't unexpected. Her sister was asking for her alliance to overthrow the balance so she could take possession of the throne. The word for it though, did not mean friendship, or a permanent alliance, but one that meant a short term combining of resources until such time that one or the other is no longer needed. Such an alliance usually ended in death for one, the other, or both. 'Now for yet another piece to move', Medri thought to herself.

"Yes, I was wondering when you were going to get around to asking that very thing. You see, Dalharil had already given me the exact same offer earlier this morning."

Medri watched as Drada's color faded from her face. She hadn't needed the light to help the goblin pack, nor to comb her hair. Her eyesight, like all dark elves, was accustomed to the total darkness. She could even make out heat patterns of objects and creatures. This would have allowed her to watch the heat drain from her sister's face without a problem, but she wanted to watch the fullest effect and so the soft light was lit ahead of time. She watched as Drada moved slightly, perhaps casting a spell to see if she were telling the truth, or perhaps just to adjust her view to get a better glimpse of Medri's face to see if she were lying. Either way, Medri was confident, her sister had in fact given her the offer earlier that morning.

"I will give you the same answer I gave her. We will have to see how the Senet pieces fall."

Drada clicked her tongue in frustration, turned on her heel and left Medri in frustration. The eyes in the skull shifted and seemed to watch Drada leave. Medri put her hand on the skull, as if to calm it down and smiled, her plan was working quite well. Her only regret was that she couldn't stay behind and watch how it all played out. She could try to scry, but most of the house was guarded against such things. She could also leave items behind that she could watch through, but that would mean trying to keep an eye on every one of them all the time so as to not miss a thing. This would mean that she would spend too much time indulging her curiosity and less time on her mission. She will have to wait until she returned. Meanwhile, she will take all the items that held personal significance, including her slave, out of the path of the fury that would follow shortly after she left.

She didn't have feelings or attachment to her slave. On the contrary, he was still a goblin. Her sister had been right in stating that most dark elves would disembowel such a creature, but she had thought differently. She believed that whipping a slave only decreased its moral and never produced the optimal effect. She had taken a goblin at random and treated it with more kindness, if one could call it that, or at least with less violence. After much time and effort, the slave gave its fullest commitment in everything it did. She didn't have to threaten it, didn't have to beat it, she just had informed it once, and only once, that any disappointment would mean that it would leave its life of kindness and be sent to one of the sisters for them to do with it as she pleased. The goblin understood completely and now she had a slave that she could depend on, one that would even defend her life, and that was something worth having, especially in the underworld.

Chapter: Drada

*D*rada angrily stormed down the hall and made her way back to her personal room. One guard had the misfortune of not moving away from her fast enough and before the unfortunate male had time to react, Drada had snapped the snake whip and caught him at the wrist. He had looked panicked, but only momentarily. Drada's mace found his skull and he dropped in a heaping pile, his blood smeared on the wall and continued to drain on to the floor beside him. If the snake venom didn't kill him then the blow would. She left him where he was. Dalharil would probably raise the guard back to life or Medri would raise him as an undead, she didn't care which.

She made her way to her room and tried to slam open the door, but it didn't budge, and she almost ran into it. Drada pulled her mace and swore.

"Iblith! Iblith! Iblith!" she screamed time and again as she beat the door by means of her mace with all of her fury. Her banging could be heard up and down the whole of the corridor. She was less upset with the fact that the door didn't open and more upset about the fact that she forgot to unlock it. After a few more bashes, the door gave way and it nearly fell off its hinges. Drada swore again and kicked the remainder of the door away from her path. She stomped into her room, grabbed her piwafwi from the floor where she had left it, and then she stormed toward the main entrance of the house structure.

As she approached the main double door entrance, the two main guards had full warning of her approaching fury and were quick enough to open the massive set of double doors well before Drada's arrival. However, just as Drada reached them, she turned, raised a knee into the groin of one of them and slammed her mace into the backside of his helmet as he bent over. She spun on the other guard. He thought of going for his sword to protect himself, but then thought better of it. If he wanted to live then he would just have to let her extract her fury as she wished. And she did.

She grabbed him by his chain mail and slammed him head first into the stone wall. She looked to them both, hoping either one of them would try to stand back up, but neither did. She didn't believe either one of them had died, so they were either unconscious or were smart enough to feign it. She turned and continued to exit the house, stomping her feet and making no attempt to hide her tantrum.

She put her piwafwi over her shoulders, clasped it with her house broach insignia, and pulled the hood over her head. She took in the fresher, cooler air from the cavern that housed all of the stalactite and stalagmite structures of the whole city, but hardly anything else. Everything was more a blur for her, but she knew exactly where she was going.

She walked past several permanent structures, turned, and found herself in one of the smaller market places. Ignoring the crowded street, the various aromas, the sounds from every direction, she kept her head low and plowed her way through the throng of merchants, buyers, sellers, commoners, and slaves.

At one turn she clipped the side of a merchant trying to set up a small stand of freshly cut underworld mushrooms. Both he and his crops went sprawling across the hard cave floor; his mushrooms bounced among the feet of several would be buyers. The merchant came up out of his fall with a roll and sprang to his feet, bringing his short sword to bear. He looked around and caught sight of the back of the individual who had just humiliated him and made his move, but then caught himself short. His eyes caught sight of the snake whip at Drada's side. She was a priestess, he realized, and quickly turned away. He hoped she didn't see him. It was a long, drawn out, painful death sentence to anyone one who even attempted to strike a priestess.

After a few more turns, Drada found herself in front of the shop she was looking for, it was the "Respite" a public spa. The "Respite" sat on top of a natural mineral hot springs that was a definite source of income to whatever house took possession of it. When she had first found this place, she knew that some serious coin went to secure the location, and she believed that it was either a combination of houses and a commission to the ruling counsel or just the ruling council themselves that had secured it. A small fee was paid to rent a time slot. Although it was a public spa, there were enough enchantments to keep out scrying, so whatever happened in the spa rooms never really happened at all, or so the advertisement stated. This was the spa's greatest appeal. Most knew, however, that word eventually did get out, but at least it would take a while, and sometimes it was that amount of time that any conspirator needed. Drada was definitely a conspirator and time is what she needed. She closed her eyes, took a deep breath to calm herself and entered.

The entry room was full of spider and web motifs and the only furniture was a reception desk and female dark elf behind it; who only barely glanced up and didn't even acknowledge Drada's presence. With her hood pulled low, Drada didn't even give the receptionist a notice. There were several doors with numbers on them leading out to the various spa rooms. Drada took a coin out of her coin bag and dropped it down on the desk. She had already reserved a room; this payment was for the receptionist's silence. The receptionist quickly pawned the octagonal black coin, etched with spiders and webbing on both sides, and put in its place a key with a number on it. Drada picked up the key, found the corresponding door and left the reception room.

The next chamber was octagonal. In the center of the room was an octagonal pool of very hot mineral water, its sulfuric smell filled the room and immediately made Drada light headed. A small table was next to the spa with various decanters of liquid. Drada knew that most of them were body oils and a few of them were various liquors. There was even one or two that were narcotics. Drada was sure that more than one body had been found in these spas, some of which were obviously murders, but some also were accidental from the mixing of several, or indulging in too much of, any one of the table's contents. She would have to keep a mental note of how much she indulged. Along the walls were several pegs to hold personal items and clothing.

Drada slowly discarded her weapons, took off her piwafwi, her priestess vestments, her chain mail, boots, and undergarments and let them fall on the ground. She was in no mood to carefully hang them up. She cautiously stepped into the gradually deepening pool and felt the warmth come over her. The soft, black texture of the pool's surface was like smooth obsidian. At the center of the pool the depth was about chest high, but she bent her knees to allow most of her body to succumb to the relaxing and penetrating heat.

She took long deep breaths letting the frustration of the day melt away.

After a few minutes she went to the side of the pool nearest the table and found one of the liquors. It was a light blue and was thought to be fermented milk from a dragon, but there was no known dragon that gave milk so no one exactly knew where it got its name. She poured herself a glass, drank it down, and poured herself another. Before she indulged herself in her second drink, she reached for one of the narcotics. After a quick smell of the contents, she poured a little into the pool followed by some of the contents of one of the body oils. The effect was immediate. The heat interacted with the oil and her pores opened up; the narcotic entered her system with great force. Her eyes rolled upward, her brain swam, her body slightly trembled and she started to hallucinate. The room began to spin and she felt like she was floating. She had forgotten where she was, why she was here, and had even forgotten her best laid plans. But this was only one of the reasons why she came.

About ten minutes later the door opened again to Drada's spa. Another female dark elf had entered the room. Lael Dalninil from house N'shtyl was expecting to meet Drada, but hadn't expected to see her in such a state. She expected to find Drada in her fullest wits and ready to confide with her the depths how their plots were moving along, but Drada seemed to barely be conscious and definitely wasn't even aware of Lael's arrival. Lael's house was only two down for Drada's, far enough away to not be an immediate threat, but close enough to be an ally. And they were allies, but only in the since of mutual benefit. Both understood what would happen once that benefit ceased to exist.

Lael was, like most dark elves, tall, slender, and had long white hair, shortened only by having most of it up, supported by two long pins. She wore thigh high boots, a one-piece leather outfit that showed off every curve and almost completely revealed a few of them. She had a rapier sword on one hip and several daggers around her belt. Upon her view of Drada, Lael believed that the time had come, that the mutual benefit had in fact ceased to exist. She was the eighth daughter of her very prolific mother, or at least everyone thought most of the daughters were from the same mother, and there was nowhere for her to move up the ladder of succession. She would have to kill off a lot of sisters to get to the top.   Her plan was to join a house with less competition, and hopefully one with a Matron-to-be on the rise. It didn't take long to find the right house, but if the plan was going as well as Drada looked, then Lael might be better off on her own.

Lael undid her belt and let her weapon slowly drop to the floor without making a sound. She was good at being quiet; she was a rogue after all since the position of priestess was filled too many times already in her house. Lael finished undressing and took the two long pins out of her hair and let it fall down to the fullest extent of her hips. The urge to put Drada out of her misery was tempting, but then she thought against it. 'Perhaps', she thought, 'I can salvage this'. She put down her long hairpins and entered the water. Drada barely stirred, still facing away from her. Lael came close to Drada and put her hands on Drada's shoulders, slowly tightening, releasing, and tightening again, massaging the obvious tension from Drada's shoulders. Drada moaned.

"What's wrong?" Lael asked.

"That Iblith of a sister."

"Which one? Medri?"

"No, not THAT bowch. It's Dalharil. She got to Medri first."

'Damn', Lael thought to herself still massaging Drada's shoulders. The plan depended on Medri joining them, or at least, staying out of the way. If Medri had joined with Dalharil then things just got a lot more complicated.

"At least she hasn't allied herself with Dalharil." Drada said as if reading Lael's mind, and for a second Lael thought that Drada might be able to. No one really knew what magic was currently active or when; and for all she knew, most of the underworld could read their minds right now.

"Oh?"

"Medri told me that she was going to see where the Senet pieces landed. I don't care about Medri. I don't care if she helps, hinders or stays away. It's Dalharil. It's always Dalharil. She's always one step ahead of me, always." Drada's voice began to rise.

"Shhhh", Lael hushed as she continued to massage Drada's shoulders. "Medri will stay out of the way; perhaps she will even join us in the end. We'll take out your mother, and then Dalharil. If Medri gets in the way then we'll take her out as well. If she helps us…" Lael shrugged and left the conversation open to get Drada's reply. She wanted to know if she was going to be the first daughter to Matron Mother Drada Olis'inth or be placed under Medri as the second daughter.

"Then we'll take her out anyway", Drada said as she turn around and faced Lael. They both smiled

An hour later Lael exited the "Respite" fully dressed and well refreshed. She had only gone a few steps, then turned back and looked over her shoulder. She hoped she had made the right decision, but then smiled. 'If not, I can always kill her another time', she thought to herself. She was going to do that anyway in order to take over the house that she wanted, but for now Drada would live.

Chapter: Dalharil

*D*alharil couldn't help but over hear Drada's high-pitched screams, her long-winded stream of obscenities and finally the bashing of her own bedroom door. She doubted anyone could have missed it. Her only hope was that Drada didn't catch a guard or two unaware since she had a habit of doing sizeable damage. It wasn't that Dalharil cared about any of them; it just took time and resources to keep the guards whole and alive. What she didn't want was another guard killed off and becoming another undead minion under Medri's control. Medri's small army of undead was becoming impressive; too impressive for Dalharil's comfort.

Dalharil was big, square shoulders, sizeable muscles and had a shapely fitness that would intimate even an ogre. That wasn't difficult to do, since she was a dark elf priestess, but sometimes size did matter, and Dalharil had bulk. Her chain mail, priestess vestments, and her piwafwi only came to enhance her size. Dalharil doubted that she would ever need her mace or her snake whip in any battle, but it was still good to know that they were always ready at the sides of her hips. Dalharil was in such contrast with her other two sisters that she often wondered if they had different fathers. Come to think of it, she didn't look much like her mother either. But her family lineage wasn't on her mind, only her heritage.

Dalharil waited and watched from a balcony as Drada stormed out of the house complex and made her way out into the city of Anarchia. She already knew where Drada was going and whom she was seeing; she too had her spies and her magic. She also knew earlier this morning that Drada would try to pull Medri into the plot to ascend the hierarchy of the household structure. Dalharil wanted to know where Medri stood in the plot, not that she minded one way or another, and she just wanted to know where all the pieces were on the board. Medri had given the answer she had expected, one that kept her options open. The meeting with Medri had a double meaning as well. She knew that Medri would tell Drada just to offend her. Drada would then use her magic to see if Medri was telling the truth, and when it was confirmed, she would have an emotional break down and make the meeting that she was off to now. Everything was going according to plan.

Dalharil touched her snake whip, closed her eyes and focused. With her enchantments between her snake whip and the one she created for Drada, she could see everything that transpired. It didn't take long to get a mental image of Drada colliding with a mushroom salesman. She touched her broach and could hear the crowd of merchants, buyers, slave traders, and any others who were in close proximity to Drada's broach. Dalharil smiled. She pulled her mind back to her surrounds and left to go access Drada's damage to the door and any of the poor unfortunate guards that might have been in her way.

Dalharil made her way from her balcony view and went down the hallway, down a set of stairs and down yet another hallway. She turned a corner, stopped abruptly and hid herself behind the corner she just passed and hoped she hadn't been seen. Down the corridor Dalharil could see Medri attending the body of a dead guard. Quickly Dalharil cast a spell and she had full confidence that she would no longer be seen.

Dalharil cursed under her breath. 'Damn, she's faster than I expected', she thought to herself. She would have to make a mental note of Medri's effectiveness, 'She must have some spell that alerts her to nearby dead bodies, like a deep dwarf to gold.'

She watched Medri take a few spell components out of a small bag and started weaving a spell. Dalharil could feel the rush of negative energy fill the air and course through her own body, she could feel the temperature drop, and for a brief moment, she could even see her breath warm up the cool air. For a short time the hall went darker. The darkness started to solidify and then entered the dead fallen guard. The lifeless guard sat up, obviously still mortally wounded. Dalharil continued to watch as Medri spoke to the new undead creation, as she gave it directions and commands. The undead guard stood up and walked down the other end of the hallway where Dalharil knew it would find a stairway to the top of the upper walls to join the other undead guards.

Dalharil thought Medri was finished, but to her astonishment, she wasn't. She continued to watch as Medri pulled a skull from her backpack.

'Did the skull still have its eyes in its sockets?' Dalharil asked herself letting a slight shudder go down her spine.

Medri got up from her kneeling position that she was in to raise the undead guard, looked down both ways of the hallway to make sure she was alone, and took care to step over the bashed door as she entered Drada's room. A few moments later Medri came out again, but without the skull. She glanced both ways down the hall, then chose the way the undead guard had went. In a few moments, Medri had turned a corner and was out of sight.

Curiously, and cautiously, Dalharil approached the bashed door to Drada's room. 'She must have been more upset that I thought', she said to herself noting the carnage of the door. But she hadn't come to inspect the entrance; she wanted to find what Medri was up to. She looked in the room to find it completely trashed.

The room was fairly large with two smaller rooms connecting from open archways. There was a large bed in the center of the room and was slightly askew with the silk sheets and pillows tossed aside. A large trunk was near the foot of the bed, open, with its contents sprawled out over the chest and onto the floor as if the chest had decided to disgorge the clothing and other items on its own accord. There were pegs along the wall to hang items on, but not a single item was hanging on them. The floor with littered with odds and ends, clothing and, to Dalharil's amusement but after seeing the rest of the room not a surprise, bits of food and dishes. A side desk was near the bed with its drawer open and papers spewed out of it obvious to any observer that it could no longer hold anything else. One of the other two rooms was a priestess room full of incense, meditation circles, a small library and another desk. The third room was a bathroom with a tub, small table with a washbasin and a cabinet. Even from this distance, Dalharil could see that each adjoining room was equally a mess with clothing, books, towels, and paper scattered across the floor.

At first Dalharil thought that Medri was searching for something and had completely trashed the bedroom. Then she realized that Medri simply didn't have the time to accomplish all of this. Drada actually lived in this sty. 'If she wasn't looking for something to take out...' Dalharil thought, then paused and smiled.

She looked around and was sure the skull was placed here somewhere, but the state of things made it difficult to walk through the room, let alone to look for something out of place. It would be easier to find something in its proper place then to sort through all this mess. She grinned again. Dalharil moved her arms through a small gesture and cast another spell. This one she aimed at the side desk near the bed. A shower of eerie green flames fell over the whole table. The fire didn't give off any heat or burned in any way, but it did outline each item, which included papers, dishes, a half-eaten chunk of cheese that wasn't even on a plate, a half drunken bottle of wine, three drinking glasses and even the invisible skull sitting on the desk near the edge; its eyes looking straight at the bed as if waiting for its occupant to arrive.

She watched as the eyes of the green flamed skull turned from watching the bed and moved its gaze toward her to observe her every movement. Dalharil had seen many things that would curl the blood of many regular individuals and was used to them, but this sight, the sight of a skull with green flames with eyes that moved and watched her had started to unnerve her just a bit.

Dalharil's smile widened. 'So, Medri intends to spy on Drada,' Dalharil thought to herself. 'It would seem that she isn't going to stay out of this after all. It would have been easier if Medri had accepted the house broach I made for her, but then again that might have made it too easy. Life isn't interesting without a challenge. A challenge I'll have to look into. Meanwhile, I'll have to check my own chambers as well.' Dalharil dismissed the flames, turned and left the room as she found it. She still had to find Sarol Jabbuk, the house weapon's master. Her alliance with Sarol would be the second time she had tried to make an alliance with a male in her household. Her first time was her brother M'elzar.

"And this affects me how exactly?" M'elzar had asked dryly.

She had always found him to be more than the regular arrogance found in most dark elf. As the house mage, he was tolerated more than the usual male would be and that left M'elzar in the position to flaunt his defiance as he wished. Dalharil had laid out her plan to kill off her Matron Mother to M'elzar in hopes that her succession would benefit her brother. It was in that instant, the instant of his response, that she realized that it wouldn't matter. M'elzar's position wouldn't change, his benefits wouldn't change, and his treatment wouldn't change. Now, however, her plan was out in the open with an individual that had no reason to keep her secret.

It took some time, effort and coin to win the trust of the high priestess of house D'Silva, Naliara. Some minor information about the security and time schedule for a few of their shops was leaked to Naliara. It was all part of the plot to silence M'elzar, and Naliara took full advantage of it. The shops were totally ransacked and a few minor slaves were killed, but Dalharil thought it was worth it.

"We should set a trap of the house that is responsible," Dalharil suggested to her mother. "A false caravan traveling through the underworld. This would lure the house out and we can counter attack with proof to the ruling council."

A raid on a house caravan was not illegal, not even frowned upon, but being caught, being sloppy was. Dalharil even nominated herself to guard the caravan and lead the attack against the unknown house. Ilharess had agreed, but since it was too close to a religious gala, it would not be wise to send any of the priestesses. Medri was still not strong enough and was in the middle of creating the undead guards that they have now. That only left M'elzar. Dalharil had given a set of guards clothing to Naliara to ensure their assassin would be able to blend in to the caravan.

After M'elzar's assassination, Naliara had contacted Dalharil. In exchange for M'elzar's death, Krenala, Naliara's youngest sister, was offered as a sacrifice. With Krenala's death, Naliara would have less competition in her own household and wouldn't have to keep looking over her shoulder for her youngest sister. This would also appease Ilharess and trick her mother into thinking the assassination had been avenged.

That was then. Now, with all the other players and Senet pieces looking in other directions, Dalharil could now get to work on her own plan. For that to work, she still needed the alliance of Sarol. This thought brought her back to where she was. She rounded a corner and found Sarol in a large chamber, a sword in each hand fending off several guards in training. She leaned against the open archway and watched.

Chapter: Sarol

Sarol had just finished his early day training session with several of the guards. They were a bit rusty and sluggish and Sarol often wondered why some other house hadn't declared war and sent their house to the abyss already. He shook his head and took off his sweaty shirt. He was very bulky for a male and the tight thick muscles only added to the bulk. Sweat dripped off his body from his work out.

'At the very least', he thought, 'I will be ready for an attack'. He ran his fingers though his short cropped white hair and sighed.

"Not bad", came a female dark elf voice.

Sarol spun around to see his newly made ally, Naliara coming out of the shadows from the back of the room. She had chosen to wear her seductively low cut green and gold dress. The top of the dress cut very deeply revealing her cleavage and the slit on the thigh ran high enough up that any false move would reveal what she had underneath, if anything at all. She had very high-heeled shoes that placed her height significantly above his. He quickly looked about to ensure all of his students had already left.

"You could have been caught," he said. "How did you get in here anyway?"

Naliara walked smoothly and seductively toward him. She held up a finger and gently placed it on his lips. "Shhhh", she hushed. "We have plans to discuss, plans about my ascension and plans about your ascension with me."

"Matron Mother Naliara has a good ring to it", Sarol said in a hushed whisper.

"And so does Consort Sarol", she replied. Her lips found his and they both retreated into a nearby room.

It was a few hours later that the both of them had been awakened by the sound of Ilharess' screeching voice. "Medri... Medri Jabbress Olis'inth!"

"Matron Mother Ilharess sounds very upset. I doubt Medri will live though this one." Sarol said as we started to put his clothing back on.

"Yes, I suppose so. As interesting as it will be to find out I'm afraid that this will be my cue to leave. We will meet again." Her statement wasn't put as a fact, or a request, but as a demand.

Sarol put his shirt back on and turned to speak to Naliara but then realized she was no longer there. 'How does she do that?' He shook his head and finished dressing.

When Sarol entered the training hall his new set of trainees were already waiting for him. Matron Mother Ilharess would have his hide if she found out he was late. 'To the abyss with that,' he thought, 'she'll have my hide if she found out why I was late.'

The eight male guards stood at attention the moment he walked in. They were all wearing chain mail armor, a helmet, leather pants and black leather boots. Sarol often wondered why, if this city was the City of Chaos and all of its inhabitants were concerned about being different, did all of the guards dress the same. Yes, it would be easier to identify them in a battle. But then getting a uniform to pretend to be a guard was easy enough, so sight of a uniform alone would never install trust in any of them. Sarol ignored the guards and simply grabbed two scimitar swords. The swords weren't sharp; he had to make sure he didn't accidentally kill any of them. Although any death could be resurrected or brought back as undead, the resources of the house were limited and he would pay for those expenses himself, one way or another. He didn't have the coin to pay for the first method and shuddered to think of how he would end up paying if it were the other.

"Today we will learn about fighting with both swords. Our focus today will be creating a feint with the first sword while going in for the kill with the second." He motioned the first guard toward him.

The guard took a defensive position within arm's reach of Sarol and watched as his Master took a similar position. When the guard realized that Sarol wasn't attacking, he took the first swing. It was clumsy and exaggerated. Sarol knew the guard to be better than this initial swing and realized a feint when he saw it. Before the guard could come back with a backhanded lower cut, Sarol made a jab with his right hand. The guard had to switch tactics and moved his scimitar to block, this left the guard's right side wide open, and

Sarol took full advantage of it and brought his left scimitar to bear. Time and again, Sarol went over and over the same feint and attack maneuver.

After a while and a short break, Sarol went into a different tactic, attacking with both swords simultaneously. He motioned two guards to attack him. The two went into their defensive positions and then both swung at their Master. Sarol sent both of his scimitars in opposite directions blocking both of the attacks. He then shifted his weight to the ball of his left foot and pivoted. His body went in tight, bringing his scimitars in close, and then as he came out of his spin, his arms went wide. He was too close for the guards to block, the speed was faster than they had expected and their defenses were down. Only at the last second did they realize that they should have taken a step back and not continue to press their attacks. Both scimitars found their marks on each guard just under their ribs. They would be greatly bruised and Sarol hopped they learned their lesson; it might save their life.

The training continued for another hour with a few more double scimitar maneuvers. This batch of guards was better than the last batch earlier this morning and started to show promise. Only one had to be sent to the infirmary, a lazy miscalculated block resulted in a broken rib. All in all, the session was productive and after a few hours he sent the guards to rest and recoup before taking their scheduled guard posts for the evening.

"Not bad", came a female voice from the archway of the training room.

Sarol froze. It was the same set of words, but a different voice. His blood ran cold with the anticipation of being caught; being found out that he was already in alliance with a different house. If he were found out, then the punishment would be far worse than death. Even if he did die, they would bring him back to life to endure yet again and again. Sarol turned to see Dalharil leaning against the open archway.

"Everything is going according to plan," Dalharil said

Sarol wondered which plan that she was referring to. There were far too many going on and he felt he was in the middle of all of them. He hoped that once everything settles, he would still be standing, which was the majority of the reason why he continued to train so hard.

"You look worried," Dalharil said as she strode over to him. She had confused his concern about his own survival to her plan of accession. She put a finger to his lips. "There is nothing to worry about, I have everything planned."

Sarol couldn't believe the similarities between the two meetings. He was taught that there were no coincidences; all were part of a bigger plot. This meant his life was in more danger than he had initially realized. But, that was part of the thrill, living on the edge. He smiled and wondered if he could make the coincidences even more similar. "Matron Mother Dalharil has a good ring to it", he said softly.

"And so does Consort Sarol". Her lips found his and they both retired for the night in his nearby room, the room he had only recently taken another priestess early that day.

Book: Anarchia

Chapter: Anarchia

*M*edri opened the house doors and took in the sights of the city she called home, Anarchia, the City of Chaos. The city sat in a large cavern about a mile wide with many large stalactites and stalagmites, several large shelf platforms, and a port that sat on an underground lake. There were four entrances into this large cavern; all were patrolled by two of households of the ruling council at each location at random. The household guards were responsible for security of the entrances and were allowed to collect any fees they saw fit, but understood that too much of a fee would leave potential merchants to find another entrance with a lower fee. Since the rotation was at random, no one knew which house was guarding which location in advance. This made bribing a house guard more difficult.

Medri felt the shift well before she saw it. A small earthquake rippled through the whole cavern. The city started to change. The buildings started to move, the streets started to wind and curve, the stalagmites and stalactites flip flopped and the whole city was in a different shape and size than what it started in. The process was only about thirty seconds, but the change was definite. The whole city was under a spell to transform it randomly. The thought was that if the inhabitants didn't know what the city looked like from one day to the next then neither would any attackers. No enemy would be able to plan a siege.

Medri cursed under her breath. She wanted to do her errands quickly, but now she would have to find the shops all over again. She understood the reasoning behind the transformation, but it didn't make it any less frustrating. With her slave goblin at her side, she set forth into the great city.

The streets were full of dark elves, mostly of the common houses. Periodically Medri could make out a representative of a major house and even one or two from the ruling council households. Several slaves were about, hauling gear, carrying bulk and even two were hauling a type of ornate cart that carried their mistress. They had to move aside a few times to make room for a lizard rider, twice for spider riders, and once they saw a giant bat rider circling the city. A couple of male escorts tried to sell their services as Medri walked by, but she merely waved them on. She didn't have time to indulge. With the city streets so full, she often wondered why the ruling council didn't find a bigger cavern.

The whole city reeked with stench. There was sweat of the inhabitants, smell of urine and feces, the smells of the nearby docks, and the greasy smoke fumes of the forges. These were mixed with perfumes, wines, narcotics, fruit, and the occasional smell of cooking and or rotting meat. The passing animals gave off their own stench as well and Medri wondered if any of them, even with a good bath, would have any form of acceptable odor. All this combined with cave fungus, the mushroom fields, and the fertilizer used with them.

They walked past several buildings, all a glow with red, blue, green, and purple fey fire, giving each building an eerie radiance. There were clothing shops that sold spider silk garments, bowch hide, weapon smithy, armor smithy, pottery, jewelry, spices, and other various goods that anyone could possible want or desire. At one point they had passed a building that had been crushed by the transformation, its mushroom wood splinted beyond repair. Such incidents weren't uncommon. Any house that lost a shop to the transformation could appeal to the ruling council. The council would have the shop repaired, but would also essentially take it over. It was easier to chalk the whole building up as a loss and start all over again. Less respectable, but not less profitable and definitely not less sociably accepted business was also present. There were narcotics, prostitutes (all male, no respectable female would stoop to such a level) and a slave market.

There were lesser structures as well. There were small stands that could be taken down, moved, and erected in short order. Here the poorest of merchants sold their wares, mostly small trinkets. There were even a few that offered some of goblin's favorite, mystery meat on a stick. Medri stopped at once such stall. The aroma nearly turned her stomach, but she knew her goblin would eat it. How it could have such a constitution to digest such a thing, she would never know. The merchant was a male dark elf who had obviously seen better days. He was old, half blind, and missing one hand. It was clearly visible that he had fallen out of status with his house and, without an attempt to heal his wounds; he was tossed out to fend for himself. She smiled. She knew that her race was thought of as a plight upon the world, but this just reminded her how tenacious they were. She produced a black octagonal coin and handed it to the merchant. The male dark elf produced a stick of mystery meat and handed it to her without making eye contact. He may be down and out, he may even be tenacious, but he still knew his place in life. To the merchant's amazement, she handed the stick to her goblin slave to eat before walking off.

Medri stopped at the slave market. Any species was fair game for the slave market, and most ended up on the stage at one time or another. Many houses were represented with potential buyers pressing forward to get a better glance at the creatures that were on sale. Any house could go out and get their own slaves, or even bread them once they had a starting stock, but it didn't hurt to check out any new slaves that the market might churn up. Sometimes it was just an ordinary goblin, sometimes an exotic and extra planar creature, and sometimes a creature definitely worthy of note. Today one such creature was being presented. On stage was a large bulky orc, strong enough to carry out most any mundane order given it, and even more than a few extra ordinary ones as well. Several guards were on stage to ensure that the orc would think twice before trying to escape, although it held by its neck and wrists by chains.

The slave driver pointed out the obvious features, trying his best to pitch his sale. He even showed the teeth of the orc, which Medri thought was quite amusing since its teeth had nothing to do with its ability to carry or smash, which was what the orc was obviously built for.

"Ten"

"Fifteen"

"Twenty"

The bids continued to climb. Medri noticed that some of the ruling council household representatives were starting to get in on the bidding. She knew that each of the houses had a fairly good-sized slave pen and that another single orc, no matter its size, wouldn't add it their effectiveness. She understood that this orc was meant for breeding. Its litter would have its strength and the next generation could be formidable. She smiled and thought it might be fun to outbid a major house and upset their plans. Medri listened to the biding and checked her coin bag. She calculated the approximate value of the orc, the amount of coins she had, and the tasks she still wanted to do tonight. She also thought about having to feed it and the time and effort it would take in breaking in a new slave, let alone keeping it subdued. She also thought about killing it and raising it to life as an undead.

Her goblin slave looked up at her. He knew that the orc would pound it into an unidentifiable mess just to prove its worth. Medri turned and looked at her goblin and smiled. She shook her head as if to show it had nothing to worry about and continued to walk toward the docks.

Chapter: The Docks

*I*t was more the smell that told Medri she had reached the docks then the twists and turns she had taken to get there. The roads were so different than this morning that it had taken her twice the amount of time to arrive at one of her desired locations. The smell of fish, ichors, moss, rotting dock wood, salt for brining, mold, and something beyond identifying, and yet oddly familiar, was over whelming as she turned an unfamiliar corner.

The first sight she saw was the expanse of the lake. It was enormous in length, beyond her field of vision. Even though she could see heat patterns in the cool underworld at great distances, the lake only looked black to her, extending beyond her sight. She wasn't found of the lake. Its cool consistent temperature was in full contrast to the ever-changing heat patterns of the cave walls, lichen, steam vents, and inhabitants that helped her see. The lake only left her blind, except when some strange fish or other creature made its way to the surface. Medri shuddered as she remembered some of the odd things that had come up from the lake, the reason why she had come.

The wooden docks stood out on to the lake like fingers with several small boats and two larger ones. The small boats were for fishing near the dock and not built for far travel. They could maneuver quite well and with a crew of two or three, a fishing trip would be short and effective. The larger boats were definitely built for further travel. Each one had a main single mast that a sail was attached to. Each boat could carry at least ten and stay out from the city for several days. They weren't, however, anything like the boats at the Wizards guild on the top tier. Those were massive, with several masts, catapults, ballista, and were able to not only avoid water travel and cruise through the air, but also travel through the planes. It was rumored that arcane wizard spell casters powered most of them, while those with psionic abilities powered others, then there were fewer that were powered by priestess casters, a few had elementals or demons or other such creatures bound to the craft, and finally a few but very rare drew on the very life force of sacrificed individuals. These boats at the docks, however, didn't have such a privilege of any of them. Although a simple spell could help move them, they were usually powered the old fashioned way, by rowing.

On the dock were several boxes, barrels, crates, netting material, fishing material, oars, and other items Medri could only hazard a guess. Among the items there were several dark elves working. Some were moving the containers, others were filling them, some were tending the nets and some were just returning from a fishing trip with one of the smaller boats. They had brought in a good haul of underground blindfish and their nets were full of squirming life waiting to be beheaded, de-scaled, and gutted.

Medri scanned the docks for the male she was looking and found him in no time. Rrosa Veldruk was a short and heavy stock dark elf male. His white hair was cut short, either to keep it out of the way, or to have less to wash the fish stench out of. His working leather outfit was cracked, old and torn in many places showing its age and wear, similar to the male who wore it. His face showed his maturity with wrinkles and scars from either hazards of the job or from old battle wounds that left him worthless to stay in the favor of any house. Despite his lack of appeal, Medri could see that he hadn't lost his touch in commanding the docks he was now in charge of.

"No, no, no. Put the fish over there and the eels over there. Hurry it up, we haven't got all night."

"Rrosa, it's a pleasure as always," Medri cried out to him.

Rrosa stopped in mid stride. He recognized the voice and talking to Medri was the last thing he wanted to do today.

"Medri, I wasn't expecting you", he said dryly. "You know it's a pleasure." Rrosa folded his arms and turned his head slightly the other way of Medri. It was a dark elf gesture. The arms were away from any weapons and the eyes away from an opponent, it meant trust, or as far as trust could be given from one dark elf to another.

Medri caught the tone in his voice. She knew that no male wanted to be stopped and questioned from any female, even if they were allies and she had paid him handsomely.

"How is business?" She asked, as she walked over to a crate nearby Rrosa, her goblin behind her in tow.

"We are doing well."

Medri sighed. 'So it was going to be this game again', she thought as she pulled a few coins and placed them on the crate.

Rrosa eyed them hungrily. He made a move to pawn them, but Medri was faster. Her hand slapped down on all of the coins, fast enough to momentarily take Rrosa back.

"I know about the Aberrant."

An Aberrant was an aquatic eel like animal. It was up to thirty feet long and had four long tentacles, two on each side that ended with padded sections full of suction cups. They were an intelligent species of underworld waters, and were on par with plots and schemes as any dark elf. The Aberrant were capable of enslaving individuals to do it's bidding, and some of the more powerful ones could cast arcane magic. The foulest attribute of the Aberrant, Medri thought, was the mucus they produced through their suction cupped pads. Not only could the mucus turn a victim into a mutated aquatic version of itself, but it also ranked a horrible smell of rancid and rotting blubber. It was this smell that Medri had identified when she first arrived

"I ... don't know ..."

"Don't take me for a fool Rrosa. Your catch is better than it has been ... ever!" She had put an emphasis on the last word and started to raise her tone. "I know we are still on shaky ground with the Ichfey, so it has to be the Aberrant."

Rrosa's face went flush. She had obviously struck a nerve and her guess had proven correct. 'Twice in one night', she thought, in reference to shocking an individual to such a state, 'best I've done in quite some time.'

'There it was,' Rrosa thought. How she could have guessed, he would never know. He knew she was good and had connections, but he didn't realize she was this good or this well connected. He couldn't let her know about his association with the Aberrant. They were horrible creatures, but there was no way out. He couldn't lie to Medri now, she found out too much as it was, she might even have abilities to detect lies. She was also a female and had the authority to deal with any male she saw fit, even if she wasn't a priestess. Although he couldn't give her the whole story, he had to give her something.

"Ok, ok," he said hesitantly, putting his hands palm forward as if to keep her at bay. He caught his breath, turned away, and continued to speak to her. He just couldn't look her in the eyes.

"We meet an Aberrant a few days ago. At first we thought it would tear our boat to shreds. When it didn't we realized it wanted our help. The Selachii threatened its society. It was willing to trade fish for gems and coin to bribe the Ichfey to become their allies. We figured we would benefit, and hopefully all three species would wipe each other from the underworld."

'Spoken like a true dark elf,' Medri thought. 'Enough plots and twists with a hint of greed.' But she knew he was lying. The Aberrant never needed anyone's help, let alone from a non-aquatic humanoid. She could deal with Rrosa here and now without any resistance from anyone, but she knew Rrosa also knew that. This meant he was more afraid of something else than he was of her. It also meant that, whatever it was, it was nearby.

Medri took her hand off the coins and watched as Rrosa tentatively picked them up and placed them in his pocket. She nodded to him, pulled up her hood, and with her goblin on her heels, she headed toward a fish restaurant a few buildings down. She wouldn't get anything else out of him, at least not through traditional questioning, though what she did get spoke volumes. It wasn't in what he had said; it was what he hadn't. There was much to ponder.

She hadn't gone far when a slim smile came over her face. She stopped and turned toward the docks once more. She was found a shadow between buildings that made her practically invisible, but the dockworkers heat was a high contrast against the cool lake. She looked down the alleyway to make sure she wasn't noticed. Satisfied that she would not be seen, she started casting a spell.

The air got cooler, the heat drained, and the darkness of the underworld grew pitch black. The poor goblin at her side felt the minor effects of her spell casting, and although he was accustomed to the negative energy that flowed around him, he still felt like death was over his shoulder draining the very life of him and he was glad when she finally let loose the spell.

A large black sphere of negative energy rolled from her palms and rushed toward the dock. At first the dockworkers felt cold and a chill ran down their spines. Not an outside coldness, but it was as if something from their inside had just left, or some wraith had passed through them. They all stopped working and patted themselves down as if checking to make sure they were still all right.

After a brief moment, noticing nothing had changed, and a few comments of "evil spirits", they went back to work.

A scream from one of the dockworkers pierced the underworld. Another and then another cried out. Rrosa turned to see what had come over his deck hands. Two of them were slashing at the barrels of fish and eels with their short swords while a third was trying to pull something off of his face. Rrosa pull his short sword, but was stopped by a sound. The sound was something moving in his barrel of fish. He looked down at some of their new haul and found that the fish were alive. 'No', he thought, 'not alive … undead. The fish had come back as undead.' Rrosa raised his short sword and started to fend off the hungry zombie-like undead fish that started to throw themselves at him relentlessly. For every one he cut, two more took their place. Their sharp teeth gnashed at him and he continued to lose ground.

Medri smiled. She didn't like not having her heavily paid ally not being totally upfront. 'Perhaps this will remind him of his place,' she thought. Then again, she thought she might have done this anyway, even if he had been upfront. She was still a child of chaos and this was well worth the effort. She stayed and watched for a few moments, smiled, and continued her journey to the restaurant she had seen. Perhaps she would have the fish, then again, perhaps not.

As Medri turned, a large eel-like creature slightly rose to the surface of the lake, not too far from the docks. It had watched the whole scene play out. Its new ally in Rrosa had served it well and not mentioned the true meaning of their acquaintance, though it wondered if it would keep Rrosa around much longer.

'Perhaps after I see how he deals with his new situation', it thought. It changed its attention to Medri, watched her continue to disappear from its sight, and continued with its own conversation.

'That one is going to be trouble, she has stumbled on too much, and we need to deal with her tonight.'

Chapter: Leithivress

*M*edri had come to the docks to check up on the trading progress of a few of the houses, but the find of the connections with Aberrant far outweighed her curiosity of the income of her rivals. Her thoughts turned away from the excitement from only a few moments ago to the realization that she hadn't eaten an evening meal yet and she had wandered throughout most of the city just to find a passage to the docks.

The restaurant was called the "Leithivress" and was to her liking. It was nestled between two warehouses. The windows were barred with boards from giant mushrooms, the sign showing a dead fish was barely hanging on to its hinges, and the whole place looked like it might fall down during the next city transformation. Medri cautiously opened the door, being careful not to pull the whole thing off, and let herself in.

The entire inside was dark and dank. The tables were far away from each other and it would be easy enough to entertain a guest and hardly be noticed. Her heat vision picked up a couple of humanoids sitting in a corner, but couldn't make out what they were. She was sure that this place would be full of ruffians, assassins, thieves, and other houseless rogues except for the fact that the city's transformation had shifted this place beyond its last known locale. She slid into a small circular table that had four chairs around its perimeter, all of which were of different sizes and shapes. Although there were plenty of chairs, she had her slave kneel on the ground beside her.

A tavern waiter made his way toward her. His clothing looked as though the poor male had worked the whole day before, threw a large gala during the evening, and slept in them the rest of the night. His unkempt and unwashed hair gave the same impression and from the tone of his voice and demeanor, Medri believed she wasn't far from the truth. A greasy stained apron was worn over his shabby, dirty clothing, and Medri wondered why the waiter had bothered putting the apron on in the first place.

"Greetings Mistress, what may I ..." he stopped mid-sentence. "We don't serve their kind", he said firmly pointing toward her goblin slave. His restaurant may be home to the scum of the houseless rogues, but at least they were dark elves. He didn't allow any other species inside. They were the superior race and his establishment was going to remain exclusive to that fact.

The goblin rolled its eyes. Although this happened quite often, Medri would bring him into a place he was forbidden to enter just to flaunt her superiority; he was always uncomfortable with it. He was certain that there were dark elves out in the shadows that would kill him just to wipe the smug look off Medri's face. That wasn't a very pleasing thought. He was sure that Medri would raise him as an undead personal slave, and that wasn't a very pleasing thought either.

Medri glared up at the waiter. "I believe my house is above yours," she said dryly, "and I am a female. Are you, as a mere male telling me what to do? Are you, a lesser ranking house, telling me what I can or cannot do?"

The waiter stood in shock. Usually he could play the 'My Matron Mother will hear about this' Senet piece but Medri's house was higher rank.

"No, no Mistress. Please forgive me. I'll ..."

"You will bring me the special of the day and it will be on the house. If there are any problems with the food or service ..." She didn't finish the sentence and let it drop with the underlying hint of full retribution to the fullest extent of his imagination.

The waiter clenched his teeth and cinched his lips into a tight thin line, but he kept his composure. He bowed, said in a gravely humiliated voice "Yes Mistress", turned and left for the kitchen.

"That bowch Iblith!" he said aloud to the other dark elf, the cook, behind the kitchen door. "Who does she think she is, barging her way in here, telling us how to run this place, telling me what to do, demanding out best food? I have half a mind ..." his sentence was cut short.

The back door from the kitchen to the alleyway slammed open. Three amphibian humanoid creatures burst through and charged toward the waiter and cook. The cook already had a meat cleaver in one hand and was ready to defend himself while the waiter turned to his side and pulled out a butcher knife from a knife holder. They were just about ready to protect themselves and their business when they heard a powerful and gripping command.

"Stop!" The voice was more of a gurgle and hadn't come from the amphibians, but from a mental command beyond them.

It was as if another creature was using these creatures as an amplifier. As if the two dark elves no longer had a mind of their own, they halted where they were. A series of instruction came to them in their minds. They were to prepare the dish that their guest had ordered and then the both of them would deliver the order with the intention of using the very knives they had in their hands to chop her into small enough pieces as to no longer be identified. There was even a message on how the dockhands could use more chum for their fishing bait.

As the three amphibian creatures watched, the two dark elves went through the motions of making the meal. It was a deep fried fish with sautéed mushroom and onions coupled with a few select fruits, a rare treat in the underworld. When they had completed their culinary art, the both of them placed their selected pieces of cutlery behind their backs held by their belts, grabbed a bottle of their best wine and, in unison, walked the meal toward Medri.

Medri was so deep in thought in the various plots and twists she had uncovered today that they had closed half the distance to her before she become conscious to their presence.

'Great! He went to get back up. No doubt so they could both deal with me,' she thought, not realizing how far from the truth she was. It wasn't until they had almost reached her that she understood her suspicions to be more than accurate. The eyes of the two were too focused, their bodies too ridged, as if they were being controlled.

The waiter threw the plate of food at Medri and brandished his kitchen knife the same time the cook brought out his cleaver. Medri had ducked just in time to avoid her head from being smashed by the plate, but she knew it was a feint. As she ducked, she saw three shapes come from out of the kitchen with obvious intention to join the fray and the two in the corner coming to join them as well. She was terribly outnumbered, even with the help of her goblin, and already at a disadvantage at the beginning of the fight. Despite this, she smiled; she knew she only had to take down one of them.

She pulled herself into a ball and rolled away from the table. She got to her feet, watched as her goblin dove under the table and began to cast her first spell.

'Maybe I don't even have my slave to fight by my side', she thought as her arms wove through the air and her words formed the arcane sounds. Her spell went off and an armor made of bone crossed most of her body and made her look as if she were wearing a skeleton on her outside.

The three amphibians from the kitchen rounded one side of the table, the two from the corner rounded the other side and the cook and waiter tried to go over. The waiter was able to go over, but just before the cook had managed to get his body on top of the table, a thin green goblin hand reached from under the table where he had been standing, grabbed his leg, and pulled. The cook landed on the table with such a thump that she was certain that the mushroom wood had split. The goblin pulled again and again and finally dragged the panicked cook under the table. A scream followed, and Medri knew it wasn't a goblin scream.

One of the three on her left took a swipe with its fish-like hands and missed Medri; the second caught her in the mid-section and the blow was absorbed by the bone armor, and the third hit her on the thigh, drawing blood. She had already lost her breath when the two on her right hit her with a body tackle that took her down and pinned her to the floor. The waiter jumped from the table and landed on top of her, his knife dug in deep through her armor and into flesh and muscle. It was a deep wound; one that she would have to take care of immediately or this fight was over.

From the side of her piwfia, in a hidden pocket, she pulled out a small skull and slightly tossed it in the air. The skull exploded in a thunderous clap and shot bone fragments in all directions. Her own resistance to spells protected her from the effect, but her opponents weren't so fortunate. They rolled off the top of her, and found they had multiple splinter bone wounds all over.

She rolled to her feet and clutched her own wound. She just needed a little time, a little reprieve. As if the goblin had read her mind, a thin green goblin arm reached from under the table again and took hold of the waiter's ankle. The waiter lost balance and went face first into the floor. There was a sickening crack as his nose broke when he hit. But before the pain of the broken nose had registered, the goblin pulled the dark elf waiter under the table to join the fate of the cook; a fate that was confirmed with another blood curling scream and then silence.

The others were caught off guard by the last few events, which gave Medri time for two things. The first was for her to realize that the two in the corner were the same species as the three amphibians from the kitchen. This was key, only dark elves had innate resistance to spells, these creatures didn't. The second was for her to cast another spell. With one hand still holding her wound, she began to cast with her other. Red streams shot out in all directions, touching each wound of her opponents. Their wounds glowed bright red and the slimy creatures howled in pain. She smiled. She knew that she only needed to kill one of them and the goblin had already taken out two. She was one piece ahead on the Senet board and now she needed to put them into play.

Her hands gestured again and at first, nothing seemed to happen. The creatures had stopped their cries of agony and recouped themselves. They attempted to make another charge at their opponent when the table from where the goblin had been hiding burst into the air. The dead bodies of the cook and waiter, each holding their kitchen cutlery, stood lifeless as undead abominations of themselves.

The undead cook went one way and attacked the set of three. His cleaver found the neck of one of them and sliced him wide open. His weapon cut through flesh, muscle and bone. Blood vessels were severed and blood shot in spurts as the body fell to the ground. A puddle of red pooled around the dead body. Meanwhile the waiter went for the set of two, found his first mark on its arm and drew blood.

The amphibians went from the offensive to an attempt at being counter offensive by switching their attacks to their newly perceived threat, the undead dark elves. One of the humanoids was already dead from its neck wound, but the others grabbed at their zombies and pulled them to the ground.

Medri started her weaving again, this time she let loose a sphere, black as the abyss and the size of a skull. It floated upward and settled in place halfway up to the ceiling. All of the inhabitants could feel the cold drain the heat from their bodies. This however, was not Medri's ambition. To the horror of the four remaining humanoids, the zombies started to heal and regain strength while the most recently slain amphibian pulled itself off the floor. Blood continued to drain from its throat as it attacked its nearby brethren.

The remaining opponents tried to fend off the zombies but found themselves at a stalemate. Both sides gave and received blow after blow, although the zombies continued to heal from the negative energy given off by the sphere overhead. One of the amphibians decided to switch tactics and turned its back on the zombie it was trying to defend against and went to attack Medri instead. Medri was already prepared. She had pulled out a small, straight, thin bone and threw it at her opponent. The bone grew into a four-foot long bone spear and impaled the creature through its stomach. Blood and bone spurted out the other side and its entrails started to leak out its front. Before it had a chance to fall, the negative energy from the black sphere triggered its undead transformation and it fell back into battle, this time under Medri's control.

Medri watched as one by one the creatures fell to her ever-increasing army of zombies, until there was one left. It held one hand in place on an open wound and she watched as it tried to hold on to its life. It muttered something, but it was too weak to hear what it said. She raised her hand, halted the attack of the zombies, and approached the creature. Only now did she realize that these creatures had the same rancid blubber smell she had smelled earlier, but it didn't really come to any surprise. She put a hand on its slimy skin. Immediately it could feel its very life being drained from its body. It tried to put an arm up to protest, but its strength failed. With each passing second, the creature became weaker and Medri became stronger. Its cheeks caved in, its skin withered away, its muscles rotted and finally its bones turned to dust. At the end of the spell a pile of ash laid at Medri's feet and her wound was completely healed.

Medri's goblin came out of its hiding place. It did its job and then stayed out of the way, he knew better. His devotion to her wasn't out of compassion, but out of self-preservation. If she died then he would be someone else's slave and he probably wouldn't last very long. He had found the dropped bottle of wine; the only remains of her ordered dinner, then walked over to Medri and handed it to her.

She popped the cork and smelled. It was a pungent and very strong mushroom wine. She tilted her head back as she put the bottle to her lips and took a big swig. It burned all the way down. After wiping her lips with the back of her hand, she waved her fingers and let all of her spells discontinue. The black sphere disappeared, the bone armor went away, and the undead zombies fell lifeless at her feet. She took the bottle and twisted her wrist slightly and let the remaining portion of the bottle drain all over the corpses that littered the area. Medri dropped the bottle and walked toward the kitchen, which she figured had a back door. A few steps from where she started, she halted, took out a fire stick, lit it, and tossed it over her shoulder. Without looking back, she continued forward and felt the heat rise from the flamed carnage. She didn't know if the fire would spread to the whole building, and she didn't care. Her dinner was ruined and she was hungry.

'Perhaps fish wasn't the best idea for tonight's meal', she thought.

She smiled and thought about the mystery meat vender she had met up with earlier as she entered the kitchen and then thought better of it. She found several dried meats, some bowch cheese, and some exotic fruits from the surface and placed them in her backpack. A short search yielded a fine wine, which she also pocketed. She was considering what else she could take when the smell of burning flesh came through the kitchen door. She decided it was time to leave and she walked out the back door with her goblin in tow.

Out on the lake a big eel like animal slightly surfaced. Its small beady eyes took in the scene. It had felt and watched every move and now its scum and its enslaved dark elves were dead. It would have to be more cunning next time, it thought, and slowly submerged into the lake once again.

Chapter: Apothecary

*I*t took longer than expected for Medri to find her next stop, a shop called "Detholar Dosst Elg'cahl", or "Elg'cahl" for short. She had walked by a procession from Olath Orbben, the second house of the ruling council. It was obvious that the house wanted to parade its members around the city to show their power and their authority to a community that had just underwent its transformation. This wasn't uncommon, since the ruling council members were usually not very confident in their own iron fist rule in the first place. And, like all dark elves, they were highly suspicious of any conspiracy that might arrive, even if it were in their own minds. There were guards in their royal outfits with long swords, hand crossbows and neatly polished armor and shields that reflected the various fey fires from one building to the next. Large ogres, unarmored and unarmed, flanked the guards and pushed bystanders aside if they were too close to the procession, and even pushed a few to the ground just for the fun of it. There were also two high priestesses with their adamantite chain mail, shields, heavy maces and their snake whips. A crack from one of the snake whips from a priestess had sent a poor orc to the ground clutching at his poison wounded arm and Medri doubted the creature would live. Finally, in the middle on a floating disk, was the Matron Mother of house. Medri didn't know her name. She thought the Matron had looked younger since the last time Medri had seen her. 'Then again', she had thought, 'this could be one of the daughters who had risen to power'. The parade had slowed her time and caused such a blockage of pedestrians that she wondered if she would be able to get to the shop she was looking for before it closed.

When she had finally arrived at "Elg'cahl" she recognized it by the signpost outside showing a beaker with a glowing green fluid. She thought the owner to highly imaginative by using green fey fire to highlight just the painted liquid to actually make the substance glow. Its windows were already closed and she was sure they were barred on the inside. She also was sure that the door would be locked. It was already late and the store was closed. She merely smiled, as if the time of day or the inconvenience of others had nothing to with her, and pulled out the same bone key she had used in her bedroom, the same one she would have used in Drada's room had her sister not bashed the door down for her. She placed the key in the keyhole and muttered a few words. Her key turned and there was a slight click. With satisfaction, she replaced the key, opened the door and entered.

The smell of the apothecary hit her strong. The scents were pungent, acidic, and rotten all at the same time.   Inside were assorted shelves around the walls at various places. They were filled with crystal, glass, metal, and clay jars some of which were labeled; some were see-through to reveal their contents, and others she could only guess. There were herbs, crystals, roots, and insects, body parts of different species, gasses and liquids. One of the eyes floating in an unknown liquid moved toward her as she entered and stared at her relentlessly. A skeleton of some other planar creature stood in the corner. It could have been almost any other humanoid except for the fact that it had four arms.

The male dark elf behind the counter was on a stool with his head lowered intently close to the mortar and pestle he was working with. It was obvious he had been in the middle of making another of his potions. His mortar had a few select minerals, some plant segments, and a little bit of animal parts all in a powder form that he had crushed together. Medri couldn't see how the businessman was dressed, but she knew him well enough to know his clothing would be in good taste. The only view of him she could see was the top of his head. His white hair had fallen out in a bald spot so the only hair he did have made a ring around the backside of his head from ear to ear. What he didn't have on the top of his head, he made up with a long well-kept ponytail. A curtain covered archway lead into an adjacent back room behind him.

"We're closed, it's late", the patron said without even bothering to look up to see Medri as she opened the door. A small bell above the door rang as she entered and gave away her presence. There was a short pause from the business caretaker, before he dared to repeat himself. He had hoped the intruder would leave before he would have to throw the interloper out. He did have ways to defend himself and his shop; ways that were not only effective, but also that left any intruder in tacked well enough to add to his collection of the macabre.

"I said we are closed. How did you get in here … ", he stopped his sentence short as he looked up and saw Medri for the first time since she walked into his shop.

"Hello Xindarl", Medri said with a grin on her face as she casually perused his wares.

"Medri! What a surprise to see you".

That was the second time she had heard her presence as a surprise. She hoped that this time her meeting didn't echo the scene at the docks or the restaurant. She smiled and made her way toward him, feigning interest in his merchandise. A few of his items would make a fine addition to her set of ingredients, but that wasn't the reason she was here. She continued to feign her interest until an odd object did catch her attention. In one of the large jars was a tuber, a root that looked very much like a small ugly humanoid. She picked up the jar and raised her eyebrows.

"It is mandrake," Xindarl said, "part of the nightshade family of plants from the surface. It usually is formed in the shape of a humanoid, but why they call it a "man" instead of some other bipedal creature is beyond me. I can't even imagine what association it has with dragons, none that I can tell at least. It has hallucinogenic qualities and is very poisonous. I can get you a good deal on it, if you would like. I acquired it from a gnome that grows them. "

Medri knew what Xindarl meant when he said he had "acquired" the plant. She doubted he had even seen the gnome, or if there was a gnome at all. She was sure there had been a raiding party that found these in a store or on a traveling merchant train and had left all the original owners dead. Xindarl wasn't one to go on such raids, he was a businessman, and a cunning one at that, but he wasn't a fighter. Even the wand of rotting he carried behind his counter didn't concern her, she was sure he was a bad aim.

She smiled at him for his information. She would have to purchase this at another time, but for now she had more pressing matters. She put the jar back and closed the gap to Xindarl so only the counter stood between the two of them. She leaned on the counter with both hands to support her weight as she drew closer to Xindarl.

"How is Agrong?" She asked.

"Who?"

Medri sighed. It was like this every time. None of her allies ever gave her a straight answer right off. Her goblin, which had remained indiscriminately by her side, had shifted uncomfortably at the salesman response. He knew Medri would deal with this one as well as she had with all of the others.

Medri glared at him. She didn't want to lose an ally but she was no longer in any mood to continue this form of banter. Agrong was a deep dwarf, an underworld dwarf, similar to the surface world dwarves. Unlike their surface cousins, they were bald and beardless, it was rumored that this applied even to their females. She had met him when she was doing one of her own scouting expeditions through the underworld.

On her way to find various plants and minerals for her collection, she hadn't traveled too far from the city when she had heard a muffled cry of pain. She drew a bone dagger, snuck through the shadows, and hid behind an outcropping of rocks. After her short journey, she came across a deep dwarf on the side of the tunnel. A small cave-in had occurred and his legs were pinned under rubble and by the looks of things, he had been there for quite some time.

When he came to realize that a dark elf had found him, he closed his eyes and resolved himself to the death that would follow. To his surprise, the female dark elf started to dig him out. After a few minutes of hard physical labor, his legs were free, but one of his hands was crushed beyond use.

"You are free to go." She had told him in a controlled and commanding voice.

"Bah, an wha's the use? Me hand is crushed, can't work no more. See? Anything I make would be nothing but scrap. Might as well as leave me here." It was obvious to Medri that it was more than the deep dwarf's hand that had been crushed; it was his spirit as well. His whole sense of being, his whole purpose, seemed to be beyond repair.

Medri knelt beside the deep dwarf and look at him. She could kill him off now and save the time of starvation and then raise him as an undead. A deep dwarf undead with a broken hand wouldn't work very well. She thought for a moment and then smiled. She revealed a plan that only a dark elf could come up with. She remembered that the spider queen had a massive metal structure at one time. When the spider queen retreated deeper into the abyss for reasons beyond anyone's understanding, she left her structure behind and over time it had turned to scrap. He would indeed go back to work and indeed make scrap. She would help him to make the pitch that the scrap was from their Goddess, the Spider Queen, and all he had to do was make an endless supply of it. Agrong had agreed; mainly to make sure he could get back to his home safely and not fall into some dark elf torture chamber. He was surprised when Xindarl came to his forge one day to collect scrap and was shocked beyond his wildest beliefs that the dark elf had actually come back a few days later with a large sum of coins to pay him for more.

Xindarl was the connection, the in-between retailer who helped pawn the scrap metal and she came here on a regular basis to collect her share. She was sure Xindarl was skimming off her profits, but it didn't matter. She would bargain down his best sales price and use her profits to get her ingredients for free.

"Oh, that Agrong." Xindarl emphasized and drew out the word "that" as if to say there were far too many with such a name that he had hadn't realized which one she was talking about.

"His business is doing well and he wanted to make sure you received your portion of the profits." Xindarl placed his hand under the counter and reached for a coin purse. The small bag was next to a wand he purchased some time ago to deal with anyone he felt needed dealing with. Although Medri was a good and regular customer, the income from Agrong could be his alone if she were no longer around. For a moment, his hand slid over the wand. Then doubt crept in. What if he missed? What if her resistance shrugged off the effects? A merchant was only worth the income he could bring in and a dead merchant was only worth something to someone else. His hand left the wand in its place and he pulled the coin pouch from under of the counter and set it beside her hand.

With her left hand Medri picked up the bag, felt its weight and thought it to be satisfactory. Her little scheme had paid off for everyone involved, and if she continued, there would be plenty more where that came from. She tied the bag strings around her belt.

"Have you heard?" Xindarl asked.

Medri looked at him questionably.

"There was a fire down at the docks. A restaurant had burned down. The local guards believe that a grease fire due to the transformation earlier today started it. A pity. I really liked the place."

Medri knew Xindarl too well. Not only would Xindarl not go on raiding parties, but also he wouldn't enter an establishment as the Leithivress. He was digging for information and she was sure he had made a connection between her and her ally on the docks. She shrugged and looked disinterested, hoping that her non-reply would let him know that she wanted the matter dropped. She doubted she could lie to him without him understanding what she really meant. The best she could do was to drop a subtle hint that the conversation was over.

"The mandrake. How much?"

"Twenty"

"Ten", she replied

"Fifteen", he said and met her halfway.

"Seven"

"What about your offer of ten?"

"Ten it is then."

"You know that is robbery", he accused. He acted hurt to her haggling him down this low, but it was really all an act. They had played this game every time and he never got tired of it.

"You obtained this for free. Anything I give you is a profit, so don't act so wounded. While you're at it, there are a few other items I would like as well."

After several minutes and some more haggling, she had picked up quite a few things, which she paid with her share of profits. The whole transaction went better than she expected and she believed she even came out a little bit ahead. Saving the deep dwarf's life was worth more than killing the poor creature. After a few more pleasantries she turned toward the front door and opened it to leave.

'It just isn't my day', she thought as she took in the sight. A large spider, with a height that was half her size, had taken the spot in front of the door to rest. It was obsidian black and, from Medri's recollection, was very poisonous. It had huddled its legs under itself and blocked the exit. She remembered the saying about 'letting sleeping spiders lay' and closed the door again. Although she wasn't one who detested spiders or even had a fear of them, far from it, she just found their constant presence to be an inconvenience. They took up residence wherever they felt like and it was by the will of the spider queen that they stayed, undisturbed. She sighed and clicked her tongue in frustration. There was just no getting around this arachnid.

"I'll just use your back door", she said to Xindarl as she walked toward the curtain-covered archway behind him. He raised an eyebrow as if to question her decision, but he knew better than to ask aloud. She may be an ally, a good customer, and her scheme is making him rich, but she was still a female and he still knew his place.

"You have a friend who decided to camp out for the night on your front door." She answered his unspoken question, although she knew she didn't have to. Xindarl nodded and then tilted his head toward the curtain as if he gave a direction to where the back door was. Then he remembered that she had used the back door several times and knew quite well where it was.

Medri pulled back the curtain to reveal the adjoining chamber. It wasn't very wide, only a few strides, but it was long enough and served its purpose as a general catch all for over stock of supplies. The shelves were wider with larger jars on them. There were also barrels and crates scattered about. To her right she saw a table with a dead orc on top. It was cut open to reveal its entrails and Medri wondered what use Xindarl could have with this poor creature. In front of her, a few steps away, was the back door, a door she had used quite frequently. She turned the handle and stepped out with her goblin right behind her into the alleyway, and as the door closed it locked itself behind her.

The alley was only ten feet wide before it bumped up against another building, but it did turn left and right. To Medri's right she could see where the alley ended and opened into a main street. This option was ruled out immediately since halfway between where she was and the street was a large spider web that blocked the passage with a massive spider in the center. Medri sighed, shook her head and turned toward her left. She could tell that the alley went quite some distance and its exit was beyond her field of vision.

She had only gone a few strides when two male guards came out of the shadows to block her way. They had hidden behind a few crates to keep their body heat from being picked up. Now, they were clear against the cool air. She could tell by the heat signature of their house symbols that they were from House Olath Orbben and she could tell from the swords in their hands that they meant to kill her. She had no knowledge that she had upset House Olath Orbben, but then there never had to be a reason for an assassination. She knew she had to be at her best since these were trained killers and not a waiter, a cook, or some amphibian fresh from the water. They approached with murder in their eyes and death in their hands.

Medri had already cast several spells today and she was running out and these guards were trained to shrug off spells so she knew she had to think of something else and fast. She unsheathed her bone dagger in one hand and her hand held crossbow in the other. The two guards closed in quicker than she could come up with an idea. The first guard brought his two swords to bare, the first one missed and the second one cut across her arm as she tried to move to her other side. She knew the attack to be a distraction since the two of them attacked in tandem. She was now in position for the second guard to sneak through her defenses. One of his swords came high toward her neck. She just barely had time to duck when his second caught her in the thigh. Her leg gave way and she was nearly in a kneeling position.

As she put her hand to the ground to hold her balance she conjured up her innate ability to conjure a darkened area around her. She then shot her hand held crossbow at the last position known of one of her assailants while she moved back and to her right. She knew that they would attack the spot she was just in so she wanted to make sure she was no longer there. Sure enough she heard the four swords cut through the air and knew if she hadn't moved that she would have died right there on the spot.

She started to cast another spell. The goblin, which had enough smarts to stay out of this fight and stay behind his mistress, could feel the familiar dark energies swirl around him. This time however, the energies started to take shape. He knew this spell and didn't have to see through the darkness that was put up by Medri to know what was about to happen. When he thought that death had breathed down his shoulder before, he knew now that it was about to take shape.

The darkness formed together and created tentacles, thick black appendages that sprang out of thin air. It was similar to another weaker spell. Not only did this spell have tentacles that attacked, held, and squeezed, but it also drained the very life of its victims. The entire area erupted in movement with the slimy appendages and a few of them caught the first guard by the ankle. He turned his attention to try to cut off the first tentacle, but another caught a wrist, then another wrapped around his waist and finally one went around his throat. He could feel his life start to drain from him immediately. His body flailed and twisted as the tentacles' pulled and moved about. His life drained, his body shrank, his flesh fell off, his muscles fell limp, and his bones withered away to nothingness. When the whole encounter was over the only thing that remained of the guard were his gear and a pile of dust.

As the life drained from the first guard, Medri could feel some of his life energy enter her and her wound healed. She was down one opponent and now had to face the other. The second guard had made his way ahead of the tentacles and was now out of their reach. He took a powerful swing with one of his swords but her quick movement that brought her bone dagger up to a parry blocking it. Although the blow was stopped the damage was done. His blow was so hard that Medri's bone dagger broke. Instead of breaking in half as the guard had expected, the dagger blew up in a thousand shards into his face. He dropped both of his swords and reached for his eyes as he howled in pain.

The goblin didn't wait for an invitation. He charged the dark elf guard and plowed into him, knocking the both of them to the ground. With his opponent prone, the goblin brought up both of his hands and started to strangle him. The guard didn't know what to do first, try to remove the bone fragments in his eyes or try to remove the hands that were around his neck. The goblin saw the dark elf try to struggle and decided to put an end to that. He used all of his might as he pulled guard's head up and pounded it into the ground. Time and time again he pulled back and slammed the head of his opponent until he heard a loud crack that signaled the breaking of the guard's skull and the end of his life.

Medri put a hand on the goblin's shoulder to let him know he had done well and that the fight was over.

'The fight might be over, but this battle has just begun. I've been set up from my first move,' she thought to herself as she scanned the battlefield. The black tentacles had faded to nothingness, one body was still at her feet and the gear of the other one was exposed for all to see. She thought about rummaging through their gear and taking what she could but then thought against it. Some of these items could by magically detected and it would not bode well to be caught with items from the second most powerful house in the entire city. She looked around and then saw the spider at the other end of the alleyway again and smiled.

Both she and the goblin dragged the body and all of the gear from both of the guards down the alley to the base of the spider web. With a little help from her goblin slave, Medri was able to pick up the guard and place him the webbing and was mindful not to get caught in it as well. The spider sensed its new prey and immediately started to wrap the body in its webbing. When they had finished, the sight was staged to look as if the guards had fallen prey to the monstrosity of the spider.

After setting the stage, her mind turned toward Xindarl. It was too convenient that the front door was blocked. She walked to the apothecary's back door and took out her bone key. After she placed it in the keyhole, she said a few magic words and turned the key. The familiar click told her that the lock was undone. She entered and wondered how she was going to deal with Xindarl since most of her spells were gone and bone dagger had been destroyed.

"Xindarl! Xindarl, show yourself" she said with a raised voice that only echoed back to her as she entered the back room. There was silence. She walked the few paces of the room and flung open the curtain. "Xindarl!"

The first thing she noticed was the absence of the apothecary. The shopkeeper probably had run off, but for what reason? Why was she set up? Then her senses registered the rest of the room. All of his possessions were gone. All the jars, beakers, containers, boxes, and even the skeleton in the corner were all gone. She did a quick look in the back room and came to the realization that this room was completely empty as well; she was so absorbed in her initial entry that she didn't even notice its lack of supplies that it had earlier. The crates were gone, the barrels were gone, even the dead orc was gone. She rushed behind the counter in the main room and looked under it for Xindarl's wand but it was also gone. Xindarl simply did not have the time to clear everything out.

She opened the front door and noticed that the spider had already cleared itself from blocking the entrance. She decided that looking for answers here was simply asking for trouble and determined it was better to think out this evening's events on the way home. She did a quick glance back into the empty room that had only recently been full of items she would have loved to fill her inventory with, shook her head, and headed back to her stalactite structure she called home.

Chapter: Valenci

Xindarl heard the back door close and was glad Medri had left. He had a few things to do before he headed home. She was good business, but she was still a female and a necromancer. He knew some of his supply was bizarre, strange, atypical, odd, abnormal, and downright extra ordinary; it was what she could do with those items that really scared him. If only she knew how much he was skimming off of her profits. He was glad she didn't know or his body parts might end up in his own inventory. He went back to his mortar and pestle and continued to mix and grind his ingredients when he heard his front door bell go off again.

"We're closed." He said for the second time that evening, twice too many by his count. He was about to look up to see who had picked the lock and entered this time when a wave of raw power shot through his mind. The room spun and he dropped his pestle as his body rocked from the mental blast that had entered his head. Before his body had time to hit the ground he watched as a rubbery light purple hand grabbed him by the neck. Xindarl could barely get his bearings to identify the creature in front of him, but he was fairly certain what was about to happen and he was powerless to stop it. His guess was confirmed when two tentacles sprang through his nose and threatened to penetrate deep into his brain. Two more tentacles wrapped around the base of his head while a couple more wrapped around his body.

'You have a choice Xindarl'. The voice was alien in nature and wasn't something he heard with his ears but something that was in his head. The Id Scourger was close enough that he could make out every feature of it. From what Xindarl remembered, the Id Scourgers were from a different plane of existence or perhaps they were just another world. They were an evil, sadistic race that enslaved all creatures they could get their hands on and thought that they were the superior race to all species. 'Such arrogance for a species to have', Xindarl once thought, but then laughed at the irony of his own thought process when he compared the Id Scourgers to dark elves who had similar arrogance.

No one knew exactly how the Id Scourgers came to be, but their foreign existence was publicized in their physical features. They were almost the same size as a human, a little taller than a dark elf, but thinner and frail looking. Each hand had five long bony fingers. Many Id Scourgers dressed in mage-like garments that flowed on the ground so no one knew exactly if they walked on any legs at all or merely floated on the ground. On its shoulders rested an oversized head that resembled more of a six tentacle squid or octopus than one would normally find on any humanoid body. Not that Xindarl knew what either an octopus or a squid looked like, but he guessed they would look similar in nature to the head that was in front of him now. The Id Scourgers alien brain was capable of blasting its enemies with a mind stunning discharge at quite the distance and only those of very strong will was able to bare a hit from one of those blasts. The Id Scourgers were also capable of charming its victims, traveling through the planes, reading minds, and worst of all, pulling brains out with their tentacles and feasting on them. The Id Scourger's bloated black orbs of eyes meet Xindarl's and it didn't have to speak, didn't even have to mind speak, to get the message across that Xindarl's brain was next on the menu.

'I am Valenci, and I will acquire your service.' The thought entered Xindarl's mind easily enough.

'At least it didn't say that it will acquire my brain', Xindarl thought, but then realized that the Id Scourger was listening to his own thoughts and the push of the tentacles deeper into his nose reminded him of that fact. Xindarl squirmed only momentarily, his heart raced beyond his comprehension and sweat broke out over his body, but the Id Scourger halted before he killed Xindarl.

'Your city is close to all of the ingredients I am looking for. It was a perfect spot to recommend to your scouting party a year ago. Now that you have settled, I have found the individuals that will do my bidding, and you are one of them. Your choice is rather or not you agree with my assessment of your abilities. If you find yourself lacking, then I will have no further use for you being alive. I am looking for someone to gather ingredients, secure them, prepare them and mix them in such a delicate fashion as per the instructions I have carefully researched and labored over.'

Valenci took out a scroll with his free hand and rolled it out on the table as if to show Xindarl its contents. The scroll was filled with ingredients and instructions and had Xindarl been able to move his head he would have been able to guess that this was a very complicated potion. Valenci then pulled out a second scroll. It was a map of great detail showing a passage to a well-hidden cavern. The cavern had several smaller caverns attached to it.

'You will reside here', Valenci said in reference to the set of caverns on his map. 'It is well hidden, away from any known passages, and highly defensible. You will have a small contingent of guards that you can find from your city's array of houseless rogues.' Xindarl could hear a bag of coins hit the counter. 'This will compensate and persuade them and there will be more to come. So your choice is this: will you or will you not give your service? Have I overestimated your ability and in so doing wasted my time?'

Xindarl knew what the real question was. He knew it was either work for this Id Scourger or die. As he put this thought process together, he remembered that the alien could read his mind very easily. Valenci made no move, no action to give away that he had heard those thoughts. This let Xindarl understand he had a short time to think about his predicament, but it was only a short time. Earlier he had thought Medri would never leave, and perhaps never come back, now he wished she had stayed, or at least would soon return.

'Don't worry about her'. Valenci's mind entered his again. 'I was employed to deal with her and I have done so. I guarantee that she will not be coming back. It was convenient for my own purpose as well; I don't need a competent necromancer getting involved in my affairs. And since I will ensure her "mission" is a success even without her, her presence will not be missed. Now, your time is over. I require an answer.'

"Yes, yes I will serve you." The answer came easier than he had expected, but then again since he was so close to death he realized this was really his only answer.

Valenci released his grip on his new potion maker. With a mere flicker barely evident on his face, he sent a mental command. The door to the apothecary burst open and in flew a dozen or so imps. These small red and black humanoid creatures had leathery bat wings and a poisonous spiked tail, like a scorpion, and they all swarmed in with amazing speed and agility. Each creature took an object, flew out the door and flew back in again. For the larger items several imps had to work in unison and it was only a short amount of time that imps had stripped the shop clean before they all flew out the door for the last time.

Valenci guided Xindarl out his door and through a blue glowing circle placed just outside. Xindarl knew a dimensional portal, a traveling gateway bridging one location to another, when he saw one. He knew the travel would be safe, his fear wasn't the travel but his destination. He swallowed hard, entered, and the dimensional portal closed behind the both of them taking him away from his shop that he would never see again.

Chapter: The Tower

*T*he dimensional portal opened to an area near the mushroom fields. At this time of hour and at the back of the fields near the cavern wall between two stalagmites where they were, Xindarl knew they would not be seen and nor would the forty foot tower that was between the stalagmites. It was smooth and black like obsidian and had no apparent doors or windows. From what Xindarl could tell all the imps had already entered, but he could not tell how they had done so.

Valenci guided Xindarl the several paces to the nearest wall of the tower. As they approached the tower a portion of the wall opened like a door. No words had been said, no magic item was activated and the tower itself hadn't been touched, it merely opened on its own as if it simply created a door. Xindarl guessed that once it closed behind them it would be seamless once again.

The door opened to an intersection of two hallways. One went left and right the other went straight ahead. The whole of the interior was lit from the ceiling as if the ceiling itself was the source of the light but Xindarl could not discern its true origin. The light was dim but bright enough for him to see down each hallway. To his left and right he could see a door set in the middle of each wall where it gave access to what Xindarl could only guess to be store rooms. The imps flew in and out of these doors carrying items, and rearranging supplies. Valenci ignored the bisected hallway and went ahead a short distance to the end of the forward hallway.

Without even a pause, Valenci continued to walk into the dead end, and at the last moment, a section of this wall opened. Xindarl followed as Valenci entered the next chamber, an empty square room. By the layout and size of the tower Xindarl suspected that this was a center room. The door closed behind him and another opened to his left and lead into another room.

Here Xindarl observed that most of the room held machinery. He had heard of delicate machinery in clockwork structures or even mechanical appendages, but these large, bulky things were beyond his comprehension. They were huge, smelled of grease, dirt, grime, and another odor he couldn't place. To his surprise, the machines ran very quietly and didn't give any evidence on their true function. Valenci glanced at a few gauges, tapped them to insure their readings were correct, and then moved to an adjacent wall on the right that gave way to yet another seamless door.

The room beyond was full of large tanks, tanks round enough to hold an ogre and almost as tall as the ceiling. Each tank was a transparent material that wasn't glass or crystal or anything he could compare it with. Inside every one of them was a liquid, a light green liquid that smelled briny. On top of each tube was a metal topper with a connecting hose linking all the tanks and then ran back to the machinery room. Inside one of the tanks was an unconscious naked male dark elf, floating in the greenish liquid in a standing position. In the middle of his forehead was a blue gem as if it were impaled through his skull and into his brain. Xindarl shuddered at what experiments the Id Scourger had in store for this poor soul.

Valenci approached this tank and studied it. Xindarl wasn't sure if he was trying to communicate with the dark elf inside or if he had made sure the tank was working properly, or both. Whatever Valenci had done, it didn't take him long and he turned to another wall on his right that revealed another door. This one led them back to the small center room.

After the wall closed itself behind them Xindarl felt a movement as if the room had moved upward. He was sure he was in a room that elevated between the floors of the tower. At one spot he received a mental picture of the layout of the floor. He suspected Valenci was showing him what he needed to know to get around if the need ever so arose. The second floor, Xindarl found through the images, held a kitchen, a dining room, a dry storage for food goods, and a cold storage. He was sure the cold storage was either magically kept cold through some sort of artifact item or through the machinery from below. Either way it was cold enough to keep meats frozen.

At the third level he received another set of images of the floor. It had a small library, an alchemist room, a study hall, and two storage chambers with various ingredients. The library was smaller than the public library he knew at Anarchia but much larger than any personal library he had ever known. The alchemy room was full of beakers, tubes, and various other devices for measuring and testing results. The two chambers held ingredients similar to his own shop, but at a much larger scale and he was glad this tower didn't stay in Anarchia and do business or else his business would have been driven out a long time ago. But his shop was now in the past and he doubted he would ever see it again.

The elevating room stopped at the next level. Like the other times it had before, the wall opened and formed a seamless door, which the both of them stepped through. He didn't get any mental images of this level, but he did get a feeling that the room he was about to enter was the only room on this level that he was allowed to have access. This room had only one piece of furniture, a singular leather chair. Across the whole side of the room ran a counter that was full of dials, diodes, switches, gages, and various instrumental controls. He figured that these controlled the machinery on the lowest floor. On each wall above the counter were windows, only these didn't look out to the city beyond, but instead seem to look at various other places or even planes. On one window he saw molten lava in a fiery place that held an iron city surrounded by an iron wall. On another window he saw nothing but white fluffy material that fell from the sky and swirled about in the foreground of a set of crystal like mountains.

Valenci took a seat in the chair and barely motioned. A few of the buttons blinked and Xindarl was left was a sense of an implosion, a sensation he had grown accustomed to whenever he traveled by teleportation. He knew this was beyond the teleportation of any wizard and even beyond the transportation of the sky ships that ran on arcane spells, and he also knew that he would never see his city again.

Chapter: Valas

Valas Velkyn had been watching the merchant caravan pull together. The inhabitants of Anarchia might be chaotic beyond the likes of even he preferred, but it appeared to him that when these citizens wanted to get something done, they seemed to pull their resources in an organized and speedy fashion. The locked carts of goods, ingredients, food, clothing, gold, gems, and various contracts were already lined up and it made him smile at the amount of worth sitting in front of him.

Valas was a male dark elf. He wore a tight black leather jacket with many pockets and straps and a set of black leather pants with similar design. The look was topped off with a set of black leather boots, soft enough to be quiet when needed but hard enough to make long journeys through the underworld. He also wore a piwafwi and a house symbol broach that held it in place just under his throat. Like all other dark elves, he had white hair, but unlike most, he kept his short. He didn't like having to fuss with it or having to keep it out of the way. His profession kept him moving and he wanted to be as unencumbered as possible. And what was his profession title exactly, he often wondered. He could be a rogue, thief, spy, assassin, or all of the above. It didn't matter as long as the pay was good. He smiled and thought himself above any of those titles. He was after all, the Leader of the House of Acquisitions from the city of Malzebowan.

House of Acquisitions was an interesting set of words for the house he lead. Yes, they were thieves, but they were also merchants and ensured all merchant caravans that reached their city of Malzebowan were well protected. Any merchant that came into his city would have his protection, for a fee of course. And those that selected the private safeguard of the inner walls of his household would spend their money on his goods or services first and the rest of their money in the city second. Those who did not buy the protection needed would fall victim to all sorts of nasty, evil, and vile activities and the merchandise would wind up in his stores.

He thought about the mission he was expected to do and payment in his coin bag. He was called in to see Matron Mother Elg'caress Barrindar, the ruling matron of house Barrindar, the second house in the ruling council of Malzebowan. She had made contact with a new rival city and made arrangements for Anarchia to send a merchant train through the underworld to establish a trade route in good faith. Valas had to control himself from laughing aloud when he heard the words "good faith" coming from the lips of Elg'caress and his suspicions were verified when she told him of the ambush that would happen. The contents of the merchant train would be hers. There was only one dark elf city worthy of the spider queens' attention and that was Malzebowan, the city of evil. His task was to ensure the merchant train reached a certain spot where the ambush would happen. The consequences of failure were the obvious threats of dungeon torture. Such threats were useless to him. He would either do his job and be paid handsomely for it or he wouldn't even bother to come back. The initial down payment of his service was substantial enough. He had estimated the time and supplies needed, and the dangers he would face and considered the payment to be more than adequate. He was even promised an item off of the merchant train of his choice, but he doubted that the Matron would let him choose. He would have to procure his choice of item ahead of time.

That was a long journey through the underworld and a few days ago. Now he sat on the roof of the stables of the riding lizards. The lizards were long, albino, big enough to put a saddle on, had a thick leathery skin, and was as dumb as any creature could get. The easiest command a lizard could follow was "stay", and sometimes it would do so even to the point of starvation. They also had suction cups their toes. This allowed the lizard to follow the contours of any cavern, even upside-down. These lizards would be the pack animals that would pull the carts or even be ridden on by some of those higher up in the hierarchy. At this time the animals were in their stable and fast asleep, oblivious to the long journey ahead of them.

All of his surveillance had made him hungry. He took from his backpack a few items he had procured throughout this city. It all started with a mushroom seller. The merchant was just starting to display his ware when Valas initially came upon him. A close inspection revealed the stand to be unstable and would fall at the first opportunity, and he was definitely an opportunist. Valas closed in on the merchant and feigned a stumble. He didn't stumble into the merchant; he knew a trick like that would be suspect. His stumble only came close, close enough for the merchant to take a step backward. Unfortunately for the poor merchant a female priestess, who was in a foul mood, clipped his shoulder, knocked him down, and in turn his stand full of mushroom came crashing to the ground. Valas had of course been a good citizen and helped the merchant gather his mushrooms, but not after collecting a few for himself.

The next vendor he came across was a one handed male selling some unknown pieces of meat. He could tell that most of the items were barely cooked or in such poor condition that not even a riding lizard would eat, but he could make out a few that were eatable. He guessed that even such a lowly creature as this cook could get lucky at some point. He was sure the cook was holding off on selling these for a higher price or even to keep them for himself. Valas waited. When he saw a fairly young and good looking female dark elf leading a slave goblin, he measured his opportunity. As the female bought her pieces of mystery meat on a stick and gave it to the goblin, Valas walked close enough to the stand to snatch the best pieces. Everyone had been busy with the transaction that he had procured his prize and was lost in the crowd before the transaction was finished.

He had thought about other items to add to a later dinner when he saw smoke rising in the distance. With the help of his magical boots, Valas jumped from rooftop to rooftop and made his way to a restaurant on fire by a fairly large lake. He had arrived just in time to watch two figures leave from the back door. We waited for a short bit, and when he was sure they were gone and could not see him, he entered the burning building. The air had gotten thin and the smoke had started to take over so Valas knew he had little time. With quick efficiency he was able to find a few bottles of wine and was out of the building before it crashed to the ground behind him. It was the thrill of near death that made him feel alive and he would savor the taste of the wine that much more because of it.

From the burning building he followed the lake and came across the docks where he figured he would continue his spree of procurement. However, when he approached he noticed the wounded dockhands were dumping their fish back into the lake.

When he asked why, they merely said it was a bad batch. A quick look revealed the fish to be rotten and he chalked his lose up to be more of a gain. As he left the dock he wondered if he should procure a chunk of bowch cheese to go with his meal items, but decided against it since he still had to find the caravan and settle for the meal he had already acquired.

Valas took the various food items from his pack and was almost done eating when he saw the parade of house Olath Orbben. He thought they had looked so humorous in all of their pomp and circumstance. Not only was arrogance a racial trait, but he also knew that it was usually taken beyond the rational. The parade only served to support his observations. As he watched he noticed that the last two rear guards had suddenly stopped. The rest of the parade was so absorbed in the display of haughtiness that no one else had noticed. The two guards seemed to wait until the rest of the parade had gone by and then they slipped into a nearby alley.

'No, they didn't seem to wait', Valas thought. That would imply conscious will. From what he had noticed was that these two had lost their will. He knew when someone was under the control of someone else, the muscles were too stiff, the eyes were too glazed, and their purpose was too focused. Valas waited and watched.

A short time after the parade, a female dark elf entered an apothecary that had initially been too crowded from the spectators to even find; but by the time she had entered the building, the streets were practically empty. This wouldn't have naturally caught his attention except for the fact that a large spider came from around the same alley that the guards had disappeared into, sat at the front door of the apothecary, and settled down for the night. This was a set up if Valas had seen one, and he had seen plenty since he was usually the one to do the setting up.

A few minutes later the female tried to leave through the front door only to be blocked and then went back inside. Valas remembered the two guards that had gone down the alley and knew that if the apothecary had a back door then she would be ambushed and his suspensions were verified when he heard the closing of a door in the alley followed by the sounds of battle. His curiosity got the better of him, one of his few flaws, and he climbed down from his perch.

He followed the sounds of combat while he stayed in the shadows. After a few strides, while he kept his head down and his back to walls, he came to the corner of the alley and peered around it expecting to find the female fighting the two guards. When he did manage to see it, he knew she was in trouble, since two highly trained guards had outnumbered her and another large spider blocked her escape route. He decided to watch the outcome since he was always willing to watch yet another female dark elf fall in battle. Yet the outcome was a disappointment as well as a surprise when the female won the battle. When it was over, she moved the remaining body to the spider web to cover her battle and went back into the apothecary through its back door.

He turned back down the main street and thought he saw the remains of a light blue after effect of a dimensional portal. The spider in the front had already left and in a short time the female exited the apothecary and went down the street, more than likely on her way back home, he thought. Valas smiled. She had taken care of two things he had needed.

He turned back into the alley and approached the huge spider web. By its base was the gear of the two guards. Valas reached down and pulled a house symbol out of the pile. After removing his own house symbol, he replaced it with the one he recently picked up. Now he would be able to travel with the merchant train as a member of the second highest house without suspicion. He then produced a small case from one of his pockets and from there, pulled out a few small fine instruments. He kneeled by the back door and within a few seconds, used his skills to unlock the door and entered.

As he thought, the store was empty. If there were anything of value here then the female would definitely have taken it. It was obvious this place wasn't hers and the owner wasn't coming back anytime soon. He did need a place to stay the night, just a few hours of meditation in a safe, secure, locked room, and here was the perfect place. He would be done before the rest of the shops were open the next day and he would join the caravan without anyone ever being the wiser. He found a place between the back of the counter and the wall, hidden and well protected with his back against the wall and went into his meditation. He had a long day ahead of him tomorrow.

Chapter: Matron G'eldlara

G'eldlara Torrret watched from her balcony from her private throne room. She was the Matron Mother of House Torrret, the first ruling house of the city of Anarchia and so she was also the Matron Mother of the whole city. Her long white hair was bound near the top of her skull, fluffed out from there and then flowed halfway down her back. She wore a red dress that hung loosely on her and cut in such a revealing way, so much so that if she were modest in any way then she would be grateful that there weren't random breezes through the underworld. As it was, she wasn't concerned about her privacy or modesty at the moment. Her eyes scanned the city as if she tried to make sense of it all, or perhaps how to bring her city into further chaos; her mind was yet to be made up on either decision.

She had already made the merchant train possible to trade with Malzebowan. The rival city had sent an emissary through the underworld and he had made his way to her. With a few modifications with the plan, she set the art of conspiracy in motion. She put out a citywide notice of a merchant train going to the other city and all those who were interested could bid on a spot on the train. This would allow any household to start an initial trade route that could potentially make anyone wealthy beyond their wildest dreams. The bids had come in and she had reaped a good portion of the income with the rest of the ruling council. For the most part the bidding had gone very well, with the exception of one house that backed down unexpectedly and gave way to house Olis'inth. She wondered what plot had transpired to ensure the transfer of power, but then it didn't really matter.

G'eldlara promised the security of the train herself, with her own guards. Of course she would never send her own guards; she had hired many of the houseless rogues to act as her guards with promise of promotion into her house and a substantial payment. Neither would happen. If all went according to plan then the train would be ambushed and its entire haul would go to Elg'caress

Barrindar. The ruling councils of both cities would act surprised by an accident that took the lives of these travelers, merchants, and guards and even the full set of merchandise, which traveled with them. Another train would be put together and be heavily guarded to make sure there were no incidents, but the new train would only do dealings through the ruling councils, just to be safe.

The Matron counted the ways she came out in the whole deal. She was paid for the slots on the train. She would secure an ally with the second most powerful Matron in the Malzebowan. She would have personal trade routes without the competition of the lower houses. The lower houses would lose funds and guards, which in turn would make them weaker and thus further away from any attempt at climbing the social ladder. She would even get rid of some of the houseless rogues that plague her city. On top of all of this, she would lose a daughter so she would have less in-house conspiracy to be assassinated. All in all, it was a great conspiracy and it brought a smile her thin-lipped mouth.

'The merchant train is ready for its departure tomorrow and all goes according to plan,' an alien thought came to her mind. She knew that thought pattern well and had dealt with this one before.

"Your payment for your involvement is on the table", she said without turning around. She knew he would take it and leave the rest of her lavishly furnished room intact, and her suspicions were confirmed when she heard the coin bag that was placed on one of her side tables removed.

'Is there ... ', his thought projection was halted by the wave of the Matron's hand. It wasn't a magical blocking of his telepathic abilities, but more a wave a dismissal. The conversation was over and he was dismissed from her presence. He bowed. Then with a slight effort he created a two-dimensional disk that allowed him to step through and appear at a great distance away. Without even a look back, she knew he was gone and she was alone with her thoughts yet again.

Book: The Mission

Chapter: The Embark

*M*edri had gone to her room the night before in disgust. She had more questions than answers, had discharged most of her offensive spells, and had broken her favorite dagger. The spells would be replenished after a night's rest, that wasn't the problem; it was the fact that she had to use them. The questions would always find their appropriate answers, but sometimes the answers came too late. The dagger was another thing all together. She had to take a femur off of the skeleton she had reserved in her room, and then sharpened it down to the right size, shape it, and then cast the right combination of spells. It was a several hour process and put her in a foul mood by the time she was ready for her meditation. She unzipped her leather boots and left them where they fell. Medri kneaded her bare feet and relieved some of her tension before she finished undressing and spent the rest of the night in meditation.

The next morning after she had dressed, prepared the spells she thought she might need, and made sure all of her personal gear was packed to her satisfaction, she and her goblin slave made their way to the stables. She decided to cut through the kitchen on her way out. This was to the dissatisfaction of the couple of cooks that were already in the process of preparing a morning meal for the ruling family. A quick scowl from Medri was enough to send a reminder the cooks that she was one of the members of the ruling family and immediately put them in their place. She was able to grab several pieces of dried meats, tubers, mushrooms and even a bottle of wine for the road before she was about to exit the kitchen. Then, on impulse, she stopped, walked back to the wine storage and picked up a second bottle before she proceeded to the stables.

Her riding lizard already had its tack, harness, bit, bridle, saddle and saddlebags set and ready to go. Of course this did not surprise Medri; if they weren't then the stable hands would pay dearly. Neither of her sisters nor her mother was present to see her off.

She wasn't sure if that was a relief or a foreboding sign, but either way she was sure they were watching her. She mounted the beast then turned the reigns and led the lizard toward the front gates of the house complex with her goblin walking slightly behind her carrying her backpack. The saddlebags were already filled with materials they had wished to sell. There were bolts of spider silk, bottles of house mushroom wine, a few magical items they were willing to part with at a nice profit, a few gems that they were able to procure from a few unsuspecting dwarves and Medri was able to toss in a few scraps of metal with a slight enchantment to pass as an artifact from their beloved goddess. Of course she had to sneak in those pieces herself. If her mother knew that the piece in her own throne room was nothing more than a scrap piece created from a deep dwarf inspired from one of her plots then there would be nothing to prevent her death.

Medri made her way through the gates of her house complex and on to the main street where she meet up with several other smaller houses in a similar state. Some also rode riding lizards, there were even two that rode large spiders but most walked. Another half block and their group doubled and by the time they had just about come to the gathering point their numbers doubled again. When they were all together she figured there were around a hundred total including guards and slaves.

"Attention" A strong looking female spoke with an enchantment to emphasize her voice. "I am Xesst Torrret, and I am here to take command. The guards are under my control and they will follow my orders and my orders only. While you are in this caravan, you will also be in my command. We will be in the wilds of the underworld and the journey will be long and arduous. We will need every one of us at our wits end to guarantee the safe journey of this excursion. There will be no house fighting." The last few words came out one at a time as to elaborate her underlined meaning. She shot a glare to two of the females in the caravan. It was obvious to Medri that Xesst had her eye on two other houses and their house rivalries. She hoped she would be able to fulfill her mission under the distraction of the other two.

With that thought in mind, she looked around for her mark. She wanted to make sure all was going according to plan before they even started into the underworld. It would be a long journey home to be the herald of bad news. After a moment of searching,

Medri found the house symbol she was looking for, the symbol of house D'Silva. She dismounted her lizard, gave the reigns to her slave and feigned an interest in the speaker as she moved closer to her prey. She wasn't going to assassinate her now, not in front of the huge crowd. It wasn't murder that was frowned upon in the city; it was getting caught doing it. Sloppiness and lack of imagination were not only a sin; they were a punishable crime. When she got close enough to the female she gasped in surprise. This wasn't Krenala D'Silva, the youngest daughter; it was Naliara, the oldest.

'Iblith', she thought to herself and with such strong emotion that she almost thought she had said it aloud. A quick glance around told her she hadn't. 'If Naliara is here then I've been set up again'.

Krenala was not only the youngest, but also the weakest. She was supposed to be the peace offering, or at least the sacrifice to their house. But this was Naliara. She was an older, stronger, and a wiser individual. House D'Silva wasn't about to offer up their best, strongest daughter. Medri would have a tougher time killing this one off which meant Medri was the one to be sacrificed. But there was no backing out now. The only thing she could do was to go forward with the assassination and bring back a greater prize and then find out who set her up. Going home now, empty handed, would not be tolerated. Medri made her way back to her riding lizard. She was going to have to make the best use and the cover of the other house rivalry if she wanted to pull this off.

Valas listened as the speaker droned on. He had made his way into the crowd, and with his new house insignia, he was given wide berth. The caravan leader continued with the same propaganda he had heard in his hometown. Nothing ever changed. It was the same 'for the glory of the spider queen' and the same 'dark elves are superior'. He closed his eyes for just a second and imagined slipping a blade between her ribs and through her lungs to keep her quiet, or perhaps between her breasts and into her beating heart. Perhaps he would get the chance later, but now he would endure her lecture on how they were the chosen race and how she was leading them all to glory.

Chapter: Underworld

*T*he caravan headed out of the city and beyond the outer sentry guards. She wished she could teleport or use dimensional portals, but as it was pointed out during the long winded speech and a few other times prior to her departure, that the underworld was full of magnetic and radioactive spots which would throw off the spell. Anyone who attempted to travel great distances by these means might end up in a rock wall or even worse yet, in some lava. With the great amount of troops and merchandise to move, the chance of anyone merging within rock or burnt alive was a high probability. Medri sighed; perhaps when this was over she would get a better pair of hiking boots for the next time she had to meander through the underworld.

The underworld is a series of underground caverns connecting through passageways and tunnels. Stalagmites and stalactites populate various areas and from time to time phosphorescent fungi and rocks gave off their eerie but natural glow. Underground streams periodically crossed the passages, some were drinkable, others were full of sulfur from nearby magma vents and others were super-heated. Blind cave fish could be seen in the more potable waters. Bats and small cave lizards were also common among the fauna found in the underworld. But these were the safest of all creatures; some horrible beasts also ran wild in the tunnels. There were large worms, big enough to swallow Medri whole. There were beasts that had hooks on their hands, land sharks, and even plants that got up and moved on their own, and worse yet.

Medri shuddered at the thought of meeting any of those. The caves gave off echoes of dripping water and bats off in the distance. There were heat differences all across the cavern walls, which showed a close proximity to lava tunnels, radiation spots, or fungi. To Medri, the whole place was lit up in such a fantastic, spectacular fashion, beyond anything they had in her city. As much as the beauty of the underworld enthralled Medri, she kept her excitement and fascination checked. She was still a dark elf, surrounded by other dark elves with dangerous creatures hiding just beyond the next turn or next shadow.

It was the second day into the journey when Medri approached Baebaste Melervs during an evening rest. Baebaste was one of the two house rivals Medri had identified on the first day. Her hair was short and in a chaotic mess, spiked in all directions. She wore a fighter's outfit with chain mail and a long sword, which she had taken out and was sharpening.

"I am Medri". Medri waited for a response, but only received a cold stare in return as Baebaste continued to sharpen her sword. "I couldn't help but notice the rivalry you have with house Zaurret. I also have a rivalry. Perhaps we could benefit from each other's company."

Baebaste stopped sharpening her sword and for a moment Medri thought that Baebaste might run it through her. "Let me get this straight. You help me take out Nathnilee and I will help you take out your rival?"

"Two can be better than one. We both gain from the benefits of each other's help and we have nothing to lose. But we should wait until the return trip. That way we may prosper from the other houses' profits after our dealing with Malzebowan."

Baebaste looked Medri over as to judge her ability to defend herself if it came down to an abrupt ending of this partnership. Satisfied that she had the upper hand and nothing to lose, Baebaste agreed and decided that they would talk more in Malzebowan, away from prying eyes.

It was an hour later when Medri was able to corner Nathnilee Zaurret.

"I am Medri". Medri said. "I couldn't help but notice the rivalry you have with house Melervs. I also have a rivalry. Perhaps we could benefit from each other's company."

The conversation was similar to the one she had with Baebaste and ended up with the same results. Now she had two individuals ready to help with her own mission, all she had to do was set the rest of the plan in action. She would set up an encounter while in Malzebowan but after all of the trading. If Naliara died during the first encounter she would raise Naliara and help her new ally to kill her rival. If Naliara survived then the first of the two rivals would be dead and she would raise her to join with the second rival to go against Naliara. Medri was sure that once bodies started to fall she would have a small army at her aid and have access to all of the profits gained at the trade. No matter how this came out, her mission would be completed with the least amount of effort on her side and she would have a bit more coin in her pouch and at least one more undead body to add to her increasing army.

On the start of the third day the caravan was attacked by a swarm of ahool. Ahool resembled a bat like creature with a monkey face with the exception of two large thin needlelike fangs. The ahool would attach themselves on their intended prey and suck the blood out of them. Where one ahool wasn't too bad to deal with on its own, these creatures never traveled as just one but in swarms. An entire swarm could drain any creature to a dried husk of a corpse in a matter of seconds. And so it was when the ahool swarm attacked. Two members of the caravan had died so quickly that there wasn't time for them to defend against the ahool. At least the cries of pain gave a warning to the attack and the rest of the caravan was able to go on the defensive and then the offensive.

Medri initially got her hands in motion and cast a spell that enveloped her in a sheath of cold, dark energy. She made sure she wasn't anywhere near her riding lizard or her goblin slave. The lizard wouldn't know any better, but the goblin had studied most of Medri's spells and knew where he had to be when each spell went off. This one would kill him if he tried to hide behind her in defense. The dark energy stole life from any living creature that touched her. He decided to hide behind the riding lizard instead. With any luck, the lizard might think some of the ahool to be food and actually attempt to eat them.

Several nearby dark elves tossed up fey fire and captured the whole swarm in painless flames. It wasn't meant to harm the ahool or even scare them away; the spell just lit each creature up and kept them lit up even when they flew away from each other. There was no way any of the ahool could get lost in the darkness, although Medri had to admit the effect was interesting and a bit eerie as she watched a swarm of ahool on fire flying about the cavern.

Medri walked into the swarm and let the ahool attack her. Three immediately caught hold of her, turned rigid and fell toward the ground. As they plummeted, their bodies were stripped back, their hides rotted away, muscle and bone were revealed and melted, and by the time the ahool hit the ground their bodies had turned to dust.

One ahool was attracted to the goblin's heat and made an effort to go after him, but the riding lizard saw the ahool thanks to the fire that was lighting it up. It was used to finding a swarm of bats and sneaking up on them while they slept. Before any of the bats would know what hit them, its long sticky tongue would shoot out, grab one, and pull it into its mouth with no difficulty. It was very easy to wipe out a full swarm of bats in this fashion. An ahool was no different than a bat, at least in the eyes of the riding lizard. As the ahool came in for an aerial attack on the goblin, the lizard lashed out its tongue. The sticky tongue easily grabbed the ahool and in a short time, the lizard was biting down hard on its new treat. The goblin cringed as he heard the crunching of bone.

A wizard in the group finally let go a fireball. It centered not too far from Medri and exploded in a hellish heat and tremendous fiery detonation. The light momentarily blinded Medri and it was all she could do to duck and pull her piwfia around her. He could feel the flames draw over her and the heat threaten to burn her skin. If it weren't for her piwfia or her resistance to spells, the fireball would have reduced her to a crisp.

"What are you doing," she screamed at the wizard as soon as she was able to get up. The remains of the ahool were still flapping on the floor in a death thro dance.

"They are all dead aren't they?"

"Yes, but you could have taken me with them", she said accusatorily as she walked up to face him.

"But I didn't. You seem to be very much alive. And you are welcome." The wizard was smug. But then perhaps not, she thought. Perhaps he wasn't just smug or even careless; perhaps he was trying to kill her. Who knew what this wizard was up to? She would have to watch her back more carefully. It also dawned on her that the greater spell casters in the group didn't even try to fend off the ahool until after the two other members had died. And if the major spell casters didn't know better, which they didn't, Medri could have been the third if she hadn't had her defensive spell up. 'Someone definitely wants me dead.' Medri thought. She went back to her riding lizard; made sure everything was still ok with it and the goblin and then set off with the rest of the caravan.

It was the end of their traveling day, as they were securing another location to settle for the night, when it happened. They choose a fairly long cavern, but not very wide. A deep stream ran the length of the cavern and from the lack of heat from it Medri could tell that it was very deep. To guarantee everyone had a fair share of water, Xesst Torrret had the caravan split into two equal halves, one on each side of the stream. Medri choose a small section with a niche where she could sit in meditation of the rest of the night. After unpacking her riding lizard, she let it climb halfway up the cavern wall where if found a small patch of fungi to feast on before sleeping nearly upside down. The goblin had found a tiny crawl space between two stalagmites that Medri was surprised he was able to fit into and wondered how he would ever be able to get out.

Medri heard the first sound of battle from the other side of the stream while her back was turned. As she spun around she saw its source. Many Ichfey had surfaced from the depth of the deep stream and was in the process of attacking the whole caravan up and down the whole lengths of the cavern.

Ichfey are fish-like humanoids, bipedal with long fin like arms and legs. They are covered in scales, have big fish like eyes and smell of rotting fish. Their teeth are small but sharp like an eel and yet for battle they preferred crude spears. Although they seemed to be more fish than humanoid, especially with their set of gills, they were also air breathers and could survive for long periods of time above water or even indefinably for all Medri knew. Their coloring ranged from purple to yellow depending on age and status in their society, but at times of emotional distress that color could change. Currently they were red.

The one Medri heard across the stream had caught its prey by surprise and had pierced a male dark elf through the stomach and out his back. The male wasn't dead yet, she could heal him with the life force of another, preferably one of the Ichfey. It wasn't that she had any affection for anyone on this caravan, she just could use any ally she can get a hold of and one extra person to help defend her on the rest of the way to Malzebowan and back wouldn't hurt either.

But that would have to wait; there was an Ichfey in front of her and ready to strike. His stench filled her nostrils. With his arms already pulled up and back, he came down hard on Medri. She was able to twist and turn and he only hit her arm instead of straight in the chest, but the hit was solid and pierced right through. She bit back the urge to scream and with all her might she let loose a spell.

The environment grew cold and she was able to see her breath as her arcane words filled the air. She shot her good arm forward and grabbed the Ichfey in the face and released the spell. Her hand began to stick to its fishy scales, but that discomfort and the wound in her arm would be over soon. The creature screamed in agony as its flesh began to boil and bubble. Its scales began to fall off and those that remained turned a dull shadow of its former self. Flesh peeled back, muscles fell off and the whole body withered as if it had aged a thousand years in a single second. All that remained was a pile of ashes, and like many of her other spells, this one drained the life from her opponent and healed the wound in her arm.

Baebaste Melervs caught an initial attack as she blocked the first Ichfey's spear strike with her long sword, twisted, and got her sword under its defenses. With a thrust she sliced deep into its flesh and a stream of greenish blood spewed out. As she pulled her sword out, her back ended up too close to another and her second opponent took advantage. She was too close for it to use its spear so the Ichfey reached out with its webbed claw, grabbed hold of her hair and yanked hard. Baebaste fell off balance, and with the aid of the blood slick cavern floor, she slipped and fell to the ground hard. Her sword fell from her hand and out of reach, which wouldn't have mattered since the wind was knocked out of her and she saw stars as she bumped her head.

With a sudden look around Medri could make out the rest of the battle. Although outnumbered, the dark elves were holding their position. She could hear the twang of crossbows being fired and the thud of the missiles slamming into their targets. She could smell ozone and knew a wizard had let loose a lightning bolt or a similar electrical discharge somewhere. Just across the stream she could see that an Ichfey had Baebaste Melervs pinned to the ground and was about to impale her with its spear. Medri definitely needed this one alive and saving her would only help her case.

Medri cast another spell. She pulled a bone shard from her pouch, pulled her arm back and threw. Immediately upon release the bone shard transformed into a sheared bone spear with its jagged sharp edge aiming straight for the Ichfey that had Baebaste Melervs detained. The necromantic bone spear flew true and hit the Ichfey in the back, came out its chest, and pushed its still beating heart five feet beyond. The Ichfey sank to its knees horrified and died before it hit the ground.

Suddenly Medri was aware of a certain smell, a familiar smell like that made by the aberrant. She looked around and saw a black liquid float down stream and with only a few moments to spare did she figure out its purpose. She turned her back to the stream and pulled her piwafwi around her as someone upstream lit the oil slick. Heat, light, and flames shot down the stream as if a dragon breathed a fiery breath. Most of the Ichfey had attacked from the comforts of the water and only a few were on land, but they were only a few feet away from the comforts of their watery home. The flames caught them all. Smell of burning flesh, awful screams of pain and a presence of death filled the air. When the flames cleared, the Ichfey had either swum off, burned to a crisp, lay dead or were dying. The battle was over.

With a quick glance at Baebaste, Medri realized her ally was not hurt so she turned her attention to those who were. There were several Ichfey that weren't dead yet and she knew she could use their life force and give it to others. Across the stream Medri caught sight of the male she had seen earlier. With a little effort, she jumped and cleared the stream, though she told herself she shouldn't do that again with the high heel boots she had on. As she approached, she found a dying Ichfey and was about to prepare her spell.

"Leave him." The voice was commanding, its presence was demanding and its weight had authority. Medri glanced up to see Xesst Torrret standing next to her.

"He's hurt."

"So?"

"So, he can be an asset. Every able body we can get can help us keep guard or carry supplies or even carry our profits back from Malzebowan."

"He is a male and therefore insignificant. You will take his guard duty and you will carry his load since you are so concerned with such things. I am the leader. I will tell you what to do, and you will do it. I will tell you what not to do and you will not do it. I am telling you to leave him. I am telling you to not heal him. Are you questioning my authority? Are you questioning the Spider queen's will? Is this a rebellion? A mutiny?" Xesst's hand was already on her snake whip and she was just seconds away from using it.

"No", Medri said in a downtrodden tone. She was defeated, at least for now.

"No, what?"

"No Mistress, I am not in rebellion, I am not questioning your authority. You are the Spider queen's will."

Xesst walked over to the dying male. With little effort she pushed him with her foot, as if the mere touch of him would offend her, and knocked him into the deep running stream. His body sank with the heavy weight of his armor and was quickly out of sight.

"His gear, his merchandise, and his profits from our dealing are now claimed by house Torrret." Xesst had said something similar when the others had died during the ahool attack. She was getting rich by default. Her face lit up in a sadistic smile. "Pack up, we are leaving."

Medri wanted nothing better than to wipe the smug smile from Xesst's face, but that would have to wait. She turned to Baebaste and could only see Baebaste shrug her shoulders. Medri sighed and went to pack up her backpack just to walk another mile and then unpack all over again.

Nathnilee Zaurret had witnessed the whole thing. She watched Medri save Baebaste's life, had even watched the exchange between them even as brief as it was. She knew where their alliance lay and she was going to make sure she told them where hers lay. At the right time she would make sure that both Medri and Baebaste were dead and she would take their profits back home. But not yet, the timing had to be just right. She turned from the shadows and joined the others to break camp.

Chapter: Ambush

*I*t was the fourth day when Medri came under the realization that the caravan was being followed. At first she thought she was just hearing things, but at times the sound grew louder and at others it distanced itself. She knew from the way the sounds of footsteps had echoed that the following party wasn't behind them, but rather in a parallel tunnel. Under her breath, while she still rode on her lizard, Medri cast a spell. The goblin caught the casting and prepared for the familiar dark, cold feeling that was usually present during one of his mistress's spells, but it never came. This was a different type of spell.

As soon as the spell went off, Medri was able to get a feeling of all living creatures in her area. She was able to pick up the members of the caravan, her own goblin, the riding lizard, and even a few small cave animals such as rats, bats, and small lizards. These she expected and ignored. It was the faint reading of the life that was ten feet behind the wall to her side that made her uneasy and put her on guard. She knew the reading was faint due to the thickness of the wall which meant the creatures were easily her size. She figured there were somewhere between a dozen and two dozen, but she couldn't really tell. She also knew that if she had heard the footsteps of the shadowing individuals then so had their scouts, which told her another set up was on the way. It was just a matter of finding out what it was, who it was directed to, when it would happen and what effect it would have on her mission.

When the caravan decided to take a mid-day rest, Medri decided to find out the intentions of her shadowy company. Medri reached into her bag and pulled out a metal dagger. Although not unusual for the common individual to have a metal dagger in their possession, the weight of the dagger just didn't sit right with her. She approached her goblin slave, and for just a moment, the goblin thought she was going to finally kill him. Instead she handed the dagger to him.

"You have served me well, very well. Take this". She put the dagger in his trembling hands. He looked at her with fear and trepidation. He knew she was a chaotic creature, but giving him a weapon was beyond his comprehension. "You will need it to defend yourself. I'm setting you free."

The creature stared at her wide-eyed. He was sure there was a mistake somewhere. Was she going to kill him the second his back was turned? Was she going to alert the others in the caravan to do the same? Perhaps it was some sort of sport where he would be hunted down.

"I'll give you the cover you need. We passed a side passage a few hundred yards back; take it. If you are swift and strong you will be able to make your way to wherever you wish. Let me cast a spell on you and you will be set." Medri fell through the arm motions of her spell and goblin felt a curious sensation fall upon him. It wasn't like the cold, dark spells she usually cast, but this one was slightly warm and tingling. She looked over her should and made sure no one was watching.

"Ok, now go. Quietly, quickly, but go … go now."

This was it. She really was going to set him free, she was serious. At first he was scared of moving, then he was scared not to move. He turned and ran fast. He small feet pounded, he slim arms pumped and he ran for his life. Medri sighed. If she hadn't cast a spell to make him invisible and another to silence him, his noisy movements he would have given every underworld denizen his exact position. She was glad she had never asked him to do anything covertly. Fortunately the spells were making up where the goblin was lacking. That is where the third spell came into play. This one gave her a feeling of the goblin's life force. She wasn't able to see him or hear him, but she could detect him just the same.

She followed his movements down the cavern. She could tell he had stopped. Was he looking back? Was it out of compassion? Was it out of fear? She never knew, but she knew she would miss him and wondered if she would ever be able to break in a slave as good as he was. He turned the corner to the smaller side passage and was gone.

He broke into another bold run. He could feel his adrenaline kick in and wasn't sure if it were out of fear or joy. He had always dreamed of leaving but never had a chance. He never had the guts to kill Medri and never had the heart to either, but now he was glad he hadn't. He ducked under a low stalactite, twisted around a stalagmite, splashed through a small underground stream and then stopped. He saw the red eyes in the darkness and heard a familiar twang and then a thud as something small and sharp hit his chest. He wondered how they had spotted him, how they had heard him, since it didn't take long to figure out the spells Medri had placed on him. But then it didn't matter. The venomous poison coursed through his system and darkness fell upon him.

She could feel his life force grow brighter and knew some sort of exhilaration had entered him, and from the direction she was getting he was on the move fast. She hoped he wasn't running from some sort of underworld beast and was killed before she could be clued into those who were following her. His reading was getting fainter and she believed that it was due to the cavern wall between them. Then suddenly, his life force faded and stopped. It wasn't quick enough to be a sudden death or slow enough for him to delve deeper into the underworld and for her to lose him. It had to be poison. That probably meant dark elf. Most male carried a poison that only paralyzed while females carried poison that killed. So it was a female dark elf that shot him, she figured, probably a priestess that led the party. A priestess would be able to turn any undead back on her if she tried to rise any undead and be able to counter-spell her negative charged spells with positive charged healing spells.

Since they had killed the goblin, their intentions were now known. A fairly friendly band would take the time to bring him back for a reward. Not this group. They didn't want to be noticed and had killed the only known witness. This was not good. Of course all of this was speculation. Any, all, or none of it could be true and she didn't know if her instincts were accurate or she was just giving into her usually paranoia.

The caravan picked up the pace and continued their way along the path that led them closer to their destination. But what destination that was she now wondered. Was this a trap? If her scouts knew about the other dark elf, then who was the trap for? There were too many other plots going on for the caravan to act as a coherent band. Going back empty handed and a failure in her mission would be worse than going forward.

The caravan walked the rest of the distance that it was ordained to walk for the day and then found a spot to settle for the night.

Guards were assigned to various posts, like they always were, and Medri decided to find a spot near the middle of the group this time, instead of near the end like she usually did. If trouble came, then the others would act as a buffer for her. As she unpacked she realized that she missed her goblin that would unpack for her, and now she would have to pack up all by herself then next morning. Yes, the goblin slave would definitely be missed.

Valas stood in his position during his guard duty. The one advantage of wearing the house insignia that he was wearing was that it gave him the opportunity to stand watch. Where most would shrug, ditch, bully, or bribe their way out of such duty, Valas took his shift with full enthusiasm, without showing too much of it least he would tip his hand. This was the night when he would make his move and he needed to have guard duty to do it.

He shot a glace around to make sure most were in their meditation rest for the evening. Once he was satisfied, he peered down a side passage that was designated his responsibility. No one else would be able to see what he saw since he was the only one who knew what to look for. His hands went through a sequence of signals, the dark elf sign language. It was a series of finger, wrist, hand, and arm gestures combined with body placement, heat variations, and speed at which it was delivered. It could deliver a lengthy message over a short amount of time in the most silent and subtle ways, and right now Valas wanted both. He waited for the appropriate response and then left his post.

Valas quietly made his way through the meditating group until he came across Baebaste Melervs. His plan had to be carefully engineered and this was one of those situations that he had to be extremely careful. Baebaste was in her meditation. Talking to any female unannounced was dangerous, waking one in her meditation, especially after a hard long walk could prove to be fatal.

"Mistress, Mistress Melervs". Valas carefully nudged her hoping to gently wake her.

She shot up with a dagger in her hand and had it precariously pointed at his throat. "You dare?"

"Mistress Xesst Torrret says it is your turn on shift."

"What? Of all the nerve she has. I have no intention of taking the position of a mere male, and you can tell her that yourself."

"Mistress Torrret says she saw you in battle against the Ichfey and that you had given her a great impression. She wanted to see if you would express your loyalty, and if such were expressed, then she would have a position that would open up in her household. At least that's what she told me to tell you. She also said that she would at least turn the other way, if not help entirely, with your rivalry."

Greed and revenge were two of the greatest motivators when it came to dark elf and Valas knew how to play them well. Baebaste resentfully gathered her gear. "The position is just over there, Mistress." Valas pointed but only received a glare in return that would put a medusa to shame before Baebaste walked off to take her newly assigned guard position.

Valas waited five minutes before he put the next part of his plan in motion. When the time was right, he made his way to Nathnilee Zaurret. His first flirtation with death went quite well, now he wanted to see if his second would pan out equally well.

"Mistress Zaurret". Valas gently shook his second sleeping mark of the night.

Nathnilee quickly moved forward and pushed Valas straight to the ground as her sword came up. A quick thrust and she could decapitate his head.

"Mistress, please, please, I bring a message."

"Speak or die."

"Mistress Torrret wants to help with your rivalry. We are almost to Malzebowan, and should reach it tomorrow. Now would be the time to strike. She only asks for half of the profit from Baebaste Melervs's trade goods."

'Half?' Nathnilee thought to herself. 'That greedy bitch has already absorbed three other house profits and now wants half of another?' She clicked her tongue in anger. She would have to deal with Mistress Torrret later, but the fact was still there, it was time to strike.

"Where? How?"

"Mistress Melervs has taken guard position over there." Valas pointed to the spot he had sent the other female, the place he had only recently stood guard himself. "The position can be taken by surprise from that angle over there." Valas slightly moved his hand to show a vantage point behind a group of stalagmites. "The other guards have been told to remain "distracted" while you take care of the situation at hand."

Nathnilee pushed Valas hard into the cold rocky ground, but her eyes were no longer on him, they were on her prey. She slowly, cautiously, made her way across the cavern like a predator stalking its prey, and came into position behind the set of stalagmites Valas had so graciously pointed out. 'The idiot male had some sense', she thought as she found the location to be ideal. She waited.

Baebaste had made her way toward Nathnilee but didn't see her behind the outcropping of rock. Satisfied, she turned and walked toward the entrance of the side passage she was guarding. She had only walked a few steps when the sword plunged through her back. She tried to scream, but a dagger cut across her throat, destroying her vocal cords and slashed across her jugular. She died quickly. Nathnilee had a triumphed smile as her rival fell to the ground, but then the smile stopped.

Two thuds barely audible caught her attention. She looked and saw two small darts in her stomach and she felt the poison start to course through her body. A glace up told her the source, a group of dark elves had entered her cavern through the side passage that Baebaste was guarding. Was Baebaste a traitor and hired these to sneak past her on this shift? Was Nathnilee set up? All the usual questions ran through her mind as her body sank and then died beside her own adversary.

Medri woke from her meditation with a start. The spell she had cast on herself was able to pick up any life forms in the area and let her know when someone died and even if undead was in the area. It wasn't just the presence of more life in the area than she had become familiar with, but also the startling disappearance of a few of them. They were being ambushed and the caravan was losing. She quickly stood and took notice of the situation. They were surrounded. The opposing dark elf raiding party didn't out number them, but they struck at vital parts in their defenses and when most were deep in their meditation. Many of her group had died; some were currently in battle while others were waking, but no one had formed any form of counter attack. She quickly went into casting and hoped she was wrong about her previous assumptions.

A few members of the caravan who had died rose from their cavern floor, their wounds obviously mortal and their life noticeably drained. They fell quickly upon their attackers with full and complete surprise. They weren't the strongest of undead, but they would work. A couple undead were knocked back down immediately; while others were able to take one of the raiding party members to the ground to rend him to dismemberment. The raiders shifted tactics and started to include the newly raised dead, but for every one they took down, Medri raised another to take its place. She knew that if the raiders continued to be as effective as they were then she would run out of spells long before she could do any real difference in the battle.

Mistress Xesst Torrret raised her snake whip up and snapped out again. There were three of the raiders facing her and were attempting to surround her. She had to keep them at bay or she would fall and all would be lost. If only she could find enough time to get her spells active. The raiders had already caught her major sorcerers off guard and they were dead and thus she was the last of the great spell casters left in the battle. There were a few others but none were close to her talent and power, if only she could access that power. The three kept their distance and stayed away from the venomous whip. It was only the guard to her left that kept them from surrounding her.

Valas pulled his rapier up and blocked another thrust by one of the three that had both him and Mistress Xesst Torrret under attack. He then scanned the battlefield to make sure all was going according to plan. For the most part it was, until his eyes caught more battle than what was expected. His men were doing battle with humanoids that weren't giving off heat, which meant undead. There was a problem after all. A priestess or other spell caster had slipped by their attack and had gone unnoticed. That would have to be dealt with; right now he had other things to manage.

Valas took the momentum of the parry and spun on the ball of his foot. The pivot put him right in line with the back of Mistress Xesst Torrret. With his sword still at hip level, he gave a thrust and caught her through the chinks of her armor and out the other side. Xesst gasped out in surprise. The guard that had taken position at her side wasn't one of hers after all and the three were only in place to get him in position and this realization was the last thought she had as her body fell dead to the floor.

"Good job", Valas said to the other three, "now let's finish this." Valas and the three raiders moved from the fallen mistress and went into the battlefield to fulfill their mission.

Medri had been able to cast the spell that placed bone armor on her and even a few more spells during the battle doing damage and kept most of the raiding party at bay, but she was now out of spells. Her back was to a cavern wall. Fortunately she had placed herself between a few stalactites that kept the raiders from surrounding her although it also kept her from a full retreat, not that she had anywhere to go. With a flick of her wrist the bone dagger she held snapped forward and became a long thin bone blade. She brought it up and parried an incoming blow from one opponent and then cut across to fend off another. If her blade were only an inch longer she would have scored a hit. She was tired and couldn't keep this up much longer. She glanced around and noticed that most of the caravan was dead and those that weren't, were going to be soon. She knew she was going to die, but maybe she could take a few of them with her.

A raider looked across the cavern for his next kill. To his right he could see two of his men having problems with one of the females and decided he was going to get credit for the kill. He raised his hand crossbow and sighted the female. One clear shot and she was his. A hand was placed over his arm and gently lowered his aim.

"She's mine", Valas said calmly. The raider was about to give protest; he had a clear shot. "Don't worry, I'll give you credit." Valas raised his hand crossbow and fired.

Medri saw the crossbow raised and the dart fired. She was in no position to defend against the dart, the two opponents had moved from her center, one toward each side, to try to flank her and the dart flew true. She heard the twang, heard the thud, and felt the sting. The hit was accurate. The poison on the tip immediately went to work and the light faded from her eyes.

Valas signaled his troop's through a series of hand signals. He was pleased with the raid in whole. He had only lost one of his men to the surprise attack of the undead and those that were wounded were to be cured with the curative potions they carried and supplemented with the caravan's potions he was sure he would find. On his command the raiding party gathered the entire caravan's trading goods. Then they added all personal gear of their victims, including their backpacks, armor, weapons, and even down to their boots. There was a quick gather of the riding lizards and within the hour they were ready to head out. Valas pointed to a few of the bodies lying on the ground and his troop included them in the cargo to be carried.

However, before they headed out, Valas decided to take his pick. He was promised one of the items and he was going to claim it before he was assigned the least attractive. He started opening boxes, crates, and rummaged through sacks. After a few minutes he found a cloak that caught his attention. He could tell it was made of spider silk, but the difference was the way it shimmered, not in a way between light and dark, but in a way between being solid and then fading away. This was a quality seen with ghost spider silk. A ghost spider, also known as a blink spider, was able to shift itself to another plane and back and its silk was able to transfer some of that power to whatever item it was made of. Of course harvesting the silk from a spider that could just blink away and reappear elsewhere wasn't easy, so the silk was rare. Bags and pouches that could hold more than its obvious volume, was made of such silk. Cloaks that were made of this material could send its wearer to the astral, ethereal or perhaps even to the shadow plane and back. Valas took the cloak and wrapped it around himself. With a nod of approval to his new claim, he signaled his men and left the cavern. He was sure all the corpses would attract various parasites and other scavengers and he didn't want to be anywhere close to this location when that happened.

From one of the ledges that over looked the cavern below, Valenci stepped out from the shadows. He had watched the scene with great interest. The whole event went according to plan. The raiding party did their job exceptionally. For a moment he thought he would have to interfere and use his mental powers to blast anyone that was giving too much opposition, but the raiders turned the situation around. He would now report to Matron Mother Elg'caress Barrindar and be paid by her as well as the other Matron Mothers that had already paid him. He wasn't after the money, but what he was after would cost him, and then there was the cost of the apothecary and the other houseless rogues he picked up. He stepped back into the shadows as the first of the carrion feeders entered the cavern to start its feast, and then he was gone.

Book: Malzebowan

Chapter: L' Elggen Cretok

Yasrae Do'tlar and T'rissvyr Do'tlar entered the L' Elggen Cretok, a rowdy tavern on the fringe of the slums of Malzebowan. Almost anything happened at the L' Elggen Cretok, including assassinations, conspiracies, slave trading, drug dealing, and fights. There was always a fight. Fortunately the owner knew a few spells to mend his tables and chairs and to clean up afterwards. This was unlike the upper class taverns that catered to a calmer, less chaotic crowd. Those patrons would do most of the actions anyway but with a flare of haughtiness and sophistication. This was also unlike the lower class taverns where most of the patrons would hide in the shadows afraid of each other. The L' Elggen Cretok always had something going on, and that was exactly what Yasrae and T'rissvyr liked about it; this was their kind of tavern.

Both Yasrae and T'rissvyr had their white hair short. Yasrae had a thin, taut, flexible and agile body. He had a single rapier on his hip and was an expert at a quick dance of parries and jabs when it came to a fight. T'rissvyr couldn't be more of a contrast. He had a huge double bladed war axe strapped to his back and two short swords, one on each hip. T'rissvyr was massive for a male and even some females. His big muscles were best when he bullied and chopped his way through a battle and then forced his way from one opponent to another. Both wore a thin, but strong chain shirt and their piwafwi were held on with their house symbol from house Do'tlar. Both carried backpacks, although atypical for a trip to a tavern, they were dark elves so the unusual was always expected and performed.

As usual the place was crowded and the whole place was interested in their conversation and ale, that no one even paid attention to their arrival. The smell of the tavern was strong with ale, sweat, and cheap fragrance. Both made their way to their selective spots in the tavern by their varied subtle or not so subtle way. Yasrae turned and twisted between customers who hardly even noticed he was there while T'rissvyr pushed individuals out of the way. One of the patrons what decided to argue the point that his drink was spilled by T'rissvyr, until he spun around to come face to face with the wall of muscle.

"My fault", said the poor scrawny dark elf as he backed away and gave room to T'rissvyr. He feared this huge bulk would simply pick him up and snap him in half, and he probably wasn't far from the truth.

T'rissvyr made his way to a selected table near a wall that was already occupied. The tables were always occupied, but that never stopped T'rissvyr before and it wasn't going to stop him today. There were two male dark elves that currently occupied the table he wanted, one was drunk and unconscious and the other oblivious to his surroundings. T'rissvyr made a motion with his thumb in the outward direction, clearly showing the conscious dark elf the way out of the table or out of the tavern whichever the patron chose. When the customer got up to complain, T'rissvyr grabbed him by the nape of his shirt and tossed him out without any form of grace. The patron slammed into a few customers walking about and nearly knocked them over as well. The patron sprung to his feet and pulled a dagger from a hidden sheath and was ready to take on his opponent when his unconscious friend came flying at him from a similar fate he had just experienced, knocked him back to the ground and sent his dagger skidding out across the floor. When he looked up, he saw T'rissvyr give a growl and a look that could kill. He then decided it wasn't worth his own death, at least not today. He helped his now rudely awakened friend up and the both left the tavern to plot their revenge. T'rissvyr slid his backpack under the table and took a seat.

"I see you found us a table," Yasrae said when he returned from the bar where he had ordered two very strong ales and took his seat opposite T'rissvyr. "I didn't recall any empty tables when we came in. Weren't these occupied?"

T'rissvyr wasn't impressed with Yasrae's banter. His friend talked too much while he was more an individual with action. He knew his friend had perfect recall and could recount where everyone had been, his talking was only to impress himself and no one else. He doubted anyone really cared what Yasrae said as long as the mission was completed.

"I assume you asked nicely this time. Or perhaps you had your own subtle method of requesting their departure. Don't tell me you resulted in tossing them out again; you know how unpopular that makes us."

T'rissvyr only shrugged. He knew he would run into those two again in some dark alley and he would deal with them as he always did with others who didn't get the hint to leave him alone. He hopped it would be tonight, he hadn't killed anyone in quite some time and he was itching to feel the rush of battle sometime soon.

"Ah, you communicate much without saying a word. This is one of your great qualities." Yasrae said as he smiled then took a drink of his ale.

"We are in time", T'rissvyr said as he put his own mug down from a hearty swig. "The entertainment is just about to begin". T'rissvyr pointed to the stage on the opposite end of the tavern from the main bar. Yasrae had to hold back his comment about how T'rissvyr drank like a dwarf; he just didn't want to meet the wrong side of his friend's axe. Instead, Yasrae turned his attention to the stage.

Several instrument players took their places on stage from a side door. They were all male and in similar purple tunics with gold trim. There was a percussionist with several hand drums in various shapes. He sat in a chair near the back of the stage and arranged his equipment so he was able to reach each one as needed. A lute player came next and found his spot not too far from the percussionist followed by individual who brought a psaltery. Next there was a flute and a zink, a reed instrument in the shape of a Minotaur's horn. When all the instrument players took their positions in a semicircle around the back of the stage to give the rest of the stage to the forefront entertainer, a female singer entered and stood in the center.

She was dressed in a light purple, completely sheer spider silk mini dress. It had thin straps across her shoulders, cut very low on her cleavage and rose high enough on her thighs to be revealing when she moved. There was a faint low fey fire of purple that silhouetted her form, but not enough to reveal every account of it. Though it didn't matter, her heat pattern that was picked up by the eyes of every male in the audience was enough to show them what they wanted to see. She had long white hair down to waist and wore some of it over the front of her shoulders to cover what her dress didn't.

The temple of the music started off low and slow, as did her voice. She barely moved to the rhythm of the beat but swayed enough for the dress to slightly seductively move across her hips. Her movements enthralled the entire crowed and even the instrument players had to do their best to keep focus on the music they were playing. After a few moments, the tempo started to rise and the singer kept pace. Her body began to sway for erotically and suggestively. She moved across the whole of the stage and continued to draw the attention of any who looked her way or heard her voice. Faster and faster the tempo went and faster and more seductive was her dance.

When the band seemed to be at an all-time fever pitch the dancer pointed to one of the male in the audience and made a "come hither" gesture with her finger. Perhaps he was enthralled under some spell, perhaps they all were, or perhaps it was just her beauty, no one knew for sure and no one seem to care. The male walked toward her, got up on the stage and looked her straight in the eyes. The female picked up her dance where she left off and spun and twisted around her captive partner. Around and around she went as if she were a spider spinning a web around him. Suddenly, with the music still in its upbeat tempo, she pushed the male to the floor of the stage and fell upon him.

Her hips fell upon his. Neither T'rissvyr or Yasrae or anyone else noticed the singer undo the male's pants, but at this time they knew it had happened. She moved up and down enjoying the dance, the music, and the company. Her enthralled partner could only lay and watch in contentment. Her neck moved wildly and her body followed to the rhythm of the music. Ecstasy could be seen on her face, as she was lost in the moment. Faster and faster she went, without indignity or consciousness of the audience. Her arms raised high and she let out a gasp.

In a heartbeat she plunged both of her fists hard on the male's skull and killed him as the music came to an unexpected halt.

She was sweaty all over and her dress clung to her, but she hadn't noticed. She simply rose from the dead corpse, crossed the stage and left out the side door with the performers on her heel. The dead corpse was left sprawled in the middle of the stage.

"She does the ritual reasonably well," Yasrae said his whispered voice barely audible under the slow rise of chatter that started up the moment the singer had left. "Poor fellow though. That is quite the way to die."

T'rissvyr closed his eyes and sighed. His heart was still beating quickly and Yasrae could tell that his face was flush.

"Why don't you just stay here and I'll deal with the package," Yasrae said as he got up from the table and headed toward the stage.

Yasrae made his way through the crowd and climbed up on stage. As he passed the dead corpse he thought about rifling through the equipment of the deceased, but then thought better of it. The owner of the establishment would claim the equipment and it would be his responsibility to dispose of the body. Yasrae shrugged, stepped over the dead body and moved to a back door that led to the tavern's basement.

The door opened to a stairway that went down a half flight of stairs then turned back on itself and went down the other half of the distance. At the bottom of the stairs was a hallway with a half dozen doors, three on each side, under the whole of the tavern. Each door was locked, but Yasrae had a key. He had to pay top coin for a key, as any potential customer would, since behind each door was a prize worth more than the entertainment. Behind these doors were captured female slaves.

Although dark elf society was a matriarchy, a captured female from a rival city was no longer part of the society. She was considered a failure. The higher class Matron Mothers turned their backs on such forms of slavery either as a way to let males release their frustrations or just to show rival cities that it was that was really in control. No one really knew, 'probably a bit of both', Yasrae thought to himself.

He could hear cries, moans, and screams of pleasure and pain behind most of the doors, all except for one. It was the one he had a key to. He opened the door, casually walked in, and then closed and locked the door behind him.

Chapter: Proposition

*M*edri watched as the male dark elf entered her room. He was thin with taunt muscles and dressed very well. This was a contrast to most of the males that came into her room. Usually they were drunk, poorly dressed, and most cases were beaten, probably from their Matron Mothers or sisters. She had been their outlet.

It was about a month since her capture in the underworld. She didn't remember her journey here, but then the effects of the narcotic from the dart she had been shot with would have messed with her memory as well as her mind. When she finally did wake, her long beautiful hair had been cut to a crop and she was in this room with her ankle shackled to floor as it was now. From what she could tell, there was no keyhole for the shackle and it was welded on while she was unconscious. Her captors meant to keep her for a long, long time.

She had screamed her indignations, made her threats, used every bit of profanity she could think of and a few others she would later be proud of creating, but these all fell on deaf ears. Medri had tried with all her strength but couldn't remove the shackle. She knew what was going to happen before the first "customer" came in to her room, but he hadn't a clue. He left only moments later. He could barely walk and yet he couldn't get out of there fast enough. He was bleeding in several places, was sure he had a few broken bones, and was almost positive he would never be able to spend any time with any female again. She paid for that though. There was a beating and, from then on in, her food was poisoned enough to keep her slightly sedated. The owner couldn't have his customers leaving in such a state; his business relied on repeat clientele. And now there was another for her to entertain.

"My name is Yasrae Do'tlar from house Do'tlar", he said as he sat on the uncomfortable cot that was barely more tolerable than the floor and the only piece of furniture in the room.

Medri had heard of house Do'tlar before. The Matron Mother's name was Irraste Do'tlar, but her appearance seemed to change from story to story. She always seemed to have a hand in something, especially with the clientele she had coming through her door. Medri was certain that the house wasn't too far up the social ladder, but was strong enough to make itself a name. This was the first person she ever heard who was actually from house Do'tlar. Then again this was the first person who ever mention his name. Perhaps if he could talk long enough, his time would end or better yet the sedative that was in her previous meal would wear off and he would regret he even laid eyes on her.

"Perhaps I should start at the beginning. Our house killed off our Matron mother, our sisters, and all females in our household some time ago. I now rule house Do'tlar. When asked where Matron Mother Irraste Do'tlar is, if she can be seen, we have always been able to make up some excuse and play ignorant of female conspiracies. Playing the idiot male fool can get a male out of more trouble than you might think. Unfortunately one can only say, "She's currently engaged in another affair", or "You are not worthy of her presence" or even "She is on a spiritual journey to draw her closer to her goddess" so often. We have now come to a decision to put a female on the throne. I will still run the house and give the orders while she is a marionette to our continued existence. I have come to make you that marionette. You would make that perfect puppet. No one would recognize you, you haven't been seen and you simply don't have a choice."

Medri couldn't believe what she was hearing. A male house was blasphemous. As soon as it was found out, all the males would wish they had been killed. That would explain why the house wasn't high on the social ladder, it would have been found out by now. She definitely had to congratulate them on their conspiracy, but it was foolish to think it would last. But now she was told. She had the secret that kept them alive and she was either going to cooperate or die.

"Oh, I see you know understand your predicament. I intend to get our Matron on the throne tonight, so it can be you or someone else. You would be given your own room and enough clothing to pull the façade off, you won't be mistreated and you will have certain freedoms within the compound, but you will still have to answer to me. Now, I do need your answer fairly quickly, I have a schedule to keep."

She knew she would still be a slave. She would have luxuries and freedoms, but she would still be confined to walls. If she were caught by another house she would die, and if these males finally decided they were tired of her she would also die. But she would die here and now if she didn't agree and without her spells, she would be powerless to defend herself. She could at least buy some time by being agreeable. She nodded her head.

"Excellent. I knew you would find our proposition satisfactory". Yasrae got up from the cot and pulled a potion from a pocket, uncorked it and poured it on the shackle around her ankle. It immediately began to foam and some of the metal was eaten away. When enough of the metal was corroded Yasrae applied some pressure to it, and the metal cuff broke free. "It's black dragon acid. It will eat through anything. Now, come with me, all arrangements have been made."

She was sure they had been. He placed his piwafwi around her shoulders, drew it close around her and hid the rags she was currently wearing. She thought about making a break as soon as she could, but she would be hunted in this foreign city. So she would see how far the plan would go before she gave up hope on it and decided that discretion was the better part of valor. Yasrae led her out of the room, down the hall, past the other doors and up the stairs. The moment he arrived on stage he made eye contact with T'rissvyr and nodded. T'rissvyr took that as the signal that he was to be given, drank the last of his ale in one gulp, left the table, and met his coconspirator at the door. The three of them left the tavern quickly and without notice.

After a few dozen paces from the tavern Yasrae stopped and turned to T'rissvyr. "You seemed to have misplaced your backpack. How careless of you. Do you have any idea where you may have left it?"

Suddenly the explosion from behind them rocked the great cavern city of Malzebowan. The tavern boards and window glass shot in all directions. The sound of the explosion could be heard from every corner of the city and flames started to consume what was left of the building. The shock was almost enough to knock Yasrae and T'rissvyr from their feet and Medri had to be held since she was still under the effects of the sedative from her last meal.

Screams could be heard from inside the tavern. Dark elves ran about and tried to keep the fire from spreading while others tried magical means to stop the fire. The major clerics and wizards weren't on the scene yet so the minor cantrips were hardly effective. Chaos was everywhere. A burning orc came running out of the blazing remains of the tavern and screamed at the top of his lungs as the fire consumed him and he feel dead in a burnt crisp.

"Yes, I know perfectly well where I left it", T'rissvyr said with a slight smile.

Yasrae pushed Medri from him. "Murderer! Assassin!" Yasrae yelled as he pointed toward Medri. She was still unable to get her bearings from the narcotic and now from the blast, that she didn't even have time to respond as Yasrae lifted his crossbow and shot Medri in her midsection. For the second time she felt a crossbow dart hit her and felt the poison course through her body. She became weak, light faded from her eyes and her body collapsed on the spot.

"What's going on here?" barked a guard from house Barrindar when he arrived only a few moments later.

"From the looks of things, L' Elggen Cretok was running an illegal female slave operation. As my friend and I were leaving, one of the female slaves apparently left some sort of potion explosive behind and blew up the poor tavern in an attempt to hide her escape. She even managed to grab my cloak as a disguise for herself." Yasrae was good at making up stories, as he needed them.

The guard nodded. He didn't buy any of that for one minute, but it was better than anything he could think of. He had to give credit to the storyteller's imagination. "I'll have my men go through the rubble and see if we can have any of the dead patrons brought back to life to verify your story".

"I'm afraid that you probably won't succeed." Yasrae pointed to the burnt husk of an orc lying just outside the remains of the doorway. "There's hardly anything left of them. I doubt even your greatest priestess would be able to get enough pieces of the bodies to bring any of them to bring back. And I doubt any of them saw anything anyway."

"Then I'll take that body", the guard said as he pointed at the non-moving body of Medri.

"She is wearing my cloak, so in a sense, that makes her my property. I'm sure you can take it up with Matron Mother Irraste Do'tlar, if she can find time for an audience or if she can convince herself of giving up her precious time to individuals of lesser status."

The guard scowled at that. His house was not of a lesser status, but he was a male. All male were lesser status to any female, especially to a Matron Mother of any house. On top of that, no one saw Matron Mother Irraste, and even if he could, by the time he did, the body would be gone. He could always go to his Matron Mother and try to put pressure on the less significant house, but the body would still be gone. He was maddened by the position he was placed in.

"Don't worry", Yasrae said, "We were on our way to the mushroom fields anyway to view the new crop. My friend here is an expert at removing body parts and we will be more than happy to be of service to dispose the body in the way that best fits her crime. Fertilizer for the fields, don't you think that is fitting?"

The guard nodded. "I'll send two of my guards to the fields to make sure that all go well and you don't run into any problems."

Yasrae knew exactly what the guard meant. If Yasrae didn't show up at the mushroom field to dispose of the body, then one Matron Mother would visit another. The guard secretly hopped it would come to that. Secretive of not, Matron Mother Irraste Do'tlar would have to show herself to the likes of Matron Mother Elg'caress Barrindar.

Yasrae walked to Medri's body and picked her up and tossed her over his shoulder. He found her to be lighter than he expected. Perhaps it had to do with how little food she had been fed lately. With a nod to T'rissvyr the both of them headed toward the mushroom fields and left the fire for others to deal with. Yasrae wasn't sure if the major clerics or wizards would actually put the fire out or not. Any of the higher houses could use this to their advantage, even as a way to clear out some of the lower houses. If they weren't careful, half of Malzebowan could burn to the ground before anything was seriously attempted to put the fire out. But that wasn't Yasrae's concern, at least not at the moment.

About a block of traveling through the growing crowd and thick accumulating smoke, Yasrae turned to T'rissvyr and asked, "Are they following us?"

"The two from the tavern?" T'rissvyr turned and looked over his shoulder and spotted the two in question. "Yes and not too far away."

"Perfect. Quickly, in here," Yasrae said as he ducked between two buildings and into an alley. The alley was narrow and void of any fey fire so it was as dark as the abyss. As soon as the two of them went deep enough into the alley they stopped and turned around. Yasrae carefully put Medri's body on the ground and pulled his rapier from his hip sheath. T'rissvyr pulled his double bladed battle axe from his back sheath and balanced his weight between the balls of his feet. The two dark elves that had followed them, the two from the tavern that T'rissvyr tossed from their seats, entered the alley. The fey fire of the city and the burning tavern silhouetted them while the darkness of the alley gave the Yasrae and T'rissvyr an advantage.

T'rissvyr ran the battle through his head and realized the outcome before it had started. Once he was secure his side would win, he waited and let the events transpire.

The two opponents wadded forward through the darkness. T'rissvyr took point about five feet ahead of Yasrae as they usually did. When the opponents were within striking range the first came at T'rissvyr with wild abandon. T'rissvyr knew the rage from the first customer he had tossed out of the tavern table would keep him off balance. T'rissvyr ducked under the wild swing and took a step toward the second opponent who was still groggy from his debaucheries at the tavern. T'rissvyr almost felt sorry for him. He was sure his friend had talked him into this fight and he was nowhere near his fighting peak, but the fight had begun and T'rissvyr was going to finish it. With a quick work of his feet, T'rissvyr charged the second opponent, brought his axe low, cut through his midsection, stopped, reversed, and came with a blow to the back of the head. There was a sickening crack as the skull split open and blood, brain, and skull fragments exploded.

Yasrae brought his rapier down and blocked the first opponent from bringing his weapon back up from his wild swing. He then smiled, took a step back and released his hold so his enemy could try again. The opponent did try again and Yasrae easily brought his rapier up and blocked that blow. He tried a jab, a vertical slice, and even tried to spin and catch Yasrae off guard, but each attempt only resulted in yet another parry. He was being mocked, toyed with, and being made out to be a fool.

"Would you quit it and kill him already? I'm already done with mine. Why does it always take you so long?" T'rissvyr said with an impatient tone. He understood his friend's style of attacking. Yasrae would outwork his opponent, force him to make mistakes and slowly wear him down until he could execute the perfect blow, but sometimes he became annoyed when Yasrae toyed with his kill instead of just finishing the job.

The voice from his back distracted the opponent. He looked back and saw his alley lying dead with his head split open and then realized he made two fatal mistakes. The first was to enter the alley. The second was to turn his back on the person he was fighting. The blade ran through his back and came out his stomach. With a gasp he staggered, slid off the thin blade and fell to his death.

"Took you long enough", T'rissvyr mocked as he put his axe away, "I thought you would never kill him. Worse yet, I thought I would have to take over as house leader."

"I had to ensure my blade hit him in the right spot to make it look exactly as we had planned." Yasrae wasn't bothered by his ally's retort; instead he immediately went to work. Once he put his blade away, he cast a spell. The slain body in front of him began to metamorphous, and once the spell was complete, the dead male looked exactly like Medri. Yasrae cast a second spell and the real Medri disappeared from sight. He then picked up the fake Medri and carried the dead corpse in his arms while T'rissvyr, with a little bit of searching, picked up the real Medri and they made their way to the mushroom fields.

Yasrae and T'rissvyr decided to take the long way to the mushroom fields. He wanted to make sure he was seen with the dead body and wanted to make sure that news was spread of his trip to the mushroom fields to dispose of it. They passed through the slum district first.

The slum areas were a place designated for the less fortunate, those rejected, those who had survived and fled a raid by some other house, or even lesser humanoids that had wandered into the city. The buildings were on the verge of collapse but that usually didn't bother a band humanoids or even the destitute dark elf to over populate them to hazardous situations. The strongest would bully his way to the top of the house structure level, not unlike any regular dark elf house. The stench and the filth would be horrible. Many creatures died here without being noticed until their body became so rancid and unbearable that they were eventually moved and two more would take its place.

This was a favorite target for house Barrindar. House Barrindar always wanted to show its might and power, but ran into political problems with the upper class houses, especially with those that could fight back. So House Barrindar came here. This is where they would take their target practice, their experiments on new spells, and master their raiding techniques. Sometimes House Barrindar would find a humanoid with promising qualities to bring back to the slave pits so its genes would be passed on. Sometimes they would find an unfortunate humanoid to practice torture or scientific and magical experiments on to see what kind of mutation could be created. Sometimes it was just a cleansing of the slums that resulted in the death of everything and everyone that house Barrindar could find. Yasrae had planned his plot for today since he doubted there would be the extra complications of a slum raid. A raid had just happened the other day so it would be at least a week before there would be another.

After a few minutes of searching, Yasrae and T'rissvyr came across the very building they were looking for. It was small, more of a shack. The walls looked as if they would fall down, the windows were boarded up and the door was barely on its hinges. The shack was located between two other buildings, halfway down an alley and concealed by various crates and barrels. It would take a lucky guess at best to find this place, but they had been more than lucky, they had magic and it was that very magic that led them here the first time. It was simply a matter of remembering where it was that lead them here today.

"Perfect. This building is exactly what we need", Yasrae said. T'rissvyr sighed. They had spied this building out the day before and Yasrae continued to annoy him with an observation that was already known, just to hear the sound of his own voice.

Once the two of them made their way into the shack, two massive ogres rose from the corners. T'rissvyr sighed again. It was going to be one of those days. The building had been empty yesterday and the chance was slim its location would be found, but in the underworld, especially in a dark elf city, anything was possible.

Both Yasrae and T'rissvyr gently placed the bodies they had been carrying down on the floor and unsheathed their weapons. They knew ogres to be dumb and stupid, lacking any form of battle tactics, but they were strong. A single hit from either of the ogres would ruin their day at the very least. T'rissvyr took his usually five feet stance slightly ahead and to the right of Yasrae. This battle position worked every time and would work now even against these beasts.

The ogre on the right took a huge step forward and swung his club in a wild arching blow. It was fast, but T'rissvyr was faster and dodged left, closed the gap between him and ogre on the left and brought his axe to cleave. The ogre was able to bring his club up in time and T'rissvyr found his weapon buried deep in the wooden weapon. The ogre yanked and pulled the axe from T'rissvyr hand, and at the same time, pulled T'rissvyr forward and off balance. But that was part of his plan. The ogre was now off balance with his club overhead and T'rissvyr was close, too close for the ogre to use his club even if it could bring it to bear.

T'rissvyr stopped his forward momentum as he stepped past the ogre. He ducked, pulled a short sword from its sheath and as he kept the blade still pointing behind him, and then pushed himself backwards toward the ogre. The short sword sank deep into the back thigh of the ogre. It hollered in pain, but T'rissvyr wasn't done. With all of his might, T'rissvyr turned his shoulder and bull rushed the ogre's good leg and made it buckle. Its wounded leg could not support its weight and the ogre went down. It was only a short matter of time before the ogre was dead once T'rissvyr fell upon it with his second short sword to compliment the first.

The ogre on the right was off balance before Yasrae stepped in to face off against it. He knew he couldn't take his time with this one as he did with the dark elf in the alley. He didn't have a selective way for this one to die and he had to be quick. There were a few spells had cast already and he wanted to make sure his timing was accurate before their duration expired.

With the ogre's arm already outstretched from its wild swing, Yasrae took a thrust to the ogre's wrist. He pierced it as his blade went through and cut tendon. The ogre yelped and let go of his club once he found his hand that had it was no longer useful. Yasrae followed with an upper jab straight to the ogre's throat and pierced flesh, bone and blood vessel. When Yasrae pulled his sword free the poor ogre gasped and started to bleed in streams. It put his hands to his throat to stop the bleeding but to no avail. Yasrae stepped out of the way as the huge ogre fell forward, its life drained.

"And I am sure you expect me to clean up?" T'rissvyr asked as he retrieved his axe from the ogre's club.

"Go ahead and dispose of these two," Yasrae pointed at the ogres. "I'll hide our package and we'll get that one to the mushroom fields," Yasrae pointed to the visible Medri body.

T'rissvyr sighed. He was always stuck with the dirty work. He understood that Yasrae was the brains of the two and he was the brawn, but still, sometimes he could just run his axe through that arrogant skull of his coconspirator.

It took only a few minutes for T'rissvyr to pull the ogres into a nearby populated building. "You can have all of its possessions," he told them. The various humanoids took no time in removing everything both ogres had. Once he returned, he picked up the visible body and followed Yasrae to their destination.

The next area they passed through was the bowch fields. This was a section of the cavern that had been fenced off using one of the rock walls as a natural barrier. Inside, the bowch were penned together. Bowch were similar to cows. They were four legged animals with a hard leather hide and provided meat and dairy as a mainstay staple to many underworld residences.

Bowch hide came in many different colors depending on the specific species. There were mostly black and brown, but sometimes, on rare occasions, there were white hide. Once a bowch was harvested for its meat, the hide would be carefully collected in large sections. The bowch farmers would sell these hides to other merchants who would work them and tan them to various leather objections. Leather armor was in the largest of demand and a single suit of white leather armor was very expensive. Other items included whips; bags, backpacks, boots and anything that could be left to the imagination of bowch hide dealers.

Bowch also had their means of making methane. While similar to any other methane producing plants or animals, the bowch made their production well known and could be heard several blocks away. This was one of the two reasons that envy wasn't given to bowch herders by any other underworld denizen. And the methane was constant. This meant the bowch had to be penned in a corner of the city where the air could be circulated back into the underworld. A deep gnome once came to the ruling council with the idea of harnessing the methane. He was initially met with skepticism and even some all-out laughter, but in the end he received funding and an abandoned house near the bowch fields from an unknown benefactor. The explosion rocked the whole city cavern, blew the house into tiny fragments that to this day they were still pulling out from nearby houses, had started a fire that burned down two more houses, and the gnome was obliterated. The methane production was never tried again.

The bowch also produced fertilizer and tons of it. This was the second reason that bowch herders weren't envied. The stench of it could be intolerable if it weren't for magical spells that would sweeten the air. This, or course, was mandated by the ruling council and unanimously approved, probably the only mandate that was unanimously approved by the whole city. But although the stench was a major drawback, the fungi grew best when it was applied to their environment. The herders would sell the fertilizer to the fungi farmers at a nice profit.

When the bowch were mature enough they were slaughtered for their meat. The best choice cuts were held for the upper houses and merchants. Usually these were steaks or ribs, but the leftovers were also sold. No part of the bowch was wasted. The pieces not worthy of the upper class were sold to the lower class while the small left over pieces of entrails, bones, gristle and all other unwanted pieces from the lower class were finally sold to the absolute scum, houseless rogues, or even slaves. The female bowch were able to produce milk, which could be turned into a fermented drink or various cheeses.

Bowch pens weren't always easy to maintain. Although usually docile, the bowch would sometimes kick and buck for no apparent reason. No one knew exactly why, since not much research went into the behavior patterns of a bowch. Where one bowch kicking wasn't much a problem, it was when several others decided to join in. At one time the whole stock had gone into such a tirade that they had knocked down the pens and ran through the streets in a stampede. Many dark elves and other denizens had been gauged and trampled. Street vender carts and stalls had been knocked down and two small fires had started. It took a huge city effort on riding lizards and riding bats with lassos to drive the herd back to the pens. Precautions had been taken afterward to run small electrical discharges through the fencing but the bowch farmers only reluctantly did this since it cut into their profits and required a mage to be hired.

By the time they arrived at the mushroom fields, Yasrae figured the news of their trip had been reported or at least rumored throughout most of the city. If all went according to plan there would be several rumors about their house by the end of the day, and all of them false.

The mushroom fields were home to a wide variety of fungi. Some towered ten feet in the air, other grew like shelves on the cave walls and some actually had feet and walked around. There were even mushrooms that shrieked when they were approached. Each mushroom held a different purpose from food, to medicine, to poison, and even for alarms. The fields were located by one of the east entrances and were tended by two different houses. At any moment several slaves were could be seen tending the fields and even spreading fertilizer to speed their growth. Since space was limited in the underworld and too many houses could rise undead, anybody that was considered unworthy to be rises as such was cut into pieces and spread with the fertilizer.

T'rissvyr and Yasrae entered the fields to find many humanoids including goblins, hobgoblins, and bugbears tending the fields. There were also two guards from house Barrindar waiting for them. From the looks of them, they weren't in pleasant moods. Of course, he could understand their point of view. They were sent on a simple errand run, a lowly assignment to watch a body being hacked in pieces. Then again, Yasrae wondered if any from house Barrindar were ever in a pleasant mood.

"Greetings fine gentlemen, what an excellent evening we have today", Yasrae said to the Barrindar guards as he approached. T'rissvyr merely rolled his eyes. Yasrae had a bad habit of opening his mouth and pushing individuals beyond their comfort level and these guards already looked as if they had reached that level before they had even arrived.

"Get on with it", one guard said, "And do it quickly before you are added to the fertilizer as well."

Both Yasrae and T'rissvyr looked at the guards and examined them. They both measured the situation in their minds like they did before any battle began. Although they were both confident that the battle would end up in their favor, they needed the guards alive. They were witnesses. Yasrae shrugged and nodded to T'rissvyr.

T'rissvyr tossed the body to the ground unceremoniously. Before T'rissvyr could begin the body dismemberment, one of the guards stopped him.

"I though she died with a crossbow bolt. The hole in her stomach is too big for that." The guard looked at the two of them suspiciously. They were told to keep an eye on these two from house Do'tlar, something was going on and house Barrindar wanted a piece of it.

"She did," said Yasrae. "We keep our crossbow bolts tipped with black dragon acid. Any hit by them would leave a larger hole and some even have a tendency of traveling through our victim. Here is a sample." Yasrae pulled an empty vial from his backpack and let the guards examine and then sniff it. Of course the contents had been black dragon acid, but they had no idea how it was used.

With the guards satisfied, T'rissvyr was given the nod to go ahead. He brought forth his axe and started chopping the body with full deliberation. The head was the first to be chopped off and the body started to drain the remains of its blood. The skull was shattered with a few more chops and was crushed into tiny pieces that could easily be mixed in with the soil. T'rissvyr had to move fast, he knew the spell that was on the dead corpse wouldn't last forever. He continued to swing and chop. Bone, muscle, sinew, and entrails splattered everywhere and when T'rissvyr was finished there was a mound of remains that no longer had any identifiable means of what it used to be.

At the end of his rage and fury, T'rissvyr put his axe away. The guards were glad they weren't asked to go against the wrath they had witnessed. This was the second thing the two from house Do'tlar wanted the guards to take notice, a horrible fury that could be released when it was needed. That should start a few stories and rumors to keep potential rivals at bay. Yasrae and T'rissvyr gave a slight bow to the guards, turned on their heels and headed back to the abandoned house where they left the real Medri.

Chapter: Malzebowan

*M*edri yawned and stretched. The bed she was on was very comfortable, soft, and warm. The silk sheets slid over her near naked body and the pillow cushioned her head like a cloud. It was all a dream of course and she knew it, but she didn't want to wake up. Slowly she put out her hands to her sides and felt the bed, the sheets, and the pillow. This was not a dream. This was all wrong. Last thing she was aware was a poisoned dart hitting her while she was battling a rival city's raiders in the underworld. No, that wasn't right. That was the first time she was hit with a poisoned dart. There was a second time; the time when she was in the rival city and being accused of blowing up the very tavern that had enslaved her. So, where was she now? She did recall a conversation about sitting in for a Matron Mother, but could that proposition actually have happened?

Medri noticed that she was only wearing a few undergarments. At least who moved her didn't take liberties. It wasn't that she was modest. She just didn't want anyone else undressing her without her being awake to enjoy it. She sat up and looked across the room. It was huge by any standards she was used to. Did her Matron Mother have a room of this size? There were dressers and desks. There were closets and wardrobes. There were even two archways that lead out of the room and into two other rooms. She was in a three-room suite. She got up and examined the first dresser. Empty. The footlocker was also empty. All of the dressers and desks were empty. The only thing that had any item of interest was a closet where a set of leather armor was stored. With a brief examination, she could tell that it would be a close fit for her. She donned the black leather boots, pants, tunic and outer corset. The fit was indeed close, but didn't hug her every curve like her original outfit, though she did appreciate the outer corset, it was a nice touch. She did have some seamstress abilities and would be able to take in the clothing for a better fit. The boots were about a size too big, but she was sure she could get a pair closer to her size.

She looked quickly into one of the connecting rooms. This was a washroom. It had a mosaic of tile with a picture of a large black widow spider on the floor instead of wood like the other rooms. There was a washbasin set in a pedestal, another dresser, a cupboard, and a bathtub. Sitting on the rim of the tub was a decanter full of water with two small stones next to it, a blue and a red. Medri suspected the decanter to be ever full and could fill up the tub without a problem and that the stones would heat or cool the water once it was poured. She examined the cupboard and dresser and found they were mostly empty, aside from a few towels.

The other room was a sitting room. It had a few desks, two sitting chairs for guests and a lounging couch for the hostess, which if her suspicions were true, and then that host would be her. The desks yielded nothing inside them. There was a door that led out and she was considering rather or not to venture out when a knock came upon it. She no longer had a weapon to defend herself and she had not yet prepared her spells for the day but she thought she could come up with a trick or two if needed.

"Come in." She said as she placed her weight on the balls of her feet; ready to spring in any direction if the need arose.

The door opened and Yasrae stepped into the room carrying a tray of food. There was cooked fish, some tubers she didn't recognize, and a few cheeses that were of color and texture entirely unknown. "Ah, I see you are awake. I thought I would time my efforts to the moment the effects of the sleeping poison would wear off." He set the tray down on a desk next to her. "Now, let it be known. This is the last time I will bring you food. We do have a community-eating hall and you may join us during a morning, afternoon, and evening meal. Meals will not be made outside of these times."

Medri sat down on a lounging couch and started nibbling at the tray of food. The poison in her system and lack of decent food from her last month of incarceration had made her ravenously hungry. But as grateful as she was for receiving a civilized meal, she was still very upset with him for shooting her with a poison dart, even though it was only a sleeping poison. Her eyes never left him and she restrained herself from grabbing all the food at once and eating like some barbaric orc.

Yasrae waited in silence on one of the sitting chairs for Medri to finish her meal. When she had finished he said, "You will now be known as Matron Mother Irraste Do'tlar. You will have no power on your own; I am the leader of this household."

"Why the deception of killing me?"

"I couldn't have any witnesses identifying you later, could I? The whole city thinks you are dead, and now with your new identity, you are."

"And you expect me to wear the same outfit through the course of my reign?"

Yasrae smiled. "Oh no, not at all. We had pillaged all of the clothing in search of every magical item the real Irraste had. We will have to go out and get you more outfits later today; that is all planned. But before we go, you will have to be informed with all the information you will need. If you would follow me."

Yasrae got up from his chair and headed out the door. Medri or at least Irraste followed. She felt like a sub servant underling all over again, and to a male. This would have to get some being used to, in the mean time she would have to restrain herself from knocking that smug smile off of his face. 'Yes', she thought, 'he would make a great personal undead guard.'

Yasrae lead her down several corridors, each with full activity of male dark elves. At her home she would rarely see a male dark elf; every one of them would make themselves scarce for fear of a female's wrath. Here, however, the males were walking about in the open and not one of them bowed, scurried, or quaked in fear, although they did eye her with suspicion. She had to remember she was the outcast here and it was she that had to watch her step. The males were all carrying items of lumber, stone, rope, and mortar. It was obvious that each one had a duty to repair and upkeep the structure. Without the help of priestesses, the mages would have to have all of their offensive spells ready, which meant they didn't have time for utilitarian spells, so the structure would have to be up kept the hard way.

After a few turns, Yasrae found the door he was looking for and opened it. Inside was a large square table in the center and all around the walls was a series of honeycombed cubicles, each held a rolled up scroll. "This is our war room", Yasrae said as he reached for one of the scrolls. He placed it on the table and unrolled it; and as he did the table magically held it in place and kept it from rolling back up. It was a map of the city.

"This is Malzebowan. This is where the high tier is." Yasrae pointed to a corner of the northwest portion of the map. "It houses all eight of the ruling council houses. Over here, beside it, is the second tier. It has the fighters' guild, the mages guild and finally the priestess' temple." Irraste didn't miss the order of importance at which Yasrae put the three training centers. Any other female present would have been prompted immediately to deal with such a male who didn't place the temple as the most important building.

Yasrae caught the look in her eye and mistook it for interest in something he said. Guessing he said, "The mages guild houses a large abundance of necromancers. From what our agents have told us, they have been collecting various body parts of different species. No one knows the full intention. I've told my agents not to investigate too much. Individuals have a nasty habit of disappearing around them and I can only afford so many agents."

Curiosity crossed Irraste's mind. This might be something she could look into herself. Danger was an attraction to many of her race and she was definitely one of them. It was a thrill worth living for, but she wondered if it was worth dying for.

His finger moved to the south. "Here is the high market place. It's full of the highest-class merchants and the high end and hard to find items. Only the very wealthy, very important, or very powerful are found here. Across, over here, the market place continues and then by this area they are of the lowest standards. North of that is Forge Alley. All of the forges and smithies are located here. By the ruling council orders they were all brought together and buffered by a silence zone. Further north is the House of Acquisitions. I guess you can call it a cross between a rogue's guild and a merchant guild all rolled into one. Across the east wall is the fungi field. Further south is the bowch farms. Between the lower market place and the bowch farms are the slums. And finally we have the docks, here in the south west."

"There are eight entrance roads into Malzebowan." Yasrae pointed each one out, although they were clearly visible on the map. "Each entrance is guarded by a ruling council house and each has the responsibility to light one of the light stones every three hours. Depending on which light stone is lit will tell you what time it is."

Irraste asked, "What if there is a house war between two of the ruling council houses? Would that leave two of the entrances vulnerable?"

Yasrae smiled. "Yes it typically does. But when that happens, one of the other houses takes on the responsibility and collects any entrance fees that come their way. Any house that does not ensure its responsibility of security is dealt with one way or another and will find its entire house severally punished."

"The second most powerful house is House Barrindar. You would be wise to remember that name. Their guards roam the streets and deal whatever form of government as they see fit. They also hire out to smaller houses to supplement fighters during a house war. House Barrindar gets paid upfront and then a continued sum afterwards. Matron Elg'caress Barrindar rules them. She's an old hag and as ugly as they get. Her temper is well known and rumors are abounding with her having the largest sets of torture chamber in all of Malzebowan, with none of them ever silent. They say no one ever dies there but kept alive to be tortured forever. Barrindar also has the largest number of priestesses including the high priestess."

"And so why aren't they the most powerful house?"

Yasrae shook his head. "No one knows why exactly. There are two reasons I've come up with that sound plausible. The first is that neither the Matron nor any of her daughters manage to tolerate each other long enough to gain a stronger grip on the city and thus on the first house. The second reason is the first house itself."

"House Torvirr is the first ruling house. It is led by Matron Orbb'Rah Torvirr. She has ruled the first house and the city for as long as anyone can remember and is as young as the day she started. She has no children, no priestesses, and if rumors are correct, no consorts. From what everyone can tell, she is completely level headed in full contrast to Elg'caress. Any who threatens her or challenges her simply disappears. That rumor, at least, has been confirmed to be true. There isn't a house war or an assassination but a simple disappearance." There was a bit of trepidation in his voice as he spoke of house Torvirr and Irraste could tell why. He could fight his way through priestesses, mages, rogues, fighters, demons, and humanoid slaves. He was probably prepared for most spells that could be sent his way. But to just disappear was something he could not fight.

"What about your closest rivals?" This was probably the most important information Irraste needed. It would tell her whom to look out for in the shadows and what she was going to lead this house against, if and or when, the time came.

"The house above us is House Phorudossa. They have kept a good eye out for us for quite some time. We even periodically hint that we may make a move and attack their house, but we have absolutely no intention to do so. It would bring too much attention to us."

Irraste nodded. The higher in the social rank a house was, the more likely a secret such as this would be found out. "So you gain status in the social hierarchy by default when two rival houses above you destroy one, the other, or both. Very wise, let your enemies do your work for you."

Yasrae smiled and nodded at her compliment. It was rare to receive a genuine compliment from anyone, let alone a female. "The house has three daughters and two sons. We also have a spy in that house. He keeps us informed on their movements and leaks information about us that we want it leaked. This keeps him trusted by house Phorudossa. Although I suspect he gets paid more from that house than he does from ours."

"So he may not be very reliable?"

Yasrae shrugged. "As reliable as any other dark elf."

Irraste knew what that meant. There weren't any dark elf loyal to any other; it was only loyalty to power. So his spy would fall into the company of who had the most power, paid him the most, or even threatened him the most. She also knew that his comment was directed at her. He didn't trust her, and she didn't trust him, but right now she needed him and he needed her. She turned her attention back to the task at hand. "And the house directly below you?"

"That would be House Harludossa. They have two daughters and only one son. Their army isn't anywhere near our strength, but what they lack in power they make up in ambition. There is no secret they have their eyes set at this house. We have been able to keep them at bay with minor scrimmages and have prevented a few plots. I must say that I do appreciate their tenacity. Any other questions at the moment?"

Irraste shook her head. She took his comment as a dismissal of the conversation. Normally it would have upset her but she was willing to take a little bit humiliation in exchange for information.

Information was power, and like any other dark elf, she was drawn to it.

"We will be heading here." Yasrae pointed to a place in the market area half way to the lower market place. "I have a connection that will give us a good price on outfits that will fit you. Are you ready to go?"

Irraste nodded. She had taken in a fair amount of information but the best teacher of knowledge was experience and it was time to experience Malzebowan. After Yasrae rolled up the map and put it away, he led her back out the room, down the hall and down two flights of stairs. At the bottom of the stairs was a grand entry hall. There was a set of massive double doors that lead outside flanked by two Minotaurs. A quick salute by Yasrae and the guards pulled on the heavy doors and let both Irraste and Yasrae out into the city.

The cavern was bigger in height and width than Anarchia. She could barely see the top of the cavern and of what she could see between her and it had various flying creatures and objects and she wondered how they didn't all crash together. She saw a sailing ship with a single mast that flew in the air and then stopped at one of the towers she realized was in the high market. Its crew tossed out several ropes to hold it in place, similar to what a water craft would do, and then placed a walking plank across to the tower where the crew started to haul merchandise to and from their trading partners.

A balor crossed the sky. It was a massive sized winged demon whose body seemed to be on fire. Irraste watched as it dove toward the ground, leveled off and landed a few blocks away. She was ready to run for her life and even Yasrae placed his hand the hilt of his sword, but the balor hadn't noticed them. It seemed to have only one focus at the moment, that of a lonely kobold. The poor thing was carrying a sack full of items, probably on its way back to its owner with the items it bought. Then again, perhaps it was running away with all the items it had stolen from its master. Either way the outcome was going to be the same. The balor quickly snatched the kobold in hand, threw its head back and let out a huge, load bellow, and flew off with the poor creature. The kobold scream in agony as its body burst into flames at the presence of the balor's fiery body.

Irraste found it interesting to watch the reactions of the nearby dark elves and other denizens. Instead of retreating to a nearby hideout to avoid contact with the demon, the inhabitants of

Malzebowan watched on and waited. Once the demon had left with the kobold and the sack had fallen to the ground, there was a mad dash for the sack. Dark elves and humanoids fell upon the lonely sack of goods faster than a carrion feeder upon a corpse. Within seconds, two goblins were dead, a bugbear was wounded, and the sack was totally missing.

Another creature caught Irraste eye, a large floating orb creature. This was a Watcher, or as her race called them, orb seers. The creature was at least six feet in diameter. It had a large mouth that took up the majority of its lower half of its body and one large eye that took up the majority of the upper half. There were many eyestalks that protruded from the top of its head, and Irraste knew that each of the eyestalk could fire various deadly rays including one that would disintegrate anything it hit. The rest of the body was covered with smaller eyes and a couple of long tentacles. Fortunately they orb seer had other important things to do than to disintegrate buildings and the populace of the city.

The two of them walked on in cautious silence. Everywhere they turned, danger was obvious. They could hear a scream in the far off distance. A mugging took place a block away. They even stepped over a murdered dark elf, its corpse still warm and blood still dripping from his fresh wound.

Suddenly a male dark elf stumbled out of nowhere and bumped into Irraste. He was clumsy, perhaps drunk at first glance. She had seen this maneuver before and was already taking precautions. She pushed him away just as they bumped.

"Get away from you dumb, stupid male. If I weren't in a hurry I would have your hide for touching me with your foul presence."

"I beg forgiveness. You're right; I am a dumb, stupid male. And I'm clumsy too." It was the most pathetic attempt at being humble she had ever seen. She wanted to flay him alive for even attempting to persuade her with this insult upon her intelligence.

"Be gone. Go on, get."

And with that, the male dark elf bowed and started to walk away. He had only walked a few steps when he screamed in pain. He looked at his right hand and watched in horror as it started to melt away and was eaten by acid. First his fingers, then his hand, and the acid kept on eating away his body up his arm. The male flung about trying to shake off the acid and then screamed loader still.

He gave one last piercing cry of pain before he fell to the ground, the acid taking the last bits of his body.

Yasrae looked at her curiously, but not condemningly.

"He had a dagger and was going to assassinate me," she said without missing a step in her stride as she walked.

Yasrae wondered if the attacker actually did or didn't have a dagger, but it didn't matter now. Word would be on the street to leave them alone. It was at this point that Yasrae took note that she may have more abilities than he had bargained for and wondered if he had made the best choice in choosing her.

After a few more blocks, they came to a store named "Nau tri'sae nau klath'ra". It was of higher quality than she had been used to. The whole of the building had a purple fey fire in the shapes of spider webs all over. Underneath the words on the sign was a picture of a bolt of cloth. Yasrae opened the door and entered with Irraste close behind him.

The single bell above the door rang as they entered and brought the sales clerk from behind a counter. He wore a pair of black silk paints with black leather boots. A bright gold vest was worn over a brilliant blue tunic. The entire outfit was meant to represent wealth and talent. Irraste assumed some of that were true, but doubted he was as rich as his clothing suggested.

The inside was as finely kept and as colorful as he was. It was full of clothing outfits of intricate designs. There were shelves of pants and folded tunics. There were racks of cloaks and capes. There were shelves with cubbyholes filled with various clothing, hats, vests, vestments, wizard robes, adventuring outfits, and all in a wide variety of colors and sizes.

"Ah, Yasrae. It has been a long time."

"Yes it has, Z'plozach. May I introduce Medri? She is a cousin of our Matron Mother Irraste and has come from a nearby dark elf city."

It was general practice for dark elves to change their names as well as their backgrounds to keep their identity from being known. This was to keep potential rivals off guard. Since this was commonly done, no one would suspect if her real name were being used or a fake one. And the background story was close enough to her own that she could remember it for the short amount of time she needed to use it. She found it ironic that they could hide the truth within the truth and it wouldn't be believed. The clerk would know some part of the story was a lie, but he wouldn't know what part. So he would have to act as if it were all true least he would offend the both of them. Some days Irraste found being a female dark elf very amusing, and this was definitely one of those days.

The sales clerk stopped in his tracks. He was so occupied with his meeting with Yasrae that he hadn't even noticed Irraste come in. He so rarely had female customers come in; usually they sent their slaves, henchmen or in the case of Yasrae, their best bargainer. Protocol dictated that he only spoke to the female and not the subordinate, but he could only speak to her if she had spoken to him first. This often made transactions clumsy and so he often looked forward to the days when a female didn't come into his shop, no matter how much money she had to spend. Unfortunately, this was not one of those days.

Z'plozach bowed to her, "Mistress Medri. It is an honor to have you in our city, and more so to have you in my store. How may I be of service?"

"We are here to … "; Yasrae started to say but was cut off by a quick glance from Irraste. He was in charge, this was his plan and he was going to protest. But he remembered, in order for the plan to work he had to play his part as well. He swallowed his pride for now. He'll have to deal with her later.

"I have come … ", she corrected, "to purchase a few items for my cousin. It's a sign of good faith between our houses and even our cities. I assume you have spider silk dresses for sale."

'Right for the expensive garments', Yasrae thought. 'Fortunately I've only brought enough coins to keep her spending habits on a leash.'

"Yes, yes of course Mistress. This way, this way please." Z'plozach tried to lead the way into another connecting room through a side archway. He took a few strides and then he stopped. Females were supposed to lead and the males were supposed to follow. But he was the host and wasn't he supposed to provide his service even if it was a direction to the next room? He took another step to lead and then stopped again. He was so confused. He didn't want to assume to lead her and then again he didn't want to be rude. The wrong choice would be devastating. It was far easier to deal with a male.

Irraste did her best to restrain herself from laughter. Indeed, this was going to be one of those days she would enjoy her rank.

After letting Z'plozach make several attempts to walk, point, bow yet again, and then again attempt to walk, she put up her hand and made him stop. She could watch that all day, but she had other things to do. So, with a sinister smile that made Z'plozach's blood run cold and left him with only a guess of what might be his punishment, Irraste found her way through the arch and into the other room.

The room was obviously more elaborate than the first, and rightfully so, it was more suited for females. There were dresses, gowns, corsets, skirts, and very lacy tunics. There were purple, red, silver, black, white, blue, green, and gold colors everywhere. She made her way around the whole room and let her fingers delicately fun over every fabric. She only dreamed of wearing something like these and now she was going to pick out one to wear.

She found a dress that caught her attention. It was a deep purple with gold trim. The fabric was sheer in most places except for the few that would conceal her femininity, but then just barely. The strapless dress would start at about half way down her breasts and then join together at the top of her hip. From there it dropped in front of her, but kept her thighs exposed. It also dropped along her backside starting at her hip and barely offered any cover.

Another was white with spun silver and would amplify her hair. It gathered at the neckline and then would go out to the sides of her breast and then cut back in just below her navel. It was backless like the first dress. The garment would gather around her waist and then drape toward the ground with a slit up both sides of the thighs.

A third dress was red and totally sheer. This one started with thin straps over the shoulders and then cut down deep into cleavage. It also had a cut slit up the right thigh that went to the waist and the whole thing would end just above her knees.

They were all very lovely and would make quite the impression on anyone who came to visit a Matron Mother. Although, Irraste knew very well that Yasrae would try to keep her on a short leash, since this was his conspiracy. She did wonder how short that leash was and it was time to find out.

"Yasrae, since you have lived with Irraste longer than I have, I'm sure you have come to understand her taste in clothing then I would. Your opinion would be highly valued."

Stephen Christiansen

Z'plozach cringed at that offer to one of his best allies. This was always a trick, a trap in the conversation. No female would ever ask the opinion of a subordinate, let alone a male. He had to watch as this played out.

"Any one of those would look very lovely and fitting for Matron Mother Irraste." Yasrae said. "I'm sure she would be very pleased at whichever one you choose."

It was a neutral answer, one Yasrae probably practiced many times with any other female. But she understood what he really meant and the answer was very clear. Yasrae had emphasized the one "one". So, that was it, she could choose only one. It didn't matter which, but she was sure he had brought enough money for only one. 'A very short leash', she thought.

"Your price, Z'plozach," she said trying to get his initial offer. She knew what game was coming next and she played this one very well.

"Two hundred and twenty five each, Mistress."

Medri looked the dresses over as if to decide which one she was going to buy, but she had already made up her mind. She brought all three to the counter as Z'plozach made his way behind it.

"One hundred for each", she said.

Both Z'plozach and Yasrae acted as if the air had been punched from their lungs. Z'plozach was the first to reply.

"Mistress", he gasped, "that would barely cover my expenses. These silks were brought from far away cities, from dangerous spiders. The harvesting is dangerous and many have lost their lives in pursuit of such fine silk. And then there is the expense of the tailors."

"And may I remind Mistress," Yasrae cut in, as she knew he would. Here came the first attempt to yank the chain. "We were given a budget and the three of these over extend our resources. Where Matron Mother Irraste would be grateful of the gift, she would not be happy if we had to dip into her own coin to pay for her own gift. If Mistress would allow me, we do have the finances to cover one of these, but only one of these."

Irraste ignored Yasrae as if he wasn't even there. Now it was her turn to put both of these male in their place. "Don't give me that, Z'plozach. From the looks of you, you are the tailor of many, if not all of these fine outfits. That means the only expense you have is the fabric. You also look fairly intelligent and no Matron

126

Mother would ever put up with a more intelligent male than she. So she would be intelligent enough to keep any expense low. This tells me you didn't buy the fabric but instead, your house has a production of spider silk and you weave it yourself. In other words, there wasn't an expense."

Z'plozach's blood again ran cold and drained from his face. This was a family secret. He often used the tale of having to barter for the best fabric from far off and exotic places to boost his prices. He could weave as good a tale as he could a bolt of silk, but now he was caught off guard and didn't have any measure left to increase his proceeds. He also feared she might demand that she could take the items for free.

"From the look on your face, I see this isn't a well-known fact. So here is my deal. I will keep your family secret safe with me so that you may keep your sale prices at the top level and you may still receive your profits. Next, I will let it be known that you have sold merchandise that will clothe Matron Mother Irraste Do'tlar and as the news spreads, your business will increase. And finally this: I have contacts in my home city that deal in arachfey and blink spider silk. Ah, I see you are definitely interested. Once I reach my home city, I can have my agents barter with you and we can have a mutual benefit."

"The new price is two hundred for all three and you can toss in a set of boots."

The price was outrageous, she was asking for all three outfits for less than the price of one. But if she delivered on her trade, he would be able to recoup his loss in no time. And the threat of his secret being revealed would destroy him. He didn't have a choice.

"The price is fair, Mistress."

"Good, very good. I'll take those boots over there. And give them to Yasrae; he'll carry the whole purchase."

Z'plozach bowed and went to work. He delicately folded each dress and then tied them neatly with a silk ribbon and gave them Yasrae along with the boots Irraste had picked out. After another small bow he saw his two patrons to the door and was glad they had left. He had much to tell his contact, Valas.

"That was my contact", Yasrae protested. "You have basically destroyed my good relationship with him by your negotiating skills!"

Yasrae was furious, but did his best not to raise his voice too loud outside. He was sure his business here would spread like wildfire; he just didn't want it to spread too soon.

"When you don't return to your home city because you are playing Matron to my house, he will realize that you have cheated him and he will take it out on me. I'm ruined because of you."

"He was your contact," she corrected him. "Didn't you notice the dresses?"

"What are you talking about? What do you mean he was my contact? And I don't care about the dresses."

"Two of them are similar, but the red one is different."

"What does that have to do with anything?"

She turned down an alley and pulled him in close. Her hand went into intricate work of the dark elf sign language. At first, Yasrae thought she was going to cast a spell and his hand went immediately to his sword.

"Your contact made the first two," she signaled in sign language, "but not the red one. He couldn't make it because he had never seen it. He hadn't seen it before because it is a style well known in Anarchia. This dress came from the same caravan that I was on during my expedition here. The person who sold him the red dress is probably the same person who sold me to the tavern where you found me. Your mention of me being from another city would clue him in to checking with his other contact, the supplier of the red dress. Together they will know I am still alive and free in your house. This will lead to your secret of a fake Matron getting out."

Yasrae swore under his breath. She was right and now there was only one thing left to do. Z'plozach had been a good contact, but now he was a loose end. He nodded.

"Stay here. I'll be right back," he said as he slipped away into the darkness.

Irraste never took orders from any male, and she wasn't going to start being in the habit anytime soon. But Yasrae had a point. This city had its own pace, its own life, and until she understood this life, it was best she stayed out of sight. For a brief time she did think about trying to make her way out of the city, through the underworld and make her way back home. Unfortunately she didn't know her way through the underworld and would probably get lost. And even if she did make it back home, those that set her up to be killed with the rest of the caravan would probably hunt her down. On top of that, her Matron Mother would be very unhappy with her coming back empty handed. This was of course, if she could make her way past the guards at the entry points. If she were going to leave the city then she would need a better plan.

Until then she had to sit tight and at the moment that meant staying put as she was told, no she thought, as she was suggested to do. Yes, that sounded better at least. She gestured with her hands and began to cast a spell. She wasn't going to take her chance of just hiding in the shadows, any help she could have she would take. The spell went off and her body became like a shadow, a two-dimensional being as pitch as night. Her new body blended into the darkness better than any ability she could attempt herself. During the duration of the spell she would also stop producing heat. As long as Yasrae didn't take too long, she doubted she would ever be seen or detected in any fashion.

Yasrae had turned down the alley and kept to the dark shadows, the last thing he needed was someone to stop him and slow him down before his mark was able to make his alternate connection whoever that was. After a few blocks and a couple of turns, he found his way back to the "Nau tri'sae nau klath'ra". From his point of view he could see Z'plozach locking up his shop as he was leaving.

It was almost immediately after Yasrae and his Irraste left his building that Z'plozach had called forth a passing goblin and had paid him to deliver a message to his other contact. The information about a female coming from a new city was just too close to coincidence, even if they were a month apart. He just had to set up another meeting to discuss his new bits of information. All he had to do was close shop and meet him at their regular meeting place. Well, as long as he didn't run into …

"Is business so slow to close so early?" Yasrae asked as he crossed the street toward his connection.

"There has been a new turn of events that I have to …"

Yasrae caught up to him and stood within arm's reach. "Where are you going, Z'plozach?"

"There's a new caravan of silk that just came in," Z'plozach was cut short. The blade pierced just under the center of his rib cage at an upper angle and cut right into his heart. The pain was red hot, but was only short lived as his life and his blood flowed from his body.

Yasrae caught Z'plozach's body before he hit the ground. A flick of the wrist and Yasrae was able to pull his sword free. With Z'plozach sill caught with one arm, Yasrae was able to turn him around and head him back to the shop door. He was able to find Z'plozach's keys with ease and in no time he was able to drag Z'plozach's body into the store.

Once inside, Yasrae took off his backpack and started pulling some of the more expensive clothing off the shelves and put them inside. It didn't take long before he had put in more into his backpack that the outside volume seem to hold and yet he continued to put in more as if the whole pack was nothing but a bottomless pit. He grabbed many of the pricy dresses, the best sets of boots, a few silk tunics and anything else that caught his eye. Next, he moved to a place on the wall behind the counter. He knew what he was looking for since he had found it many months ago and he was able to find it with little effort. A small-concealed button was exactly where he remembered it. A quick push and a hidden panel opened to reveal a concealed niche. He reached inside and pulled out two large bags of coins. Fortunately for him, Z'plozach was always a creature of habit.

After a few minutes of looting the shop, Yasrae placed a few of the garments he had no care for over the corpse of Z'plozach. He then pulled a fire stick from one of his pockets and with a flick of the wrist tossed it on the heap of clothing. It didn't take long before the fire caught, was burning on its own and with a little luck, the rest of the shop would go up with the body. It was better to make it look like an arson instead of a hit job. Whoever Z'plozach was in contact with would investigate a murder, but probably not an arson gone badly. When the fire was burning well on its way, Yasrae quickly gathered his seemingly limitlessly spacious backpack and left, making sure he locked the door on the way out. He may be a murderer, he may be a thief, he may also be an arsonist, but he wasn't rude.

After a few more minutes, retracing his footsteps back through the shadows of the alley, Yasrae made his way to the spot he left Irraste. "Iblith. I told her to stay here!"

Irraste dropped her spell and her body gained thickness while the shadow features faded. "I'm not too unwise as to travel this city without someone who could watch my back. I assume the job was a success?"

Yasrae had just returned from killing off one of his best contacts and wasn't in the mood to hold a full conversation, let alone answer to a female. He merely shot a scowl at her and let her assume the fullest extent of how he dealt with the situation.

"There are a few more items I would like to pick up while we are roaming the city," Irraste said.

"We spent our entire budget on your outfits. That is all I brought for you to spend." Yasrae wasn't about to tell her that he had raided the store and was able to recoup his expenses with interest.

"Not to worry." Irraste pulled a pouch from her side.

"Where did you get that?" Yasrae's mind raced as he retraced his steps. And then it hit him. "You picked it from the assailant from earlier."

Yasrae smiled. She wasn't going to let him dictate her spending habits. "I need an apothecary. Quite a few of my spells rely on ingredients I can find there."

Yasrae wasn't in the mood to argue either. With a sigh of surrender, and a shaking of his head, Yasrae headed deeper into the city with Irraste behind him.

Valas Velkyn stood in his usual meeting place, a spot on top of one of the forge buildings. It was the only place in Malzebowan that he could view the whole city. He often wondered if the proprietor knew about his secret rendezvous. He had received the message from the terrified goblin about his contact, Z'plozach, wanting to meet. It wasn't like Z'plozach to ask for a meeting; usually he waited until after hours of his shop. This must be a significant piece of information.

Valas saw the reddish glow off to his right before he noticed the smoke. A fire had started somewhere in the city. Although a fire breaking out in a random location wasn't of any significance, Valas was quite used to the unexpected in the City of Evil; he just had an ominous feeling about this one. The timing was too close to his meeting, the meeting itself was unexpected, and the tardiness of his contact was too much to be a coincidence.

Valas climbed down from his spot and merged from the alley between a few of the smithies. He made his way, winding through the streets to the source of the fire. His steps were full of confidence, there were few to challenge his authority. As he got closer to the source of the fire, his suspensions were confirmed, the Nau tri'sae nau klath'ra was burning and from the look of things, the entire store would be a loss. As he stood and watched the fire consume the building, despite the efforts of various wizards attempting to use their magic to put the fire out, he was sure he would find Z'plozach dead, and not from the fire. He was sure his contact was murdered. Someone else got to him before he did. The only question was what the information Z'plozach was going to pass on. It must have been very important and Valas was going to find out.

Chapter: House Do'tlar

*I*rraste was able to pick up a few more items that she needed from the apothecary. With the extra income she was able to pick up from her assailant earlier that day she was able to pick up a whole skeleton, several herbs, a couple of potions, a jar with a set of eyeballs floating in some form for liquid, a set of mortar and pestle, and finally a small utility knife. The knife wasn't designed for offense or even defense use and would prove to be useless in combat, but that wasn't the function she wanted it for. While they were purchasing her rather odd items, Irraste took note that Yasrae put all of the objects into his backpack and she kept in mind the backpack's very function of holding more than seemingly possible.

Upon their arrival back to house Do'tlar, Irraste realized she was hungry. She did have a huge meal prior to leaving for her shopping spree, but utilizing dark necromantic magic usually had its toll. She had heard stories of individuals who couldn't control necromancy and the darker arts wound up consuming the caster. Although she was wise enough to stick to spells she could control, the practice still took quite a bit out of her and fortunately she was able to recoup through a good solid meal and a little rest.

Yasrae led her to the common eating hall. She was used to having a noble dining room for those who were part of the ruling family, although she usually ate in her own private room with her goblin bringing her food to her. Now she would have to get used to, not only eating with other individuals, but with males and commoners as well as well as humanoids that were considered slaves. Yasrae found the archway that lead into the eating hall and entered.

Inside Irraste found a very large room that was wider than it was long. There were two long sets of tables paralleled to each other and each set was full of chairs. Nearly every chair was occupied by male dark elves and to Irraste's surprise, quite a few slaves. There were goblins, orcs, kobolds, hobgoblins, bugbears, a few ogres and even a couple of Minotaurs. Each individual had a plate full of food and a set of utilities accompanied with a goblet. Irraste suspected these dishes were probably matching at one time but now were totally random and mismatched.

There were meats, some form of mashed roots, steamed mushrooms, and some baked breads in serving bowls that were passed around. Irraste was surprised to find some form of civility in the creatures. She suspected and assumed they would fight each other over the pick of food, that they would show their dominance over each other. But that was not the case. They were still showing their barbarianism through their eating habits, eating with their hands, tearing the meat off the bones with their teeth, tossing food to each other without passing the bowl, and even the freely release of bodily gas.

As they entered, the room that was once full of noise of various conversations, the sounds of utilities clanging on the plates, and the occasional screeching of chairs moving, suddenly silenced. There had been rumors of a female in their house, a female that was going to be their new Matron Mother. A few of them had actually seen her, but that was only in passing. Now all of them were able to confirm the rumors. None knew exactly how to take this change of their society.

As Yasrae and Irraste crossed the room to a set of chairs at the head of a table all eyes followed them. After a few moments of keeping the audience in suspense Yasrae announced, "Greetings my fellow household members. I am sure you have heard the rumors of our house receiving a new Matron Mother. Well, I am here to tell you that it is true. This is your new Matron Mother Irraste Do'tlar. Rest assured, your status and your freedoms will not change. I am still the house leader and you will follow me. This female will act like your Matron Mother during a visit from another house. You will treat her as such if you wish for our conspiracy to continue. If you have any problems with this, you may talk to me personally. Are there any questions?"

There was silence. Yasrae was sure there wouldn't be any problems or any questions, especially since he had mentioned that they could speak to him personally. They knew what a problem with any of the house rules meant. It meant that they could leave and find another house to stay in. This was certain death for most of them. No, there wouldn't be any problems.

Irraste found her seat next to Yasrae and found that she was next to another male dark elf on her right side. The male dark elf on her right simply turned his side so his back was slightly to her as if she wasn't there. She had noticed that the conversations started back up but this time in only murmurs, slightly beyond her audible range. She sat feeling watched and yet very alone. Instead of focusing on her newfound attention she decided to go ahead and eat, but she wasn't sure how she should ask for food from the serving bowls. It was Yasrae who used a few dark elf sign language gestures and a few of bowls came his way. After he had served himself, he gave her the bowls to serve herself. She was nearly infuriated and definitely irritated at having to scrve herself, but when her stomach protested with a growl, she ended up serving herself and eating with the commoners and the slaves of the house.

Once she was able to get back to her room, and after Yasrae dropped off the items she bought at the apothecary, she started immediately on working on building her dagger all over again. She still couldn't believe she had the same dagger for many years, but in a short amount of time she had gone through two of them. She sighed. They weren't too difficult to make they were just time consuming.

First, she called forth her racial ability to cast fey fire and placed the flames on top of the desk she was going to be working on. The light was bright enough for her to see but soft enough not to hurt her light sensitive eyes. She then took the two thighbones from the skeleton she bought and used the utility knife to shape the two daggers she wanted. It took some time to get the look of them correct, but through her perseverance she finally finished to her satisfaction. Both were perfectly balanced. She started casting her first spell on the first dagger. What little light that was coming from the non-burning fire seemed to dull down and a cold chill came through the room. It was a spell similar to the one that made a skull explode and was the same spell she had put on her first dagger. This one would explode the bone dagger into a thousand shards and injure if not kill any in a small radius around its focal point.

Once the first dagger was done she went upon her task to magic the second one. She cast a second spell and let its magic aura fall upon this dagger. Again the light faded and again a chill came through the room. Anyone who came into the room at such a time would think some form of undead creature had entered just before them. The spell drained the life from its victim and sent it through the dagger and into its wielder. Whomever the dagger hit would not only take damage from the blade but also from the magic that would in turn heal the owner. Between the two of them, Irraste felt more comfortable. She would have to make sheaths in her new leather armor, but that would have to be another day. She wasn't sure when she would be able to wear the armor again, since it was not something a Matron Mother would wear, but she was more comfortable knowing it was in existence.

Next she pulled a pointer finger from the right hand of the skeleton. She had not only lost her bone dagger from her capture but also her bone skeleton key. It had served her well in the past and was easy enough to make. She laid the finger on the desk in front of her and used the dagger to cut notches in the side so it more resembled a key. When she was satisfied with it, she went into another casting. This spell didn't create the same darkness, the same gloom, or even the same chill as the first two. It hardly had any effect at all, but Irraste knew the spell had been cast correctly and its effect was now imbued upon the skeleton finger.

Finally she brought forth the skull and jar full of floating eyes. These eyes were blue and she wondered from which poor creature they had been taken from. But then it didn't matter; they would serve their purpose one way or another. She cast another spell and could feel a bit of her own life force leave her body. This spell required her to give up a bit of herself but she found it was always well worth it. When the spell was done, she took the floating eyes out of the jar. Again, she cast a spell. This time the spell was the same she used to bring dead bodies back to life. When she cast the spell on the eyes she could see the eyes start to move in tandem as if they were looking around, taking in its new view, its new life. Carefully she scooped them up with her hand and gently placed them in the eye sockets of the skull. The spell was complete. She closed her eyes and she could see herself through the eyes of the skull.

Perhaps she could make a new start for herself, she thought. This was just the beginning and tomorrow was another big day. Yasrae had promised to give her a tour of the house so she would know her way around. But that was tomorrow and now she was tired. Tired from all of the walking and tired from the entire spell castings; she was truly exhausted. She unzipped her boots; the new pair that fit better, tossed them into her closet, and completely undressed. She was aware that anyone could burst in on her, but she was armed now and her undead skull would give her warning. She doubted that these male were that stupid.

She made her way to the washroom and took up the vase of water. As she poured it into the tub, the water continued to flow out as if there were no end. And she was sure there wasn't since more than likely there was a little pinhole into the very fabric of the elemental plane of water. When the tub was about a quarter full, she dropped in the red stone and immediately the water started to warm up. She could see the steam start to rise and the heat felt wonderful on her body. At about the halfway mark she dropped in the blue stone and the water started to cool a bit. Once she reached the three quarter mark of the tub, she stopped, placed the vase back, and eased her way into the hot soothing bath. The water was fantastic and soothed every stressful muscle.

After about an hour of soaking in the tub, Irraste got out and dried herself off with one of the towels. She found a plug in the tub and pulled it and let the water drain away, but where the water went, she didn't know, and at the moment she didn't care. Perhaps that would be another time. She crossed to the bed; it was definitely time to rest. Normally she would meditate for a few hours, but with all the activity she had, and the fact the bed was the best thing she had ever slept in, she decided to lie down and enjoy the pleasure of slumber. Within a few moments she was fast asleep.

The next morning, she dressed in her leather armor outfit. She thought that would be wiser than any of the Matron Mother outfits. She was sure her role as Matron Mother would only be brief when she was required to fulfill the role, so there wasn't any reason to announce it to the whole house, especially when most came here to remove themselves from the presence of a Matron. She went to the mess hall and made sure she sat in the seat she had taken the evening before. This time there wasn't anyone next to her, but she was getting used to the way things were done at this house. She made a few dark elf hand signals to individuals who were near serving bowls and they resentfully passed a few of the dishes her way, although none spoke directly to her. At least they weren't trying to kill her. The dishes held scrambled eggs of some creature, thin bowch steak strips, and one had a type of bread roll she had never seen before.

After a few moments of eating alone, when she was nearly done, Yasrae entered the room and sat at the head of the table next to her. He found it to be a welcome sight to already have the bowls next to him so he didn't have to wait for them to be passed.

"Ah, how thoughtful of you to have this waiting for me," he said to Irraste as he dished himself.

Irraste was about to say something to the effect of his conceit, but she thought better of it, though she did manage to get off a dirty look. She sat and listened to him go on and on about himself and realized just how conceited he really was. She only rolled her eyes and endured.

When they had finished breakfast, he got up and led her out of the mess hall and on to the promised tour of the house. "Before we go too far, there is someone I would like you to meet," Yasrae said to her. She continued to follow him further down the hall and up two flights of stairs. The traffic of inhabitants of the house was fewer the further up the levels she went until there was none down the stretch of hall toward the room Yasrae took her.

The entrance was a curved archway and entered into a series of joining rooms. The first room she could see was the center room, with another flanking each of its sides also connected by curved archways. This room was a library and it was lit, although only barely, by green fey fire torches in each of the four corners. There were shelves on as much of the wall space that was available as well as free stranding shelves in the middle of the room. Every shelf was covered in books. There were even book in piles on the floor. There were two round tables with a few chairs around each, most of which were empty, all except one, which was occupied by a male dark elf.

"Irraste, this is Alton Rinna Do'tlar, our house mage."

The dark elf was almost entirely bald, except for a ring of hair around the backside of his head. From here his hair grew long and flowed to half way down his back. There were various markings on his face of blue, green, red and purple. She wasn't sure if these were magical markings or tattoos. He wore mages robes, a multi-pocketed set of robes that would allow any mage to reach for material items he needed quickly for components for his spells. Although he had changed his clothing and artwork on his face had been added, she did recognize him from the table the other day; she sat beside him during dinner. During that time she thought him to be of little or no importance, but now that she understood his position in the house, she wondered why Yasrae didn't introduce her to him at the time. She was sure Yasrae was controlling the situation as he saw fit, but to what extent would be something she would have to find out.

"Alton is in charge of keeping up the magical defenses of the house as well as keeping an arcane eye on everything that happens around here."

Irraste wondered if his arcane sight included the bathtub in her washroom or her bed in her bedroom. She did not like being spied upon.

Alton didn't even bother getting up to great them. He stayed seated and crossed his arms over his chest and glared at her with penetrating eyes. Irraste now wondered what else his arcane eyesight could see.

"Ah, well, looks like we have caught Alton at a bad time. Perhaps he's researching a new spell that would shake the very foundations of our enemies no doubt. Come on, there are a few other places of importance to show you." Yasrae led Irraste out and back down the hall they had come from.

"Such a pleasant disposition", Irraste said dryly in reference to Alton.

"One could hardly blame him, I suppose. He used to have Irraste's ear and she depended on him for advice that she couldn't get from her daughters. From his point of view, he was the power behind the throne and all other advice, especially from Irraste's daughters had to be taken with suspicion of conspiracy. We deliberately withheld our intent to over throw the females from him in fear he may want to stay in the powerful position he was in. Now, he simply has a job to do and I have my own advisors. Don't get me wrong; I still listen to his opinions, but not as strongly as he was listened to during the Matron Mother's reign. Of course he had obtained his position through hard work, study, manipulation; in effect, his own accord. With the current situation, he is the same level as everyone else, including those who used to be slaves. And now, of course, I have brought in another advisor to listen to, another to put on the throne. I can understand his less than accommodating disposition."

Irraste could understand and appreciate the wizard's stance. On top of being ousted from his power, he was replaced. And now it was being flaunted. To add another wound to the already injured, she was also another arcane caster. Although she was a necromancer and not a conjurer, she was still a spell caster of competent ability. The house mage would not be happy to say the least. She would have to watch for him.

"And his facial markings?" She asked.

Yasrae shrugged. "Some say it is a tattoo he did to himself or one that the last Matron Mother insisted he have, and that he uses magic to disguise it from time to time. Others say it was an incident when he was too close to the weave and only appears as he casts magic."

They were silent again as the passed the stairway that led back down the way they came. After a few more paces, they reached the end of the hallway that ended in an archway leading into another room. As they entered, Irraste could see that this was the throne room. Like all other throne rooms she had known, this one was octagonal. There was a massive black throne on a raised dais at the far end of the room and Irraste could tell that an occupant of the throne would have full command from that position over anyone who entered. To the left there was a balcony overlooking their part of the city and all across the room were motifs of spiders and webbing. Aside from these though, the rest of the room was empty.

"It is rather sparse. We took anything and everything of value when we initially took over. Of course we will have to spruce it back up again if you are to have company; we must definitely keep up the charade. Alton keeps several wards on the balcony and I would suggest you not getting too close."

Yasrae was speaking, but Irraste didn't hear a single word. She had crossed the room with one thing on her mind, the only thing she had ever dreamed of, but never in her wildest imagination did she think she would actually have the opportunity to do. At first she just caressed the throne with her fingers, feeling the smooth ebony like surface, as if making sure it was real. Then, with purpose and deliberation, she eased herself onto its seat. She eased her palms out to each of the armrests of the throne and look across the room to Yasrae. 'Yes', she thought, 'I can really grow accustomed to this.'

"Don't get too comfortable, you are only supposed to be for show. The last female to get comfortable in that throne, well, it wasn't a very pretty sight once we were done."

Irraste smiled and closed her eyes to enjoy the moment for just a brief time longer, then slid graciously off the throne to join Yasrae on the way out.

They returned down the stairs where they came from, descended three flights total and took a hallway to their right. Here the traffic of the house had increased and she felt once again as an equal to the previous slaves, in complete contrast to how she felt just moments ago in the throne room. After Yasrae passed a few doors, he came to one on his right and walked in with Irraste right behind him.

Inside was a small room, lit by a single floating orb of red fey fire. It was furnished with several cabinets, a desk, a chair and one occupant. This male dark elf wore very fine clothing, a gold colored silk tunic, and a set of black leather pants and leather boots. His hair was neatly kept, combed, and tied neatly, falling most of the way down his back. Currently he was looking over a set of ledgers.

"This is Uhlszyne. He is our financial advisor. Were I the one in charge of finances, I'll have run the house into the abyss a long time ago. I am definitely the dreamer, but Uhlszyne here keeps us on solid ground."

"Well met, I'm sure," he said to Irraste, and then turned to Yasrae. "I hope you didn't spend too much on her the other day."

"Actually I think we made out quite well. Speaking of expenses, how are we doing?"

"With your substantial deposit from the other day, we are doing quite well and should continue to do so for a short time. But we still need that trade agreement if we are to maintain our level of expenses."

"I'm working on that. And with Irraste's help, it will be finalized."

Uhlszyne nodded in agreement with that statement as if he had approved and Yasrae nodded back in acknowledgement. Irraste saw there was a financial plan that revolved around her, but they were going to make her wait to be brought into the plan. She knew that a conspiracy was best when it was kept to a minimum amount of conspirators until the right time. With the nod, Irraste saw the discussion to be over, and Yasrae confirmed this as he led the way back out.

Yasrae continued to lead the way as they found another set of stairs and went down several flights until Irraste knew, for almost certain, that she was at the very basement of the house. The bottom of the stairs opened up to a small landing but beyond that was a large archway. Yasrae noticed this would be the dungeon to any other house. She could imagine a large set of bars here that would restrict entry or exit, except for the cell door. She could even make out some of the holes from where the bars were. There would be a couple of guards stationed here for further protection. Now, it was devoid of all of that.

As they walked in she could see her suspicions to be correct. But instead of cells blocked off by walls and bars, she saw the walls and bars were dismantled and the entire area was open with only a few pillars to hold up the ceiling. Inside she saw various weapons, swords, daggers, maces, morning stars, and other weapons she had never seen before hanging along each of the walls. But instead of the usual metal, these were made of wood. All around the room were mats, obviously intended to break a fall and soften the impact of the stone floor. In the center of the room was T'rissvyr Do'tlar. She had only seen him briefly after she was released from her imprisonment.

Currently he was training two ogres. He had a wooden long sword in each hand and was naked from the waist up. Irraste could tell that T'rissvyr took great pride in keeping himself fit since he looked as if he could take on the ogres barehanded. The ogre to his right took a lunge with his fist. T'rissvyr stepped to his left, letting the blow swing wild. As he stepped aside, he charged the ogre to his left and caught it while it was in mid stride into its attack. The blow knocked the wind out of the poor creature, but T'rissvyr wasn't done with him yet. With a quick spin he caught the ogre in the back with one of his wooden swords and then charged for the first ogre. This one reached with both of his fists meaning to catch T'rissvyr if he attempted to slip past him. T'rissvyr was already deep into his charge and hit the ogre in the midsection with a lunge of one of his swords. If it were metal and sharp, the blade would have gone right through the ogre and out the other side.

T'rissvyr put his hand up to stop the mock battle. "You two are still working as individuals; you need to work in tandem, together.

Your initial charges were off, that is how I slipped past you. You must trust each other and help each other and you must realize that you are each other's best asset." T'rissvyr didn't know how much of the instruction the ogres understood, they were after all only ogres. He waved them a dismissal, "Go practice, we will try again tomorrow."

Yasrae clapped. "Two new recruits?"

"I picked them up at the docks; part of the slum brood is my guess." This was a saying of any who were born to the slum area or any who were lower than a slave, a slum brood.

"Ah well, the more for us. I was just showing Irraste, our new Matron Mother, around."

"And how do you appreciate our house?" T'rissvyr asked her.

Irraste hadn't missed the exact verbiage of T'rissvyr. The real question was rather or not she was appreciative of all of their hard work, and if not, then she would end up being insulting to their egos. "You have done an excellent job."

"For being males?" Yasrae added. The two male dark elves laughed. They had heard that expression far too often. Irraste, however, didn't find it amusing but she feigned a smile.

"Well, that's all the main rooms for now, why don't you get some rest?" Yasrae said to Irraste. "I have some plans to attend to and if they all fall through then we shall have quite a substantial income."

Yasrae bowed and left the training room while T'rissvyr shrugged and headed over to a wooden full blade sword to continue practice, both of them leaving Irraste to her own accord. She would head back to her room and think about, not only the main characters of the house, the passages, the main rooms, but also all of the subtleties she had picked up along the way.

Chapter: A Straightforward Contract

*I*t was the next day, during breakfast, when Yasrae caught up with Irraste again. She continued to find the one seat beside Yasrae's and continued to eat in silence, neither making nor receiving conversation in a room full of occupants. The early morning meal was similar to the one she had the other day and she wondered if most of the meals were going to be the same throughout her stay. Perhaps she would travel into the city and find a tavern she could frequent, in disguise of course.

"Good news." Yasrae said as he emptied one of the serving bowls on to his plate. "House Phorudossa has agreed to a mutual trade agreement. I have been working on this for weeks and now it is finally about to happen. They intend to send an emissary from their house to meet with our dear Matron Mother Irraste Do'tlar."

"That is where I come in," Irraste said with a small pout. Although she would thoroughly enjoy the station of Matron Mother, even if it were for a short time, she now knew how far this house had, and were going to continue to, use her. "My rescue from the slave ring was all part of your process to ensure this trade agreement. The agreement could be binding, if that could be said of any dark elf agreement, only if a Matron Mother signed it and the other house witnessed it. I am only here to forge a signature on a document."

Yasrae stopped eating. Irraste was smart, perhaps too smart for her own good. "I'm sure there will be other instances where we could use a Matron Mother. Or perhaps you would like to return to your former life you had only a few days ago?"

Irraste's eyes cut into Yasrae as if to say "Go ahead and try it." Yasrae simply laughed and continued eating. He had no intention of giving up his newest asset, but he didn't have to let her know that.

"When and where is the trade agreement to be dealt with?" Irraste asked.

"It will be tomorrow evening. First, House Phorudossa will send their emissary with two copies of the trade agreement. Of course the seriousness of the trade agreement will be stressed by who the emissary is. He, or she, depending on the importance House Phorudossa has with the agreement, will bring it to you in the throne room. We will have to spruce up the place a bit of course, add a few items to make it look as if you had always been there. And there will need to be some guards, a few on the balcony and a few outside the throne room, if only for a show of power. Once you have signed the documents, I will escort the emissary back to House Phorudossa and present the document to their House Matron Mother. She will then counter sign both documents, if she is pleased, and then keep one and one will be sent back with me. It is a fairly simple and straightforward contract."

Irraste wanted to laugh, but she controlled herself for fear of harming Yasrae's ego. It wasn't that she cared about his ego, she simply knew better than to mock the only power that kept the house in check, something she learned from her own Matron Mother back in Anarchia. The laugh wasn't about the plan itself, no the plan did seem rather straight forward, but it seemed that Yasrae was too close to the plan to remember that any dealings with any dark elf was never simple and definitely never straight forward.

Valas Velkyn had made his way to the "Elghinyrrok Veldrin", a tavern between the docks and the slums. Its fame was noted as a place to gather and give information, if one could afford the price. The outside hardly showed any signs of the building being a tavern. The windows were completely boarded over to block any outside light source to reflect in or any onlooker to peer a gaze. There was a sign post above the door with a painted picture of a cloak that took up most of the sign and a small glass of ale under one of its folds, barely visible. There were no words on it and it was only by word of mouth that anyone could guess the function of this building. Anyone passing it could guess that it might be a tailor shop, perhaps even unoccupied. The door was of thick wood with iron supports and a small panel was eye level, a panel that could be opened or closed from the inside so a sentry could tell who wanted entry and rather or not it would be granted.

Valas knocked twice, once, then twice again. He was fairly certain there were different knocks for different levels of guests, and depending on the current occupancy, the sentry would know rather or not to even bother looking through the panel. Valas knew he was always welcomed despite the current occupancy count; that is if the tavern wanted to see another day of prosperity. The panel opened and Valas could make out a set of red eyes peering back at him.

"Password", the voice said in a commanding tone from behind the door.

"K'lararl Xan'ss." The panel slid closed and the door opened cautiously to his response.

As Valas entered, he noticed the tavern to be as he remembered. It was pitch black. Only his ability to see heat allowed him to notice anything in the tavern. There was bar on the left wall as in most taverns, but that's where the similarities ended. The rest of the tavern was sectioned off with partitions to form small cubicles. Each small section had a table and a couple of chairs. The partitions themselves were magically silenced so any information communicated between patrons was kept to the table. This made the "Elghinyrrok Veldrin" ideal to pass information secretly. The only disadvantage to the environment was that either the informant or the recipient could be assassinated without notice or a sound and it wasn't uncommon to find a dead body sitting in one of the cubicles at closing time.

Valas made his way through the maze of partitions. He had frequented the establishment enough times to remember his way around even without the use of his heat vision. After a few twists and turns, he found the cubicle he was looking for. He had heard through various informants that there was a witness who had information he was looking for and was willing to sell it for a price. The informant would meet him here. Valas slid into a chair opposite a deep dwarf.

If there were light, Valas would have been able to see that the deep dwarf was bald. He was dressed in a smithy gear with a light brown leather apron over a dark brown leather tunic and he wore a pair of black leather pants with black leather boots. There was a grimy, greasy, dirty, dusty smell about him. In front of the deep dwarf was a pint of ale already half empty.

"Ye must be Valas", the deep dwarf said with trepidation and apprehension. Valas didn't answer, but he did pull out a few black adamantite octagonal coins and placed them on the table between them.

"Hey this aren't the price ah 'greed on".

"It is half. If I like the information you have then I will pay you the other half."

"An if ye don't?"

Valas just stared at him and didn't elaborate; he was sure the deep dwarf wasn't that stupid and left the consequences of wasting his time up the deep dwarf's imagination.

"Fair nough," the deep dwarf said. He nodded as if to confirm his own statement, more than likely to himself than to Valas, and then took another swig of his ale to gather the courage to continue. "Well, there ah was, mindin me own business, as ah always do, when ah saw them. Them two. It was that fancy one, Yasrae, from that house Do'tlar. And he had a female with him."

"She was leading the way?"

"Ah, nah. 'E was. She was followin."

"Did you get a good look at her?"

"Sure did. She was smallish for a female, less endowed if ya know what ah mean. And she had not much hair, cropped short."

"Are you sure?" Valas look at the deep dwarf straight into his eyes as if trying to see deep into his soul.

"Oh yeah. Couldn't miss that. Most ye females have long hair, ya know, it would get in the way of any forge. But she had short. Not a very good cut neither. A real hack job."

"And all of this was just before the fire?"

"Huh? Oh yeah. The place went up in flames. Well, they came out first. Didn't see much after that; had me own business ya see. But yeah, all before the fire."

Valas sat back in his chair and absorbed the information. The deep dwarf had no idea what information he had just passed on. It wasn't just who the potential murder and or arson was, but there was something else. Something he had to make sure before he acted on it, if he acted at all. He could always keep it to himself or sell it later, but he would have to see how this tangled web was woven. Valas reached into his pocket and produced a few more coins and placed them on the table next to the first few and then left. He had another agent to contact.

Irraste sat in the black throne in the throne room as any Matron Mother would. She had chosen the red dress to wear for the trade agreement ceremony. She wanted to give the emissary a sense of understanding of who was in charge. The red fey fire she had cast in two small globes on either side of the throne would give just enough light to see the color of the dress and to show how sheer the dress was. She would also keep her tone in a commanding fashion and remind the emissary where his place was. And she was fairly certain the emissary would be a male. The house they were trading with was one house higher in the social rank and therefore would not view this as a need to send a female. A male emissary would send the message that the lesser house was just that, a lesser house. So if the higher-ranking house was going to play their little power game, then Matron Mother Irraste was going to play hers.

The decorations had come along better than she had anticipated. Tapestries were brought in and hung around the room and a large rug was rolled out. Each of these depicted scenes of horrific torture upon surface elves by large spiders, Arachfey, and dark elves. To help amplify the existence of the balcony, two deep red curtains were hung flanking the archway opening. And finally a small table was brought in through Irraste's instance. Yasrae had thought he would have a problem with Irraste demanding too much, like she had while she was picking out a dress a few days ago, but he had no difficulties in obtaining a small side table. Upon this table, Irraste placed her skull, the skull she had worked so hard on, the magical skull with those undead blue eyes. The guards were a nice touch as well. She could see two outside on the balcony and two inside the balcony flanking the entry. There were also two guards flanking on the outside of the archway that lead into the throne room, two more on the inside also flanking the archway and two flanking her but were far enough away to not be on the raised dais. Each had matching adamantite chain armor, a long sword and a hand held crossbow.

"Matron Mother Irraste Do'tlar, may I present Tanth Phorudossa, second son to Matron Mother Yaszyne Phorudossa, and house mage of House Phorudossa." Yasrae had given the introduction, as Irraste was sure he would since Yasrae had a tendency of enjoying his own voice and the fact that he wanted to make sure everything went as planned. He had too much at stake and spent too much time and effort to just sit back and not be part of the ceremony.

Tanth had long white hair like most dark elves and his was tied in the back. He wore a set of mages robes, deep purple with bright red swirls. He also had a piwafwi held in place with a pendant of his house symbol.

T'rissvyr and Alton were also invited to join in on the signing of the document. T'rissvyr had accepted and was flanking Tanth and was slightly behind him. He was armored in a breastplate and armed with the battle-axe he was known to carry, although it was currently sheathed. This would give him the best opportunity to strike if the situation called for such a tactical maneuver. Alton, however, declined to join and this did not surprise anyone. This would only remind Alton of the power he once had and that he was no longer the power behind the throne.

"Greetings Matron Mother Irraste Do'tlar. Matron Mother Yaszyne Phorudossa also sends her greetings and passes on a bestowment of Spider queen's blessing to you and your entire house."

Irraste closed her eyes. She let herself drift slightly and was able to see through the eyes of the magic skull and undead orbs. The eyes were able to see magical properties and auras around the rival spell caster. She could tell he had an enchantment that acted like armor and another like a shield; very similar to spells she had access to. He also had a resistance to fire that would reduce any damage he received. Neither of the three was necessary, but they were practical for a cautious and paranoid race.

She opened her eyes and looked directly at him forcing his gaze to the ground. "It is an honor to have an emissary from House Phorudossa. I am sure we are both busy so let's skip the rest of the pleasantries shall we? You did bring the documents?"

"Yes Mistress." Tanth walked forward toward the table at Irraste's side, trying his best not to stare at the naked figure under the sheer red dress and took out the contract he had rolled up and tucked into one of his many pockets. He was so focused on Irraste that he didn't even notice the skull sitting on the table until he arrived. Both T'rissvyr and Yasrae had followed him, keeping him flanked; they were just as paranoid as any other dark elf.

"Put it on the table and unroll it," Irraste commanded.

Tentatively, Tanth followed the instructions but all the time being mindful of the skull watching his every move. Once he had unrolled it, the eyes of the skull started to scan the words over. If there were any hidden curses or wards then the skull would take the damage. The document was safe and since Irraste could read the document as the skull did, she was satisfied with the contract.

Irraste nodded to Yasrae, a nod of approval of the contract. This was his signal and he reached inside his pocket. Tanth quickly turned, seeing the movement out of the corner of his eye and was too late; too late if Yasrae had pulled a weapon. But Yasrae hadn't, he had only pulled a feathered quail with refilling ink so the document could be signed. Yasrae might have thought about killing off this rival house mage, but that was only a short-term gain, if any, and a long-term loss.

Tanth sighed in relief and accepted the pen. Then he turned back to sign the document under the glow of the fey fire. Suddenly he stopped, turned and looked at Irraste closely. "Do I ... do I know you from somewhere Mistress?"

Irraste's heart skipped a beat. She couldn't make out his detail from across the room, but now, under the glow of the fey fire, it was evident. She muttered something under her breath, something barely audible to even Tanth who was standing an arm's reach away.

"I'm sorry Mistress, but did you say something?" Tanth was still trying to figure out where he had seen her.

The look of confusion on his face shifted. Still confused but no longer trying to place the memory of the woman he was looking at, he started to scratch a spot on his chest. Then again he scratched, this time on his left arm under the sleeve of his robe. Furiously his arms started to move around his body, smacking, and trying to flick off things that were crawling on him. He jumped up and down and tried to shake his robes and only managed to shake a few of the maggots off of his flesh. They were covering his whole body. They were moving on him, biting him, and eating him alive. Tanth screamed in pain, in anger, and in revulsion. He tried to cast a spell but the swarm had broken his concentration. He swayed, fell to his knees, then went face down and stopped moving with the exception of the maggots that continued to eat his body.

"What did you do? What have you done? He was going to be a financial lifeline! He was going to solidify our partnership with house Phorudossa, and now his house will fall upon us! You will pay dearly for this!" Yasrae's anger was unmistakable and even more so as he drew his sword and approached the few strides to her.

"He recognized me." She said flatly, looking more at the dead corpse than the dark elf intent on murdering her on the spot.

Yasrae stopped. "What? What do you mean he recognized you?"

"From the tavern, the slave pits." Her eyes finally met Yasrae's. "He would have destroyed your entire house with a single word to his Matron Mother."

Yasrae had frozen and for the first time in his life he didn't know what to do. Irraste's tone was serious enough and the means of which she had killed the mage was evident at the anger she had toward him. He believed her. There was always that slim chance that one of her previous customers would recognize her, but he thought he had covered enough precautions to take care of that. With the mage dead, house Phorudossa would destroy them. "What are we going to do?" He asked more to himself than to those in the room.

"Get rid of the body," Irraste said. "Toss it into the mushroom fields. His body will be eaten soon enough by the maggots and will be unrecognizable by the time you get there. Meanwhile, Yasrae, you will go to the house Phorudossa and tell them that their emissary is late and that your Matron Mother isn't in a happy mood. They'll send someone else with a copy of the agreement and well get the document signed." Irraste was in full command. She had never really wanted to be a Matron Mother, never wanted to lead, but now the time had come to take charge. She knew it wouldn't last, Yasrae would take his position back, but for now she was the one they looked to.

Chapter: House Phorudossa

Valas knew exactly where to go to next, his contact in house Phorudossa, Rhylaxle. Valas knew that Rhylaxle was on Yasrae's coin so if Yasrae was up to something, then Rhylaxle would know about it. Valas had made his way through town and then to House Phorudossa. He had stopped just across the street to observe the house, to get a feel of its movements, and staked his look out at the "Dra'ena To'zoe".

The "Dra'ena To'zoe" was a salvaged novel bookstore. The owner had decided to collect already read books and tried to resale them. This process had just about made him break even in his financial endeavors, but it wasn't until he had decided to do something unique that his financial income had taken a rather steady incline. He had made a deal with a few of the necromancers and even a few taxidermists to acquire amphibian frog hide skin. Most of these came from Pollywogs and other bipedal amphibian creatures that had died under whatever reason from the hands of the dark elves. Now their skin was used to recover the books in an attempt to keep them dry from underground dampness. It had worked quite well, so well in fact that most individuals who bought books wanted only amphibian hide covers, if not for the added protection against moisture, then at least for the prestige of having one. Of course Valas didn't see the cultural necessity to spend free time reading a book simply for pleasure, but he was sure there were those who did.

Valas was on the verge of summoning the ability of his newfound cloak, the one that would enable him to walk through the realm of shadows, and perhaps even the astral plane, in order to appear inside the guarded perimeter of House Phorudossa, when he saw Yasrae out of the corner of his eye. He could tell, from the direction he just came from, that he had just left his own house, house Do'tlar. This was the person of interest to Valas, the person he wanted to question the most. But he knew he would never get any information out of Yasrae. Besides, it was never the dark elf's way to deal with something in such a straightforward fashion when one could get the same information by being more indirect, subtler, and more cunning. It really wasn't the destination of the information that was the appeal, but the process, the journey, to get there.

Valas watched as Yasrae passed him by, his eyes straightforward and a strong steady gait. Yasrae was obviously focused about something, something that had changed his usual cautious movements. Yasrae had purpose, and that purpose lead him to the house across from Valas, straight to House Phorudossa. Valas continued to watch as Yasrae talked to the guards. After a short time, one of the guards left and entered the house proper. Valas knew that a guard leaving his post better has some reason to do so. Yasrae was definitely seeing someone of great importance and Valas would wait for Yasrae to leave before entering and finding his contact to learn about the Yasrae's meeting.

The guard returned a short time later and with a swift nod to his companion guard, the main gate was opened and Yasrae was let in. Yasrae's heart was beating like he had never felt before. All he had to do now was not to tell this Matron Mother that he is on a conspiracy that killed her son, destroyed the body, and then sent it off to the mushroom fields to rot, and oh, by the way, can you send another of your offspring to take his place. The guard that had delivered his message had come back, walked beside him and escorted him into the main complex.

They went through a set of massive double doors that lead into a reception room. From there he could tell the house went further back and there were two sets of stairs, one on each side of the room, that lead up and down. His guard chose the one on the right and went up and Yasrae followed at a weary pace. After three flights of stairs up they turned off of the stairway and went down a long hallway. The hallway was wider and higher than normal passageways and decorated with motifs of spiders. At the end of the passage the hallway stopped in front of another set of double doors, not as massive as the initial front doors, but was elaborate never less. Two female guards were stationed here, one on either side of the doorway, and they were dressed in black adamantite chain mail, shield, helm, a mace in one hand, and finally a morning star at their hip. Upon their arrival, one of the female guards stopped them, then opened the doors and let them in.

"Matron Mother Yaszyne Phorudossa, Yasrae Do'tlar, first son of Irraste Do'tlar from House Do'tlar, has arrived and has come in request of an audience," the female guard introduced him.

The throne room, like most dark elf throne rooms, was octagonal. There were red tapestries with white webbing on each wall, which was in great contrast to the ebony black walls. At each corner was a female guard who wore identical items to the each other and to the guards outside with adamantite chain mail, a shield, a helm, a mace in one hand, and a morning star on their hip. At the far end of the room was a double raised dais with a black ebony throne. On the throne was Matron Mother Yaszyne Phorudossa.

Matron Mother Yaszyne Phorudossa was a voluptuous female who was very well endowed to the point of her red dress barely giving her the support she required. It was obvious the dress was several sizes too small as it cut deep into her cleavage, opened back up under her breasts to reveal her bare stomach, and then cinched up again at the waist. The dress ended high on her upper thigh, high enough that as the Matron sat, her dress barely gave descent enough cover. To top off the outfit, Yaszyne wore a pair of red heels that ended with laces, which ran up her calf and tied off just below her knee giving the expression of boots.

Matron Mother Yaszyne stared with irritation at Yasrae. One simply did not call upon a Matron Mother, let alone a Matron Mother from a superior house. And, to wound her pride even further, he was a male, a male that should have been with her son signing an agreement that would financially benefit them both. "Ask him what his request for my audience is about," Yaszyne said to the female guard.

"Matron Mother Yaszyne Phorudossa would like to know the purpose of your request for her audience."

'So, this was the way it was going to be', Yasrae thought to himself. While still looking in the direction of Matron Mother Phorudossa, without looking directly at her, he said," Matron Mother Irraste Do'tlar would like to know when the emissary would be joining us today. He has yet to arrive and Matron Mother Irraste Do'tlar does have other matters to attend to if the emissary or if House Phorudossa does not wish a financial agreement."

"What?" Matron Yaszyne shouted in a voice powerful enough to unhinge the guards and with a strong enough force that it could be heard half way down the hall leading from the throne room. "What do you mean he hasn't arrived? He left an hour ago."

"Matron Mother Yaszyne, it has come to my unpleasant duty to report that your son Tanth Phorudossa, house mage to House Phorudossa, has not arrived. House Do'tlar does express our concern for his well-being and hopes that another rival house has not found him as an opportunity to forward their agendas."

"I knew it! They have been planning an attack and rumors had been heard that it would be soon! They will mourn their own loss when we are through with them! Their house will be crushed and sent to the abyss to rot!" Matron Mother Yaszyne sat back in her throne. There were many houses that didn't want the document signed and would have done anything to stop it, she even had an idea which house it was. She had just lost a son, and a house mage. This was war. But she couldn't go to war yet; she still needed that agreement to be signed. "Fetch Dilayne."

The guard bowed to the Matron and left in search of the Matron Mother's first daughter. The Matron sprang from her throne in such frustration that Yasrae feared for his life, but instead of taking her anger on him, she paced the throne room and mutter obscenities. He had heard such verbiage before and usually after a male had a rough day within his household, and then even after he had a few drinks to loosen his tongue and dull his wisdom. But he rarely heard these choice words from a Matron Mother, let alone a full barrage as such as this. When he was certain that the Matron had gone through the whole list of known obscenities several times, and with a few he was sure she made up on her own, Dilayne had appeared, escorted by the guard that had fetched her.

Dilayne was wearing her armor and was already dressed for battle. She had a breastplate over a chain shirt, a set of plate greaves over her chain trousers, and a helm already on her head. In her left hand she had a shield and in her right was a very heavy mace. On her hip with a two-headed snake whip which showed her status as a priestess.

"Mother what a surprise to have me fetched. Truly you have everything under control and don't need help from an individual of less stature and less ability than you possess." Dilayne was playing her usually game, a game that was very dangerous, but one she played often.

155

"Don't play with me today, Dilayne! I'm not in the mood! Your brother is long overdue with the financial agreement he was supposed to deliver. Either he has been assassinated by another rival house or he went rogue. Either way, I want you to deliver the agreement yourself, and take two guards with you." The two of them continued to talk as if Yasrae wasn't even in the room with them or even had ever existed.

"I have no intention of doing a simple task that should be passed off to a subordinate male. If he was incompetent enough to get himself killed or to have a foolish idea of going rogue enter his mind, then give the task to another more competent male, if there is such a thing."

Matron Mother Yaszyne crossed the room and stood with her face nearly pressed against her daughter's. "You will do as I say! Fetch a copy of the agreement and have it signed or I will find a more competent daughter to take your place!"

The threat was understood, the game had finished and she had lost this round. Dilayne bowed. "Yes Matron Mother," Dilayne said dryly. She motioned to the two guards that were standing guard to her mother's throne room. Her mother did say to take two guards, but she didn't say which ones. She may have lost the banter to her mother this time, but that didn't mean she couldn't get in one more blow before she left and taking these two guards would do just that. And with that, she and the two guards set out for the documents room where every document ever created for any agreement was kept in multiple copies in case of such contingencies. And if the rumors were correct, then there weren't just multiple copies of each document, but also multiple versions. Yasrae bowed to Matron Mother Yaszyne and followed Dilayne. He knew he had been dismissed and he wasn't going to wait for a special and more elaborate dismissal command.

Outside, Valas watched as Dilayne Phorudossa marched out of the main building with two of her elite house guards and with Yasrae following close behind. It was obvious that Dilayne was not in a good mood, but then again, he really didn't want to be around any female when they were in a good mood. He had caught some of her conversation to herself as they walked by, something to the effect of her anger in her brother's disappearance. She thought he might be in some tavern in the slave pens or even possibly had turned rogue. Valas remembered there was a son of house

Phorudossa who did frequent the L' Elggen Cretok, and wondered if this was the son she had been talking about. There were two sons and he had to make sure the connection was correct before jumping to a conclusion, and the time to get that information was now.

Valas closed his eyes and visualized the room inside the structure he wanted to enter. He had been there plenty of times before to become familiar with it. When he was satisfied of his recollection, he took his cloak and draped it over himself. He could immediately feel a coldness that permeated his skin and muscle and went straight to his bones. The landscape changed before his eye, a reversal of colors but only in black and white. All of the buildings, the items, the creature, and the inhabitants looked only like a shadow of themselves. This was the shadow plane. It wasn't just a reflection of the solid real world he was accustomed to, but he also knew that there were creature that lived on this plane, creatures that were made of shadow but were real enough here as he had been in the other reality. He had to make his presence here quick and unnoticed.

He quickly walked toward house Phorudossa. He could see individuals pass on the street and couldn't help but run into one of them since they had no way of knowing he was there. It was an orc on some important errand. Once his shadow body collided with the orc's, the orc straightened and tightened his muscles, then rubbed his body as if something cold had passed through him. Valas nodded to himself. He could barely manipulate the real world, but without the aid of magic, no one would know he was there.

Upon reaching the main door, he saw two guards flanking and guarding the entrance. He knew they couldn't see him, but he still felt cautious. With some effort of mind he put his shadowy hand through the slit of the door and let his two-dimensional body slip through. He was getting the hang of this mode of transportation, but he still had to keep the room he wanted in the front of his mind or he could wind up lost, traveling the whole shadow world in futility. He continued down the hall and made his way to a set of stairs that lead down. He followed them, and even passed a female dark elf who was heading up. Like the orc, she shivered as if a cold breeze had passed her by, but suspected nothing else and continued to move on.

At the bottom of the stairs, Valas found the hallway he wanted and followed it down. It was the third door on the right he wanted and reached it with no problem. Like the front main door, Valas turned his two-dimensional body sideways and slipped through the crack between the door and the wall.

Valas saw the room as he remembered. It had only a small cot and a few wooden pegs for clothing as furniture. It was hardly anything closely resembling a bedroom, more like a cell, and yet it was in fact a bedroom. The room had a rancid odor to it and Valas didn't know if it came from its occupant, the empty wine bottle on the floor, or the half eaten chunk of cheese in the corner. On the cot sat the occupant of the room, a male dark elf, Rhylaxle, the one he was seeking.

Rhylaxle was on the small side, even for a male. His short white hair was slicked back in a greasy fashion over a high forehead. His nose was elongated, as was his cheek bones and the rest of his face. The entire appearance gave him the appearance of were-rat or at least of some were-rat in his lineage. It was rumored that the original house he had come from did have one of the biggest collections of were-rats in the whole city. But that was some time ago. The house had been destroyed in one of the common house wars and Rhylaxle had found a place in house Phorudossa. He wore a light brown tunic with dark brown leather pants and black leather boots. 'If his physical appearance didn't make him look like a wererat, then the choice of clothing did', Valas had thought as he uncloaked himself and brought himself to the physical world.

"Valas! How did you get in here?"

"I have my ways, as I have my ways with everything I do." It was as much of a dismissal from that line of the conversation as Rhylaxle had ever heard. "I have come for some information."

"When haven't you?"

Valas smiled for a moment, and then let his smile disappear. Enough with the niceties, it was time for business. "What is going on with House Do'tlar? Especially with Yasrae."

"I don't know what you're talking about."

"Don't give me that, I'm not in the mood. There is rumor about a new Matron Mother for house Do'tlar. Has one of the daughters risen to power?"

"I really don't know. Yasrae hasn't said anything to me, I just report to him about house Phorudossa."

"I see." Valas stopped and thought a moment. He wasn't getting anywhere this way, and Rhylaxle probably didn't really know what was going on. There wasn't even enough time for him to find out through his usual persuasive measures. He would have to change his line of questioning. "So, what new events have happened here to House Phorudossa?"

"Recently? House Phorudossa and House Do'tlar are making a financial agreement. However Tanth has gone missing with the agreement. Probably turned rogue if you ask me. Fortunately Matron Yaszyne kept a copy of the agreement, she keeps all of her agreements locked up safe."

Valas placed a hand up to stop Rhylaxle from talking. Getting information from him was easy; it was shutting him up that was hard. Valas already received the information he was seeking; the brother was in fact Tanth.

Valas had only a few dealings with Tanth. His last one was about a month ago at the L' Elggen Cretok. They were celebrating the victory that Valas had just had with his major conspiracy with a neighboring city's merchant train. He had not only delivered goods to Matron Elg'caress Barrindar, and pulled a great cloak for himself, he was even able to acquire a few female survivors in on the deal and sell them to the owner of L' Elggen Cretok for his underground slave ring. Tanth was going to be the first customer and Valas had a toast to celebrate Tanth's upcoming victory, one that would involve a new sex slave. Unfortunately the victory was short lived when, only moments after Tanth had gone downstairs to visit one of the cells, he had returned in a desperate attempt to put as much distance between himself and whatever she-devil had worked him over. That desperate attempt was greatly hampered by Tanth's inability to walk from an obviously, and well placed, blow to a very sensitive area combined with several other wounds.

Valas had told the owner that the sleeping drugs of his darts may have started to wear off, but the owner hadn't listened to him. Valas had also told the owner that it probably wasn't the best idea to crop the females' hair. It was one thing to degrade them this far, but to further the humiliation to such a degree was an insult that might do less than break them but do more to enrage them. And there was nothing fiercer than an enraged female dark elf. Tanth had obviously learned that lesson all too well. And then the L'

Elggen Cretok had burned down not too long ago. Perhaps the owner had learned the same thing as well, only a bit too late.

There were far too many connections, too many coincidences to be ignored. It wasn't just things that were said, but how they were said, and the things unsaid. There were subtleties in behavior that were off, behavior that would have gone unnoticed to the untrained eye, but to Valas, these told volumes. He now fully understood the whole conspiracy, not just for the past few days, but also over the past few years. But he had to make sure, absolutely sure. If he was right, there was one dark elf he had to talk to who could and would confirm his suspicions. Of course there would be a price, but he already knew what it would be and he was sure he could deliver. All he had to do now was to meet with his new best informant. He knew where this male would be, and when he would be there and he didn't have much time to meet up with him.

"You have been more than informative, so I will give you something in return." Valas spoke to Rhylaxle as he started to pull his cloak around himself. Rhylaxle had expected coin payment from Valas, like he usually received. House Phorudossa never paid him, but instead it had always been by Valas. "Prepare for battle." With those last words, Valas disappeared from view of Rhylaxle and was gone like a shadow in the night.

Dilayne Phorudossa had made her way through house Do'tlar under escort from Yasrae and to the throne room where Matron Mother Irraste Do'tlar and T'rissvyr Do'tlar were waiting for them. From what Irraste could tell, Dilayne was not in the mood for pleasantries nor was she impressed with Irraste's choice of dress. Irraste decided to cut to the chase.

"Well, it's about time House Phorudossa sent an emissary." Irraste's tone of being impatient was very clear. Yasrae shot a glare toward Irraste, but she simply ignored him.

"Don't take that tone with me. I'm not some mere male that you can attempt to bully. I am Mistress Dilayne Phorudossa, the first daughter to House Phorudossa, and you would do best to not forget it."

"And I am Matron Irraste Do'tlar, the Matron Mother of House Do'tlar. And even though we are one house lower in rank, I am still a Matron Mother and you are not. So let's skip the rank pulling and get down to the business at hand. I assume you have a copy of the contract?"

Dilayne didn't even respond but walked forward toward the table beside Irraste. The skull was still sitting in the place it was earlier and next to it was the pen that was left behind. Dilayne unrolled the contract scroll and laid it upon the table. She was taken back and showed her surprise when the skull's eyes fell its gaze upon her and then the scroll. She watched in amazement as the eyes scanned the agreement as if reading it and decided to take note of the magical necromantic skills it would take to make this happen.

When Irraste was satisfied that this was the same agreement as the last one she had read, she nodded to both Yasrae and T'rissvyr. She got up from the throne, stood in front of the document and signed. She had noted that Matron Mother Yaszyne Phorudossa had already signed this copy. Obviously Yaszyne wanted the agreement made as much as Yasrae did. When Dilayne produced a second copy, Irraste signed that as well. Dilayne rolled up her copy, gave it to one of her guards, and promptly left, without a word.

Yasrae Do'tlar breathed a sigh of relief. The contract was signed. It had almost fallen apart; the house mage was killed, and the attention of one of the priestess was caught as well as armed guards were brought in. Yasrae was sure they would go to war and his secret would be discovered. Even if they had won the war, their house would be an abomination and every household would ban together to destroy them. But Irraste had played her part well and was able to get the document signed without further conflict. He would have to celebrate, find a way and celebrate. Perhaps he could find another slave ring and this time indulge himself instead of rescuing the first one he came to. That would just be too ironic, but he was still a dark elf, and irony was one of the attractions that drew a dark elf.

Alton watched from the shadows. His eyes grew red with fury over the giddiness of Yasrae. Alton had lost his power from behind the throne. He had lost his favored position of importance as house mage. He was reduced to having meals with creatures that used to be his slaves. He was being replaced with another mage and a necromancer at that. A new Matron was put on the throne as a reminder of the power he used to have. His contact and good informant, Tanth Phorudossa was dead. On top of all this, he had to endure watching Yasrae laughing aloud, dancing and spinning as he was doing now. It was too much for Alton to bear. He had enough.

Alton made his way down the several flights of stairs, across the entry hall and through the main doors to the outside. He didn't know where he was going or what he was going to do, but had to put distance between him and the house he used to call home.

Chapter: Revilement

Valas appeared next to the "Dra'ena To'zoe", where he had started only a few minutes ago. He made sure, as he did last time he was in the shadow world, to keep his mind focused on the spot he wanted to venture to. And also like last time, no inhabitant of the real world had noticed his travel. He only hoped he was in time to catch the individual that would confirm everything, that would change everything. A quick glance toward House Do'tlar told him that he had. From the main double doors he could see Alton Do'tlar exit in a rage of fury. His suspicions were correct. He didn't even have to talk to Alton to make sure, but he was going to anyway and he would pay the price that Alton would ask.

"Alton Do'tlar. House mage to House Do'tlar, if I'm correct."

Alton eyed him suspiciously. "You are Valas, from the House of Acquisitions. I have heard of you. What could you possibly want with me?"

"How about a drink and a proposition?"

Alton thought he could use a good strong drink at this time. And a proposition with the city's most important contact was something better than the position he just left. "We should find some place quiet", Alton said. "Have you heard of 'Elghinyrrok Veldrin'? It's not too far from here."

Valas nodded and signaled Alton to lead on. He was going to let Alton take the lead and feel like he was in control of the situation. This way Alton would divulge more information in a relaxed atmosphere.

After their drinks were ordered, and Valas had paid for them, the two of them had found an empty cubical in the Elghinyrrok Veldrin. A quick sip of his strong wine had put Alton in much better mood; of course it helped when Valas had placed a potion in his drink while he wasn't looking.

"What do you need to know?" Alton asked.

"Everything, from the beginning, but first let's talk about price. What did you have in mind for payment?"

Alton shook his head. "I doubt even you can pay me what I want. I want my power back, my position back. I want to be house mage again. I highly doubt you can do that. Can you?"

'So,' Valas thought to himself, 'Alton has lost his position which only confirms my suspicions.' "Actually, Alton, I can. I know someone who needs a house mage and the position would be available by the end of today if all goes well. Do we have an agreement?"

Alton raised his eyebrows in amazement. He knew Valas was good, but didn't realize he was this good. Valas hadn't even given the house mage position a second thought; it was as if Valas knew he would ask and that he had already arranged the position ahead of time. Alton nodded. "Ok, I'll tell you everything."

After another round of drinks and a long winded and whining tale of loss of power and eating with slaves, Valas had parted company with Alton. He had told him to go back to House Do'tlar as if nothing had happened. It would even be wise to find a room and stay put for a few hours. Now, he had made his way back through the city and back to house Phorudossa. He had finally had full confirmation of what he suspected and now he was certain who he was going to tell, and for what price.

"Would you be so kind and tell Matron Mother Yaszyne Phorudossa that Valas Velkyn from the House of Acquisitions would like council with her?" Valas had asked one of the guards. The guard clicked his tongue in disgust, but left his post to have an audience requested from his Matron Mother. There had been far too many of those today and he hoped she wasn't in too foul of a mood.

It was several minutes before the guard returned, but Valas knew the wait to be worth it and he had already known the outcome. He even suspected why she would grant him the audience. Not only was he the leader of the House of Acquisitions and no one turned down an opportunity to see him, but also she would expect that he would have news of her son. That information he did have, but it wasn't what she expected.

After being escorted through the house and to the throne room, the guard introduced him to his Matron Mother. "Matron Mother Yaszyne Phorudossa may I introduce Valas Velkyn from the House of Acquisitions." The guard gave a slight bow, a glare shot from his eyes to Valas for interrupting his guard duty, and he left the throne room.

"Valas Velkyn, what brings you to my throne room today?" Yaszyne didn't miss the coincidence of him being here. She was sure he knew something of her son's disappearance; the only thing she was sure she didn't know was what his asking price was for the information.

"If Matron would permit, I have a long winded tale to tell that all started a few years ago."

"Does this concern my house mage?"

"Yes Mistress, it does. It also has to do with the agreement you just signed with House Do'tlar."

The speed at which Valas had gathered his information was quicker than Yaszyne had expected. She was sure the ink hadn't even dried yet on the signatures of the agreement. "What price are you asking?"

"I believe you will soon come into a new house mage, and a competent one at that. All I am asking in return for both the information and for the replacement of your house mage is a simple enchantment placed upon my rapier."

"And would this new competent replacement be able to place such an enchantment upon your blade, if he was accepted into our fold?"

"Oh yes Mistress, I know he can."

"Then I don't see a problem. But that also depends on the information you give. It had better be good."

"Oh yes Mistress, I assure you it is." And with that, Valas indulged the secret of House Do'tlar and the murder of her son to Matron Mother Yaszyne Phorudossa.

Yaszyne had sat on her throne and listened to the whole story with astonishment. To think that any house could wipe out all of their females, to be run without a Matron Mother on the throne was beyond anything she could imagine dreaming of. Then to fake a Matron Mother with a common sex slave was completely out of her comprehension. But to finally kill off her son, her house mage, and to think they could get away with it was a personal slap in the face. House Do'tlar was an abomination by spiritual and social standards and it was her duty to destroy them. They had also declared war on her own house with the assassination of her house mage and it was therefore her pleasure to destroy them.

"Fetch Dilayne", Yaszyne said to one of the guards at the door. The guard turned and walked out yet again to go find the daughter of her Matron Mother. She only hopped that Dilayne wasn't in a foul mood to be summoned twice in one day.

"What is it this time, Mother?" Dilayne had asked the second she entered the throne room of her Matron Mother. She had already lost a repartee with her Mother today; she wanted to make sure she won this one. "Did you lose another son?

"Shut up and think, for just one second. Let some form of intelligence enter that empty head of yours and think. How many females did you see in House Do'tlar?"

Dilayne looked at her mother in disgust, but only for a moment then let her memory float back to earlier today. "Well, there was Irraste."

"Yes, I know that, but how many others. Come on think hard. It can't be that difficult."

Dilayne thought for just a moment, and then got a curious look on her face. "Come to think of it, none. But I'm sure they were all at some ceremony held by one of their priestesses."

"Oh? And how many priestesses have you known from House Do'tlar? You are a priestess yourself and surely you can remember at least one to show up for any of the major city ceremonies. Perhaps during an abyssal coupling?"

Dilayne remembered the abyssal coupling ceremony, and smiled at the mention of it. The abyssal coupling ceremony was an annual gathering of the all of the city's priestesses. They would all gather in the main audience chamber of the chapel. From the stage, either Matron Mother Elg'caress Barrindar or her first daughter would draw a summoning circle. A chant would rise from the entire congregation, they bodies would sway to the rhythm of the chant. After about an hour of chanting and swaying, the priestesses would remove their clothing and the summoning would begin. A balor would be summoned. Its fiery presence could be felt as far back as the back tier of the audience. The demon would step forth and gaze upon the chamber. It would pick a priestess at random and attempt a coupling right there on stage, in front of the whole congregation. If the priestess survived the ceremony and if she survived the birthing then she would be blessed with a half demon fiend offspring. If she didn't survive the initial ceremony, the balor would pick another priestess. The entire ceremony could last all evening with several priestesses' dead.

Dilayne had never been picked for the ceremony and had often wondered what it would be like. Perhaps this year she would. Her mind came back to the present, there was a point being made and she had to make a connection if she didn't want her mother to continually think she was totally incompetent. Dilayne had not seen a priestess of house Do'tlar for quite some time.

"It's been years since I've seen a priestess from house Do'tlar."

"That's because they are all dead. Their Matron is dead, their priestesses are dead, and their females are all dead." Yaszyne let the impact of her statement sink into her daughters mind.

"But that would mean ..." The thought was almost too incomprehensible for Dilayne to speak aloud.

"That would mean we are going to war. Summon the troops. You will lead them. And once you wipe them from the underground and send them to the abyss, the house is yours to rule."

The move to send her daughter into battle was her finest idea yet. If her daughter failed then the ruling council would kill her. If she died in battle then the Matron would finally be rid of her. If her daughter succeeded then she would still be rid of her daughter. "And take Rhylaxle with you."

"Why would you have me take a single male into battle? There is no single male that could turn an entire battle in our favor. I am sure I can handle this alone without his assistance."

This was another move on Matron Yaszyne. She wanted to be rid of the disgusting creature. It would be all-the better if he died as well. But if he didn't, if he survived, then he would be Dilayne's problem. "Use him as fodder if you wish, but you may find that he has his contributing abilities. Take him and go. Go now."

Dilayne bowed, turned on her heel and left the throne room. She would have the troops gathered and ready within the hour.

Book: Annihilation

Chapter: War

*I*t was during the evening shift when it happened. The guards on the upper wall had barely noticed the initial placement of the spheres of darkness. At first, the darkness blended in with the natural darkness of the cavern. But then the guards noticed that they couldn't even see the fey fire from around the city. An attacking army would cover their targeted house with globes of darkness to seal off the view from prying eyes. House Do'tlar was definitely under the initial stages of a siege, they were at war.

An alarm was attempted, but well placed spheres of silence contained their sounds. The guards on the top battlements could only hope that some form of inner alarm had been set off and that reinforcements would soon arrive. They readied their crossbows and waited for the first wave to hit. A small army of kobolds rushed the walls of the compound and immediately their bodies fried. Electrical and fire runes exploded all around the house taking out the majority of the kobolds. These were fodder, and the guards knew it, their crossbows were held in check.

The second wave came. These were goblin archers. Arrows came at them by the hundreds and the guards fired back. Fortunately the goblins weren't very accurate, but what they lacked in accuracy they made up with sheer numbers. The guards did their best to return fire, but they were outnumbered and were soon to be over run.

Dilayne had led the troops into battle. It was her tactics and her command that would take this house down and she would see it to the end. She sat on her riding lizard and commanded her troops with sure domination. Her Matron Mother may have made her lose focus when she was in her presence, but this was her place, the place she felt most comfortable, leading troops into battle. She had surrounded the house well. The troops came in from different directions, down different streets and out of formation as to not draw suspicion. Riding lizards with their riders had come around the sides at various heights and even a few giant bat riders were in the air. From the initial stand point, it would look like any other ordinary day in Malzebowan. Yes, she thought, she concealed her troops well.

She had sent in a few male dark elf close to the house on what would seem like a usually and casual saunter. It was at her mark that they all turn and cast their innate special ability to send for spheres of darkness to conceal the battle from any other spectator and to conceal the guards from the on rush of the troops until it was too late. The plan went off perfectly. She sent in her kobolds with the promise that if any made it through the wards and runes that they could keep going and run free. Of course she knew that none would make it and none did. Her goblin archers were next and they were doing the job they had intended to do, to keep the guards busy. Now it was time for the next phase of her plan.

Dilayne gave a signal through a series of hand gestures and one of the giant bat riders took that as his signal. He immediately turned his giant bat and made a strafe run at the Matron's throne room. There was a balcony, and if he could just get to it, then he could get the others in. This was the job appointed to him, and if he succeeded there was an honor of increased rank, or at least he hoped that the promise would be kept. The alternative was not something he wanted to think about. This was a do or die mission. If the balcony were protected like any other throne room balcony, then it would also have glyph runes that would ruin his day. But he put his plan into action. His strife run came in hard and strong. He could hear the twang of crossbows come his way and more than a few had just missed him. He heard a thud and thought for a second that he had been hit, but when there wasn't any form of pain, he realized that it was his giant bat that had been hit. It didn't matter. The goblin archers would cut down the guards that had come out from their cover to make the hit and the bat was expendable.

The rider made sure all of his magical rope was secure. Just before the bat fell unconscious and just before the bat hit the balcony, the rider jumped. His momentum carried him right into the wall, just above the balcony. The impact was hard and he saw stars, but he held consciousness. The enchantment that had been placed upon him activated and his body stuck to the wall like a riding lizard. The giant bat, however, was not so fortunate. It had careened into the balcony; its limp body hit was tremendous force. A series of explosions went off and the giant bat fell in a fiery mass toward the ground. It had served its purpose; the rune wards were discharged.

The rider climbed down the few feet until he landed safely on the balcony. He tied off the ends of half dozen or so rope he had been carrying and tossed the remainder of the rope to the cavern floor below. Soon, he would be joined with other male dark elves and they would take the upper floor into their command.

Dilayne watched as the giant bat crashed into the upper balcony. The plan was going better than expected. She turned to Rhylaxle to send him in next, she was eager to be rid of him and add him to the ever-increasing fodder that was falling around her. To her surprise, Rhylaxle had already left. Perhaps he had run off and become rogue. It didn't matter, he was gone and she was grateful. She went through another series of hand dark elf gestures. A full squadron of giant bat riders took off from their positions on the cavern wall and went straight in for the guards on the roof. Most of the goblin archers were killed or wounded and had done their job of not only keeping the guards busy, but to thin most of them out.

The giant bat riders, about a dozen of them swooped in their aerial attack. A house guard was hit hard and was knocked from his position; another guard was lifted from his feet and dropped to the cavern floor below. A third guard was speared through with a riders' lance. Most of the giant bats landed on the roof and the riders were able to attack the guards on their own. Crossbow bolts were fired and counter fired. Those who were close enough for melee attacked with their scimitars or lances. By the time the attack was finished, only four of the riders had died, but the roof was taken. All the riders had to do now was to stay put and keep it.

With another set of dark elf hand signals, Dilayne sent in another set of elite dark elf warriors. A dozen male dark elves charged toward the ropes that had been dropped from the balcony. These were infiltrators, dark elves accustomed to entering a building and systematically taking out the inhabitants room by room. They weren't very good in mass combat, but excelled in stealth and shadow combat. The infiltrators hit the ropes with speed and accuracy and climbed as if their lives depended on it. Perhaps their lives did depend on it, but it didn't matter, this is what they lived for. Within moments all twelve had climbed to the balcony and entered the throne room. The initial giant bat rider would stand guard and keep the balcony in their possession while the others entered and did their job.

Dilayne again went through her hand signals. This time, two massive Minotaurs ran full strength, in full stride and hit the massive front doors. If the inner complex hadn't figured out that they were under attack, they did now. The doors buckled, slightly. These two turned and headed back to their starting positions as two more Minotaurs hit the massive double doors. The doors buckled again, a bit more, but not enough. These two also looped back and a third set of Minotaurs took their turn to ram the front doors. There were three sets of Minotaurs in all and each set would take turns in an attempt to knock down the door. They were promised a fairly large amount of coin for the set that had succeeded and each set of Minotaurs was determined that they would be the ones to take to door down. Of course Dilayne figured that the first set of Minotaurs to break through would be slaughtered by any existing guards in the main entry chamber, she would not have to follow through with her payment promise if all went according to plan.

Chapter: Irraste

*I*rraste woke with a start. She could sense bodies dying, too many bodies. They were under attack; they were at war. She wondered if it was House Phorudossa, and if it was, then where had she had gone wrong. She was sure she portrayed the right amount of arrogance, of haughtiness, to pull off her role. But there wasn't time to contemplate any past errors; there would be plenty of time later, if she survived. She immediately pulled herself from her bed and went directly toward her leather armor outfit. With efficiency and speed, Medri donned her armor and armed herself with her two daggers. She hadn't rested enough to have all of her spells replenished; she would have to make do with what she had.

She heard a sound from the washroom. She spun and entered with a dagger in each hand. 'How in the abyss could anything get in here?' She asked herself. At first glance nothing seemed out of place, but then she heard the sound again. It sounded like little claws under the tub. Her eyes fixed on the tub and she saw a small rat exit the drain and enter the tub. She looked at it queerly and the rat stood on its hind legs and looked back.

Suddenly the rat grew in size. Its body increased in mass, its arms and legs elongated and within a brief amount of time the rat had assumed the size of a humanoid and stood slightly taller than Medri.

'Great, a wererat.' Medri thought to herself.

Rhylaxle jumped from the tub in an attempt to tackle Medri, but only managed to dig one of its claws on her arm before it fell to floor on all fours. With his body at the disadvantage, Medri plunged both daggers into its back. She could feel the effect of one of her daggers take effect and the wound that she had suffered closed and healed. She was grateful it had only been a claw that struck and not its horrible teeth. A bite from that thing could give her the same disease that inflected this creature and eventually would turn her into a wererat as well. She had heard that lycanthropy was deadly to elves, but she didn't want to find out either way.

Rhylaxle roared in pain, stood back up on his hind legs, spun, and delivered a backhanded blow to her face. The blow knocked her down and stunned her as she hit her head on the floor. Her stomach knotted with the urge to get sick, but she was able to overcome the sensation. She attempted to crawl away, but he grabbed her by the ankle and pulled her toward him. She kicked out with her other foot and nailed him twice in the face, but his grip was like iron and he wouldn't budge.

When she was in range he reached down with his other claw in an attempt to grab her by her throat. Medri brought one of her bone daggers up. Rhylaxle thought it was a desperate attempt for a defense and considered laughing at the feeble gesture but decided to simply bat her hand away. It was his hesitation that let Medri make her move. With a flick of the wrist her dagger extended and the bone sword pierced his neck and came through the other side. Blood splattered everywhere and the tiles ran slick with it. Rhylaxle tried to scream, but blood was caught in its throat along with the bone sword. Medri retracted her dagger and pushed the creature off of her. Immediately she bolted for the door.

Wererats, like all other lycanthropes, regenerated unless they were hit with silver and at the moment she didn't have any. The best she could do was to harm it, but not kill it. In a short amount of time it would be back to full health. She had to put some distance between herself and this creature. She slipped a bit on the blood slick tiles, recovered and had just about made it half way through her sleeping quarters when the door to the sitting room burst open.

Two male dark elves in Phorudossa outfits came through the door. 'They must have picked the lock', she thought as she continued toward them. They each had leather armor and only armed with daggers. She knew what that meant; these were rogues or assassins. She would have her hands full very shortly. She was outnumbered, but not outsmarted. She continued her sprint for the door and the two infiltrators simply stood on her side of the door with grins on their faces. Perhaps they had plans for her before they killed her, or perhaps they wanted to keep her to themselves.

'Not today, and if I can help it, and not ever again', she thought to herself. She pointed at the skull that was sitting at the desk next to the door. It was the skull she had worked so hard on and one she would miss. The skull exploded in a thousand shards and the two rogues went reeling to the ground. Medri shot past them and slammed the door behind her. But instead of running further down the hallway, she turned back on the door. She inserted her skeleton key into the lock and said a few arcane words. 'That will hold them. They might be able to pick a regular lock, but let's see how they fared with a magical one and with an angry wererat at their backs.' And with that she turned and sprinted down the hallway.

Chapter: T'rissvyr

*T*he front main massive doors to the structure burst open as two of the Minotaurs plowed through and stumbled. The force of their bull rush and the shards of the remains of the doors had left the Minotaurs off balance. Their response to the entry was of excitement for the payment they would receive, but it soon turned to concern. Four goblins were waiting for them, each with a spear set to receive their charge. Their massive bull bodies, still carried through with momentum were too much to try to stop. Their torsos found the spears and they were impaled as each spear found their mark. The spears cracked, broke and the goblins found they could not hold the weight and momentum of the Minotaurs. The elation of stopping the Minotaurs was short lived as the massive bodies fell on top of them and crushed the life from them.

The other four Minotaurs rushed the door behind the initial two. What had remained of the door from the rush of the first two was shattered into splinters when the next four hit. They took in the scene and realized that they were more fortunate than they had first thought. On the floor was a tangled mess of bodies and blood was pooling on the ground. They were only able to get their bearings when they heard clicks of crossbows and the sound of thuds as the bolts hit their bodies. A quick look and they saw several dark elves further down the entry hall reloading their crossbows. Each Minotaur tried to move forward, but the poison was fast and one by one they fell to the ground and added their bodies to ever growing pile.

T'rissvyr had just finished training with the two ogres he had picked up at the docks. His muscles were sore and he was tired. Sweat ran down his body. He was on his way to retrieving his shirt when he heard the battle upstairs. Swords were clanging on metal, creatures were howling in pain. They were at war and the battle was heading his way.

"Quick, you," T'rissvyr pointed to one of the ogres, "over there, behind the column. And you behind that one." With haste

T'rissvyr gathered his axe and made sure his two swords were in balance on his hips. He wished he had time to study his opponents, to see the full extent of what he was against. He knew that if he could win and get the ogres in motion up the stairs, he could make his was to the main battle. There would be passageways, stairways, and doors he could use to his advantage. But here, he was trapped in a single room with no way out. He had to get upstairs. Perhaps he could find Yasrae and together they would fight like they usually did. Together they made a great fighting pair, each understanding the other's abilities. Now, he had to fight alone. He did have the two ogres, but he didn't hold out any hope that they would survive for very long.

Two bugbears came down the stairway with their morning stars at the battle ready. T'rissvyr was sure they weren't his and their appearance confirmed his suspicions. The bugbears were so intent on T'rissvyr that they walked right past the two ogres. The ogres sprang into action. Each grabbed a bugbear by the arm and with a quick spin, smashed each one into a supporting column. The crack from the impacts was loud as their skulls broke. Blood, bone, and brains splattered on the ground and the bodies went limp.

Unfortunately the ogres had left their backs to the stairway. T'rissvyr had barely time to see the two dark elves enter and no time to warn the ogres. The dark elves shot their crossbows with complete accuracy and the ogres went down. T'rissvyr didn't have time to think; there was no time to plan as he usually did. The two dark elves were already loading their crossbows and he had to hurry.

Before the ogres had hit the floor, T'rissvyr was already in motion. He passed the two ogres as they fell and were upon the two dark elves before they had time to finish their reloading. T'rissvyr hit the first one with his shoulder and knocked the wind out of him, then spun and took a great arch swing at the second. The second dark elf was faster and had backed out of the way. He immediately dropped his handheld crossbow and pulled a long sword out to defend himself. As his sword came up, T'rissvyr had reversed his blow and came down hard on the sword. The sword snapped in two. T'rissvyr knew he didn't have time to finish this one off before the first one had recovered, so instead of going in for the kill, T'rissvyr grabbed the dark elf, spun, and tossed him right in the path of the first. The first dark elf had gotten to his feet and pulled his long sword out to initiate an offense but only found his partner tossed in his direction and ended up impaling his own ally. The sword went through the backside and out the stomach.

T'rissvyr charged his remaining adversary. His one hand pushed aside the impaled victim, and the sword that had impaled him went with the dead body leaving the last living enemy weaponless. It was all the intruding elf could do to watch T'rissvyr bring his axe to bare, a full swinging high arch, and to feel its sharp bite on his neck. His body collapsed with his head almost completely severed.

T'rissvyr knew the battle wasn't even close to being over, he had heard the other footsteps before he had charged his last opponent. He ducked, hit the ground and rolled under four more crossbow darts fired by the new opponents. His roll brought him close to his first and he brought his knee high. That one dropped to the floor in pain. T'rissvyr spun low. While he ducked under a swing of a scimitar, and under the reach of this combatant, T'rissvyr hooked his axe on the combatant's ankle and yanked. The opponent fell with a thud. With his spin still in action, T'rissvyr brought his axe up and sliced open the chest of the third opponent and cracked through his rib cage. But that was as far as he got.

The smell of ozone and a crack of thunder permeated the room. One of the four was an elite infiltrator and had knowledge on how to use minor magical wands. The one he had in his hand was a wand of lightning bolts. The bolt hit with expert precision and pierced through T'rissvyr's magical resistance and brought him to his knees. With cat like reflexes, the infiltrator pulled a dagger, took a single step forward, and slashed T'rissvyr across the neck with deadly precision. Blood spilled and T'rissvyr fell dead.

Chapter: Yasrae

*Y*asrae had just left the ledger room. He had gone over the numbers again with Uhlszyne and had to make sure his profits were accurate. The agreement with house Phorudossa was what their house needed to get on their feet and stay that way. His financial worries and concerns were over. As he closed the door behind him, Yasrae looked up and saw two goblins. At first he thought nothing of it, and then he realized they were wearing House Phorudossa collars. He barely had time to get his rapier up to start a defense when the two goblins rushed him.

'Where did these two come from?' He thought to himself. Then he heard the battle coming from downstairs. He could hear the cries of pain and the sound of metal against metal. He also thought he smelled flesh burning as if someone has cast a fireball. 'We must be at war with House Phorudossa, but why? What in the abyss went wrong?'

The goblins charged down the hall. If only he had T'rissvyr. T'rissvyr would take the lead and knock the first one off balance and then take out the second, but now he was by himself. He settled on the balls of his feet, turned his body slightly sideways and raised his rapier. The goblins wouldn't live long enough to regret their decision.

Upon seeing Yasrae, the goblins both rushed him but their attacks were uncoordinated. They both wanted the funds that were promised them for each male dark elf they killed and this was going to be their first. The first goblin to reach Yasrae took a right hook swing. Yasrae ducked and let the goblin's momentum over extend its swing and the poor creature almost went face first to the floor. The second was able to slow and shorten his stride upon seeing the speed of Yasrae, but it was too late. Yasrae had taken an unexpected step forward and the thrust of his rapier caught the goblin in the throat. It grabbed its throat to try to stem the flow of its own blood to no avail. Blood spread from under its hands and the creature fell.

Yasrae turned back to the first goblin that was still off balance. With two quick jabs Yasrae was able to pierce an artery at the top of each of the creature's legs. The goblin yelped, his legs buckled, and it fell to its knees. Yasrae took no time to take his opportunity. He did a quick backhanded slash and a deep red cut fell across the goblins throat and fell to the floor.

"If we are under attack from House Phorudossa, then they will have to do better than that. Now to find T'rissvyr and get out of here."

His plan was simple. All he had to do was make his way through a war that had permeated his house, find T'rissvyr in the populace of both houses and make their way to his quarters where he had a hidden secret passage that would lead them out. Except he didn't know how many he was up against, what their strengths were, where he could find T'rissvyr, if they would be able to make their way to his quarters, or even if the secret passage had been compromised.

He let his mind dwell on that word for just a brief moment. They were compromised. But who was behind the conspiracy? Was it T'rissvyr? He couldn't believe that, he had known T'rissvyr all these years. He did say that he would make himself the new leader, but Yasrae always thought T'rissvyr was only joking. There was a saying "L' Velkyn velve harventhen l' alurl" or "The hidden blade cuts the best". Had T'rissvyr bid his time to be that hidden blade? Would it be wiser to leave without him? He could use T'rissvyr's fighting skills, but he would not risk his life, T'rissvyr's fighting skills just wasn't worth it, even if he wasn't the conspirator.

Or had it been Irraste, or Medri, or whatever her name was? She had been too conveniently placed in the slave pens. It was too much a coincidence that her room was the only one available. And hadn't she been too trusting, too accommodating? She would definitely not be someone who would follow a household full of males. But when did she have time to send a message to House Phorudossa? He had her watched at all times, even while she was sleeping, and yes, even when she had taken her bath.

The conspirator could be anyone. He was letting his paranoia get the better of him. He would make a little effort to retrieve both T'rissvyr and Irraste, but only a little effort. It would be little enough that if questioned he could honestly say he had tried, but he wouldn't risk his life on either of them. Even if they were innocent, he had his own life to consider.

He made his way toward the stairway just in time to see three orcs come up. He could hear the battle below and from what little he had seen, he knew there was no way to cross the floor below. He turned and went to sprint down the way he came from only to find two adversaries dressed in leather armor and only armed with daggers with three more orcs behind them. He knew that there would be reinforcements from the stairs any second. He was surrounded. He took a deep breath and resolved to make this his last stand.

Yasrae spun quickly on the first three orcs and caught one in the stomach with his blade, then ducked. His instincts had proved correct. No dark elf could resist making a shot at an enemy's back and these two took the bait. Two daggers flew right over him and hit the one he had just wounded. He spun back around and let his rapier go wide and caught a flanking orc in the face. The orc wasn't going to die from that unexpected wound, but it was out of the fight for a while.

Yasrae then sprinted toward the dark elves. They were the most dangerous; he had just wanted to reduce the number of opponents behind him. As he approached, the two infiltrators steadied their stance on the balls of their feet and readied their counter attack. Yasrae came in a high arc on his right and it was met with a double dagger block. Then Yasrae spun and came low to his left and was met with another double dagger block from the second infiltrator.

'Perfect', he thought. He then feigned a spin back around to the first again. But instead of following through with the spin, he took a play from his weapons master and plowed down the middle between the two dark elves. Their daggers were on opposite sides and they didn't have time to react, and neither did the orcs behind them. He shot his hand straightforward and delivered a jab right into the belly of the center orc. Again, this one wasn't going to die from that wound, but it was out of the fight for a short time.

The two infiltrators had Yasrae right where they wanted him, in the middle. They fought best when they were flanking their opponents and they often trained in tandem to learn each other's strengths and weaknesses. They had played this strategy out many times and all they had to do was execute it. The first one came in high towards Yasrae's neck and then low with his other dagger toward his stomach. If Yasrae didn't move then one, the other, or both would hit and probably be a fatal blow. But neither was designed to inflict damage. The feints succeeded and Yasrae moved closer to the second infiltrator, the one that was now behind him.

The second infiltrator brought both of his dagger straight in towards Yasrae's back. It was a killing blow, a blow that would have gutted any opponent; that is if it hit. Yasrae had seen the move before and knew what to expect; he had also trained in the ability to flank under the leadership of the first Matron Mother. He crouched low with his chest to his knees and let the daggers glide over the top of his back. With a quick spin, Yasrae planted a well-placed elbow hard into his would be assassin's groin. The infiltrator doubled over.

Spinning back toward the first dark elf, he came up hard and shoved his blade deep into his throat. The dark elf was over confident at the belief that his partner would make the kill that he wasn't able to get a defense up in time and the blade cut deep. Air escaped the tiny whole and blood started to flow. He backed away, slid off the blade and hit his back on the wall behind him. There he slid into a sitting position and died.

One of the two orcs from this side of the hall tried to grab Yasrae as he came out of his spin. Unfortunately for the orc he hadn't spent enough time sparring with the infiltrators, or perhaps he wasn't allowed to. 'If he were in my house, I would have taught him everything he needed to know before going into a war like this', Yasrae thought to himself. Yasrae dodged back to his right, toward the orc that was left standing near the stairway. As he did, the infiltrator plunged his dagger straight ahead. The blade would have cut deep and the blow would have knocked the wind out of him, but instead the dagger found the orc's body. Both orc and infiltrator were shocked and surprised. But then the infiltrator shifted his emotion to anger and frustration. His second dagger went up and slashed the orc through the throat and killed it on the spot. He was sure that the orc had now learned its lesson the hard way to keep out of his reach and never again to interfere with his kill.

Yasrae had reached the orc that was content on guarding the stairway. He figured he was wise enough to stay out of the battle and let everyone else die and soften up this enemy. He hadn't counted on Yasrae doubling back at him, and by the time he realized what was happening, Yasrae had already closed on him. With a quick kick to the orc's knee, Yasrae shattered the kneecap. The orc howled and his leg buckled. But that was where Yasrae wanted him. With all of its weight off balance, Yasrae caught hold of the orcs body and tossed him back toward the onrushing infiltrator.

The infiltrator pushed the orc aside to keep it from knocking him over. However, knocking over the infiltrator wasn't the plan. As the rogue moved his attention to the oncoming orc, Yasrae had doubled back again. Just as the orc cleared the rogue's sight, Yasrae was too close. The rogue couldn't defend himself and Yasrae plunged his rapier into the infiltrator's chest, piercing his heart, and killing him instantly.

'I'm going to make it', Yasrae thought to himself. The entire combat had lasted only a short amount of time and he was sore and tired. All he had to do now was take down one more orc and he would be in the clear to take the hallway behind it. He had decided not to try the secret passage in his room, but to go up instead. If he could make it, there was a clear shot up the stairs and either to the throne room and out the balcony or up to the roof. Yasrae bolted for the last remaining orc.

But Yasrae didn't hear the footsteps coming up the stairway that was now behind him. Just before Yasrae reached the orc, he heard a crack of thunder and a smell of ozone. He was momentarily blinded, but that wasn't his major concern. He body had lost all control and every muscle went into a spasms. His knees buckled and he fell flat on his face. His arms went limp as he fell and his rapier fell out of his reach.

Yasrae was still alive, but hurt badly. He couldn't move; his muscles weren't responsive yet. All he could do was lie on the floor and hear the clicking of booted footsteps from behind him. 'At least it won't be an orc that kills me,' Yasrae thought. For a moment he thought perhaps the killer wouldn't finish him off, but then he felt the hand grab his hair and pull his head back exposing his throat. The cut was clean and he died quickly.

The door to the ledger room burst open. Uhlszyne pointed his wand, said his arcane words and fired. An explosion filled the hallway. The fireball burned flesh and clothing, and small fires broke out from the flames on the dead bodies. The remaining orcs that were still alive screamed in pain and died in a crispy charcoal form. The heat of the flames flew back into the ledger room and several of the papers lit up in fire.

'If these aren't put out soon then the entire room will go up in flames,' Uhlszyne thought. But that was the least of his concerns. The ledgers were his life's work, he spent most of his time here with the numbers; he knew how much coin came in and how much went out. But despite all of this, his main focus was the rogue, the rogue that was missing. He had seen him just before he let loose the fireball, but now he couldn't see him at all. He did realize that the heat of the blast had temporarily blinded him, but the rogue couldn't have gotten away that quickly even if his innate spell resistance had held.

Almost on cue the rogue came into view. He had placed his back against the wall that held the door. Unless Uhlszyne has stuck he head out the door completely to look down the hall, the rogue was out of his view. He almost wished Uhlszyne had stuck his head out. But he couldn't wait for the accountant to wise up. He twisted and spun and came face to face with Uhlszyne. The accountant was caught off guard. Uhlszyne gasped. At first the rogue thought he had caught him so much off guard that the accountant had cried out. But then he realized that his own reflexes were faster than his consciousness and he had already stabbed Uhlszyne in the chest. He pulled his dagger out and plunged twice more to make sure the job was done. Uhlszyne collapsed to join the ever-growing body count.

Chapter: Escape

*I*rraste ran down another hallway. She had been doing her best to avoid the battles and had to duck into several rooms to go unnoticed. She had to get out, she didn't know where she would go, anywhere would be better than here. She did remember the map that Yasrae had shown her. He had been very selective on the map he had shown her, there were no secret chambers or passages marked on the map. Most structures did have secret doors and hidden passages. She knew the structure she had called home back in Anarchia did. If her memory served her well, and it usually did, she remembered Yasrae's personal bedroom. There had been a spot that didn't make sense. The walls didn't quite match up. This was a tall tell clue of a secret door, and if her hunch was correct, it would lead outside. Of course it made sense that Yasrae would have his own private entrance and exit. If she could only make her way to his room then she was free. Perhaps she would be able to find him and he could help fend off the intruders and they could work together.

She had thought of using the shadow spell she had used several days ago to hide in the back alley. It was an effective spell to keep her from being unnoticed, but it was a dangerous one as well and had its risks. The spell didn't just make her look like a shadow; it momentarily took her to the shadow world. There were creatures there that could do considerable amount of damage if they found her. Even if she did manage to remain undetected, traveling the shadow world could leave her lost. If she was just standing still or moving only a short distance, the risk was a minimum. But she had to transverse the whole of the structure and she wanted to wait until the last possible moment before she took that risk. She had another spell that made her invisible to all living creatures, but any spell caster could drop that spell and she would still be vulnerable to attacks, including area of effect spells and the random attack that wasn't even aimed at her but might hit her never the less.

Her mind came back to the task at hand when she looked down the hall. There were two bugbears and they had seen her. She thought she could try to double back and try a different set of stairs, but that meant these two being at her back the whole way. She would have to deal with them. This was the quickest way to Yasrae's personal chambers. She let the two approach her.

Once they got close enough the first took a swing at her with its morning star. His spiked ball just missed her as she moved to her side. Unfortunately the companion's morning star didn't miss. His heavy weapon clipped her back and sent her to her knees. They had obviously been underestimated and were going to deal with her with a vengeance, a vengeance she was sure that originated from their treatment from their own Mistress. They were going to let out every ounce of frustration and humiliation they had ever experienced at the hands of their dark elf Masters, and especially from their Mistresses.

Pain was not a stranger to Irraste. She understood it; she had at times even welcomed it. Pain sharpened the senses, pain got the heart to pump, and pain shot adrenaline into the system. This was one of those times she had accepted pain. She knew the blow would come and she knew she had the discipline to fight through it. She hadn't underestimated these creatures. In fact she had them right where she wanted them. With her body bent over, they couldn't see her hands, and from the position she was in, they couldn't defend themselves.

Suddenly her hands shot out with a bone dagger in each hand. Both blades struck hard into their thighs. The creatures cried in pain. One of them, the one on her right, continued to scream more though. It was a higher pitch, a louder scream. He was in agony. His leg started to wither away, his flesh stated to rot off and his muscles shriveled into a husk. As she drained the life from his body, her body repaired itself. The pain she had momentary felt was gone.

The other bugbear pulled his thigh from the bone dagger and looked on in horror as his companion continued to whither, crumble and fade into a husk and then into dust. He was too much in shock to see Irraste make her second move and continued to be in shock as she plunged her right dagger into his heart. He would share the same fate and in moments there was nothing left of them but two piles of ash.

Irraste continued to sprint down the hallway. She could hear battle up ahead and screams of pain. She still had a trick or two she could try before she attempted to turn herself into a shadow. As she rounded the corner, she could see two ogres and a male dark elf dressed as a rogue. This battle would be tougher. She could outsmart the ogres and even be quicker than them, but she would probably be on par with the rogue. If the rogue slowed her down for just one second then the ogres would have enough time to utilize their great strength to their fullest advantage. She had to think of another way.

The hall was blood stained with the last of their victims and two dead bodies lie strewed across the floor. Only one spell came to mind, a spell she hadn't tried due to its dangers. If she didn't cast this one correctly it could weaken her, kill her, or worse, turn her into an undead. The thought made her shudder. But despite the revulsion and risk, her hands were already in motion and then with a quick flick of the wrist, she pointed at one of the dead bodies.

The rogue had half expected the body to get up and fight on her behalf. He had heard rumors that there was a necromancer in the house, and if she were the one, then she would be able to summon undead. He didn't want to fight undead creatures, they no longer felt pain, blood no longer flowed through their bodies, and his tactics to exploit these areas in living creatures would no longer work. He didn't have to worry; the corpse did not rise to fight him. Instead the corpse blew up in a fantastic explosion that rocked the whole of the hallway. The blast could be felt several floors below and parts of the ceiling crashed down.

Irraste doubled over in exhaustion. The spell took more out of her than she had expected. A wave of nausea and dizziness overcame her and for a moment she thought she would either get violently ill, loose conciseness, or both. But she was able to gather herself and the feelings passed almost as quickly as they had arrived. When she was able to observe the hall, she was pleased with herself. The three that had blocked her way, the three that had such arrogance as to block her way, were now blood splatters on the wall. There were outlines of where they had stood and a blood splatter pattern was splashed across the wall from there. Yes, she could see where they had been, but their bodies were now vaporized. She smiled and continued down the hall.

At the end of the hall she came to a stairway. From below she could hear a great battle. A quick look revealed the whole room below her was full of fighting. She could hardly tell whose side was winning. The only thing she could tell was that bodies were falling and falling fast. She had only her one spell left and she was further from the room she wanted to travel to than she wanted to be, but this would have to be where she made her casting. Her hands went into motion and she felt the familiar transformation from a solid female dark elf to a cold and dark shadow.

As soon as the spell went off, she immediately focused on Yasrae's room and the route she needed to go to get there. She walked down the stairs. She knew no one could see her and even if they detected her, she doubted anyone could harm her. Still there was the chance that any of the weapons could be enchanted to do her damage while in this form or that a spell would go off and affect her even in the shadow plane.

At the bottom of the stairs she could see the battle in its fullest. The room was full to capacity and others were still trying to get in. She saw an orc get dragged down by a bugbear. There was a goblin split in two by an axe of a Minotaur. A male dark elf fired off a hand crossbow at some enemy across the room. A kobolds body was lifted in the air and thrown, its body smashing into several other creatures.

Irraste cautiously stepped into the melee. She could see all of these things as if their shadows, and not their physical bodies, were actually doing the fighting. She held her breath and continued forward. A hobgoblin was hit and his body fell through hers. An arrow was fired and its path continued as if she was only vapor. On and on items and creature passed through her space, through her body as she carefully walked through the battle. If any had noticed, if any had felt the cold tinge of her presence, they hadn't shown it.

Once she had reached the end of the room, all she had to do was go down the hallway and it was the second door on the right. She continued to move slowly, one foot in front of the other. As she came to the door, she thought about dropping her spell and walking in, but thought against it. She still could be seen. She placed her body between the door and the wall and let her shadow-like structure slip through.

The blast knocked her off of her feet and against the wall. She had felt the impact as if someone had punched her, hard. Her breath was knocked out of her and she saw stars. She also felt the wall and the floor. For a moment she had forgotten where she was, and then it all flooded back to her. But if her recollection was correct, she shouldn't have been hit, unless …

"Ah, I'm glad you came," Alton's voice helped bring her back to her full senses. "I was wondering if I would be wrong about you. Of course I hoped you would have brought Yasrae with you. Did you leave him behind to die? Did you kill him yourself?"

The room she had entered was spacious, almost a spacious as hers. This room had a lounging couch and a couple of dressers, all in prestige condition and of excellent taste. Irraste suspected that Yasrae had taken these from the previous Matron Mother, or at least one of his sisters. The room was probably one of the sisters' as well, more than likely the first daughter by the size of it.

But spacious rooms or prestige dressers couldn't hold her attention. She had a dangerous mage to deal with, and the spell that had brought her out of her shadow plane and into this one. Although most items would have passed through her while she was in the shadow plane, magical weapons would have been able to hit her as well as powerful spells. And whatever spell that had hit her was powerful. She had a new respect of Alton.

"It doesn't matter. I'll just kill you." Alton's hands went through their motions as Alton's facial markings lit up and another spell shot out. Irraste could feel the ozone in the air and saw the room light up as the lightning bolt left his hand and hit her square in the chest. She expected the blast to punch a hole through her chest, and for her muscles to contrast, but her innate spell resistance held this time.

She could have, at any other time, tried to trade spell for spell with this mage. But that might have proven futile with their resistances to spells. Now, however, she was out of spells and had to do with what she had. She sprang to her feet and launched herself at the mage. His hands were already weaving another spell. As she hit him square on, his spell launched and the entire area that she was in was covered in sticky strands of spider webbing. Had she not moved she probably would have been stuck to the walls or the floor and at his mercy; although she doubted he had any.

Their bodies hit the floor hard and knocked the wind out of the both of them. They both rolled trying to gain the upper ground, trying to grapple the other. She had to stop him from casting any more spells and he had to stop her from reaching a dagger. She was able to bring her knee up and place it well enough to make him release his hold. With that opportunity she grabbed her left dagger and brought it forward.

Although in pain, the wizard reached forward and grabbed her by her wrists. His strength had been empowered by one of his earlier spells he had cast while he was waiting for her. She struggled against his grip, but he pushed hard and pinned her to the ground. His body was on top, his face just inches from hers. Her dagger was still in her hand and he needed her to be rid of it. He brought her wrist up slightly and slammed it hard against the floor. Then, when that didn't give the result he was after, he brought her wrist up again for a second attempt.

If Alton wasn't so busy trying to get his own way, had he thought for just one second, or even stopped to be observant, he would have seen a smile come across her lips. She knew she couldn't overpower him, she also knew she probably wouldn't be able to bring her dagger up and penetrate any defensive spells he might have place upon himself. But she did have a plan and he had played right into it. As her wrist was about to hit the ground, she twisted it and let the blade part of the dagger smash into the floor.

Bone shards exploded into Alton's face. He screamed and let go of her. Both of his hands went to his bloodied face. Her dagger was useless and ruined, but it was worth it. She quickly rolled him off of her and puller her other dagger. Immediately her dagger went to his throat and made a slight cut. She could see his life start to drain and feel some of her own strength come back to her. Before she had drained him completely, she pulled the dagger away.

"No, I'm not going to kill you Alton. I have something more devious for your life; you are going to live. Either Yasrae will find you, or whichever house has attacked us will find you. One way or the other you will wish you had died by my hand today."

Alton scarcely heard a word. He was barely even conscious and didn't even notice when she took his piwafwi, his house insignia and his coin purse. She was going to leave him there, as he was, on the floor. Anyone could find him like this and who knew what he would face. She was right; he would have preferred a quick death than to be found by either of her scenarios.

Leaving Alton to his fate, Irraste went to the back wall. If her guess was correct then the secret passage should be around here.

After a short time, she found a small button that looked like it was part of the wall. A quick push of the button and a part of the wall opened up. Beyond it she could see the outside, it was near a cavern wall and she could enter the city without being seen.

She looked back for one last look. She had been Matron for just a short time, and now it was gone. She thought that Yasrae was probably dead, and if not, then he soon would be. She nodded to herself in an agreement. If the house had fallen, if the coconspirators were dead, then Matron Mother Irraste should die as well. She would leave that name here and be Medri once again. The name suited her for now, but she would take another later. Both lives were gone and she would take another name to suit her new life, whatever, and whenever that might be.

With a sigh, she wrapped Alton's piwafwi around her and stepped into the darkness that headed deep into the city.

Chapter: House Maelyl

*D*ilayne had played her strategy well. She had secured the roof, the balcony and the Matrons throne room quickly enough. The door had come down and her shock troops were deployed. Her next wave was her expendable troops. This consisted with goblins, hobgoblins, ogres, orc, and other troops. After they had gone in for a few minutes and had softened the battle, then she sent in her male guards. Now she was satisfied. The time had come. She made a few hand gestures and the elite female warriors surrounded her. She dismounted from her lizard, and while under the protection of her elite female guard, she walked into the house she was ready to claim for her own.

The entry room was strewed with dead or dying bodies, but there were plenty of living as well. The fighting was over and those that were living bowed to her as she entered. None had shown any form of aggression toward her. But were all of these her troops? She wondered if some of the troops from House Do'tlar had turned their alliance and blended in with hers. It wasn't an uncommon practice of self-preservation and those that did were welcomed of course, provided they follow her rule. Her ranks would soon be replenished.

She made her way up several stairs and finally to the hall she had sought. This, too, had bodies, but nowhere as many as the entry. She would have to have someone clean up this mess. As she passed down it, one of the bodies started to groan, to move. It was a male dark elf and he wasn't dead yet. She didn't stop to find out if the male was one of hers or not, and she didn't care. With a flick of her wrist and the snap of her arm, she let her snake whip flick out and struck the male. The poison took hold immediately and he fell. She needed to show that she was in charge and she had no mercy. She was the new Matron Mother.

At the end of the hall she came to the room, the room she had dreamt of owning, even if it were of a different house. It didn't matter which house it was now; the throne room was hers. She casually walked to the throne and took her place upon it. A smile came across her face. 'Matron Mother Dilayne,' she thought to herself.

It wasn't long before she heard footsteps coming down the hall. The female guards took ready with their morning stars drawn and their shield in battle position, but Matron Mother Dilayne placed her hand up to stop them. She could see that it was two of her own male infiltrators dragging a mage.

"Matron," one of them said. He was a fast learner, perhaps too fast. "We found this one hiding in one of the bedrooms. It looks like he was trying to escape through a secret passage."

"Look who we have here," she said. "I do believe it is Alton, the former house mage. Whatever shall I do with you?"

"You will do nothing." The male voice came from the balcony. Dilayne turned to view the intruder who had infiltrated her house, the male who would soon be dead for telling her what to do. It was Valas.

"How dare you…" was all she was able to get out, before he interrupted her.

"I dare because I bring a message from your former Matron Mother, Mistress Yaszyne. The mage is promised to her. He is to be her new house mage."

Dilayne's anger flared. Then she controlled herself. Her house was too weak right now to take on another conflict. She decided to let her mother win one more battle. There would be time later when she would win the war. "Go. Take him and go."

Valas crossed the room and took Alton from the two infiltrators. He was able to help Alton to his feet, but still had to support the majority of his weight. "Oh, one more thing before I go. She did mention her congratulations on your successful raid and your accession to Matron. But she was wondering what you would call your new house?"

Dilayne hadn't thought about that. After a few moments she said "House Maelyl. Yes, I like the sound of that."

Valas smiled and slightly bowed to the best of his ability while still supporting Alton's weight. He then turned and left for House Phorudossa.

After they had left, Alton said "You amaze me at the speed at which you have delivered your promise. I can now be a house mage once again." His words came hard between his breathing.

Alton was in a lot of pain, but he would have his power once again. "One could almost believe you had this planned for quite some time now."

Valas only smiled and continued to lead him to House Phorudossa.

Book: Underworld

Chapter: Commencement

*M*edri was tired. She may have taken some of Alton's life force to heal her wounds and her exhaustion, but she was still emotionally drained. And she was drained of all of her spells as well. She needed a place to stay and recover her spells. She also needed some food.

The passage between the house and the cavern wall had dumped her near the slum area. She could blend in here, at least for a short time. Everything she needed was here; all she had to do was find it. First thing she needed to do was find food. She relaxed and smelled the air. Above the stench of the slum area she could smell food cooking. It would have to be a street vender, since she doubted any restaurant was anywhere near her location. She made sure her hood was pulled low on the piwafwi as she followed her senses.

Her guess had proven to be correct. She had made her way through the quiet streets of the slum area and she wondered how these buildings continued to remain standing since they looked as if they were put together by kobolds with no construction skill what so ever. The streets were practically empty at this hour, and were probably the same for most hours, thought Medri. Except for the smell of urine and an occasional hooded figure disappearing into the shadows, she would have thought the area to be deserted. 'Most likely all the inhabitants have themselves secured for the night from the fear of the upper houses', she thought. But just when she was sure the area was totally deserted, a turn of a street corner had proven to be beneficial. There was a street corner vendor selling cooked fish.

The vendor was an orc. From the looks of the creature it had seen better days. Scars were abundant about its body and for clothing it only wore rags. But Medri didn't care. She was more concerned about the portable grill it had and the hot fish it had for sale. Medri plopped one of Alton's coins down. The orc looked at her curiously. She mistook the look to be a misunderstanding of what she wanted so she pointed at one of the cooked fish slabs. But just as she pointed, the orc grabbed the coin and ran. Although curious at the transaction, Medri let her curiosity pass and she took a few pieces of cooked fish. Then she thought better of the situation and grabbed them all.

Now she needed a place to rest. She thought about getting an inn. She definitely had enough coin, but she was more afraid of being noticed. An innkeeper with a big mouth and a need for coin wouldn't turn down any opportunity as to turn in a runaway slave, a spy from a rival city, and a failed Matron. No, she would have to stay hidden. She thought about bullying her way into one of the shanty shacks, but that too had its problems. Any of the residences might kill her while she was trying to meditate. That left only one place remaining.

She made her way past the slum area and then through the bowch fields. If her memory served her correctly, there was a spot along the cavern wall between two of the main gates and on the other side of the bowch fields that would be out of the way. She doubted anyone would patrol this area, and upon reaching it, her suspicions were proven to be accurate. She found a place between two stalactites to settle down and eat her fish and then meditate for the night.

Once her meditation had been completed and she had received the several hours she needed to clear her mind and rest her body, she woke. Although no longer in pain from the battle, she had found her body had different pains. Her muscles were sore from the uncomfortable rest she had during her meditation. On top of that, her stomach was in knots and she felt violently ill. It was the fish. If she ever caught up with that orc then she would feed him the same fish just to watch as his digestive system rejected the poor excuse of what might have been called food. Although, she thought, the orc probably could eat that stuff all day and not feel a thing.

She sat for a little while longer and mentally went through the spells she thought she might have use of during the rest of the day. Sometimes it was a Senet dice roll to try to guess which ones she might need, but she knew one of them at least. She needed one that would let her get past the city guards, and there was only one that would let her do that without risk of being caught.

She had thought about her immediate future and where she would go from here. She couldn't stay. She would be recognized sooner or later in the middle section of the city. She didn't know enough contacts to fit into the higher status. She didn't have the strength or provisions to hold up in the slum area for any length of time. She didn't have an income for any sort of living. She couldn't go back to Anarchia and face failure, even if it wasn't her fault. As far as she could tell she only had one other option, the underworld. Perhaps she could find someplace where everyone wasn't plotting against her; perhaps someplace where everyone wasn't trying to kill her. Perhaps even the surface world. But she had to take things one-step at a time. First she needed supplies, and then she needed to get past the guards.

After her reflection of her spells, Medri got up and started toward the heart of the city again. She would have to be quick. The streets were starting to fill with merchants, buyers, sellers, entertainers, guards, bowch herders, commoners, slaves, and anyone else that might have any business on the street that day. Her initial quiet street eventually turned into a bustling thoroughfare. Fortunately it wasn't long before Medri found the store she wanted and quickly entered.

The sign post on the outside of the store simply read "Ugulen Delmah" and didn't give a picture of what it might suggest to sale. In fact, the only way Medri had guessed what it could be was when she saw a customer come walking out carrying an arm full of rope, climbing gear, two backpacks, a bedroll, and a grappling hook.

Inside Medri could see shelving on every wall with free standing shelving in the rest of the store. The shelves were full of all kinds of gear she could imagine. There were various sizes of backpacks, barrels, chests, sacks, and pouches. There was rope made of silk, grappling hooks, and climbing gear. She saw flint and steel, candles, tinderbox, and fire sticks. Row after row was a new item, everything she could ever want in a common or adventuring usage. To her right she could see a stairway that went down and she suspected even more items were for sale. The only problem was that the grade of the items was poor. She wouldn't trust any of these, especially with her life. But she only had a few things to buy and she didn't have time to find another store.

She was able to find a suitable backpack that wasn't in too bad of condition. On top of that she was able to find some dry rations that weren't half eaten or half rotted. When it came time to pay for her items, she was surprised at the outrageous asking price. She would have negotiated, bargained, threatened but she didn't have time and she didn't want to draw attention to herself. With reluctance, she paid the hefty fee and left. She had to tell herself that it was really Alton's money and not hers, but she wanted to make the coins last longer. She didn't know if she would need them again, it was just the feeling of having something to barter with.

With her backpack on, her rations stowed, and her hood pulled over her head, she headed for one of the south gates. She figured since this gate was the closest to the slums she had a better chance of getting past the guards, especially with the spell she had in mind. She doubted any spell casters, if there were any at this gate, would be looking for individuals entering or exiting via extra planar travel this close to the slum areas.

Once she was close enough to the gate to get a good view of it, she stopped and studied every bit of it. It was wide enough to move a large merchant caravan through, perhaps thirty feet of so. There was a station on each side of the gate that housed several dark elves each and at least one Minotaur. She suspected two other similar stations on the other side of the gate.

When she was satisfied with the distance she wanted to travel and the layout of where she wanted to go, she put her hands into motion and cast her spell. Once again her surroundings turned into a shadow of itself and every creature she had recently seen as solid, she now saw as a silhouette. She carefully placed one foot in front of the other. Slowly she made her way and covered the distance to the gate. With trepidation she walked past them, hoping they didn't have some magical means of detecting her. Her hopes and suspicions were proven correct and she passed them with ease.

She continued down the tunnel. What she needed to do now was to go far enough so she could drop her spell without being noticed. But this was a section she hadn't studied since she couldn't see it. Shadows went in all directions and she didn't know if they were part of the tunnel or adjoining tunnels or passages to other planes or other parts of the shadow plane. She had to take one of them; she was just too close and would be seen. She went right.

The tunnel darkened and she fell. She thought she saw some solid shadow creature fly past her and hopped it didn't see her. Suddenly she landed hard and her breath was knocked out of her. She wanted to lay there in the darkness and let it take over, but she had to get out of the shadow plane fast. She let her spell fade and took stock of her surroundings.

She was in a small cavern with several stalactites and stalagmites. She couldn't tell how she had fallen into the chamber, but the shadow plane didn't work the same as the solid world. There was only one way out, a small tunnel. She was lost and she wasn't sure if that was any better than being in either of the two cities with individuals trying to kill her. At least here she could make a stand. She took the tunnel and headed out.

She spent the first day meandering through various tunnels trying to guess which direction to go. It was difficult to pick directions when she didn't know where she wanted to go in the first place. The only thing she did know is where she didn't want to go. The tunnels yielded their usual forms of flora and fauna. She had startled a group of bats at one time and another time it was a pack of small cave lizards. Fungus and algae were periodically abundant, and then at times they were virtually non-existent.

On her second day she had found a small cavern with a small pool of water. She had thought she was in luck and the water might have been potable, but unfortunately it was bitter from mineral drain off. She placed her pack down and decided to take a rest and meditate. She had to do something better than just continue getting lost.

Suddenly she was hit and hit hard from behind. The blow nearly took her breath away and before she was able to recover, she felt some form of strand entangle her ankle. Medri was yanked from her kneeling position and found she was upside down. She couldn't get her bearings as her body spun freely until yet another strand and then another lashed out. Medri was caught along the waist and on her thigh. As the extra appendages held, she stopped spinning wildly and she was able to see her opponent. It was a stalagbeast.

The creature looked very like a stalagmite or a stalactite depending on how it wanted to blend into its surroundings. It was at least feet tall and had a stone coloring. She knew that the creature could change its color and heat temperature to blend into its surroundings. The creature had several appendages that grew from the sides of its upper torso and three of them already had her grappled. She knew that they had the ability to sap her strength, but her knowledge did little to stop the effects. She felt weakness wash over her. Medri could see a gapping mouth open in the beast and knew she was being drawn in. If only she could hold on to consciousness for a short time.

The creature pulled her in toward its mouth. It had been awhile since it had fed; hardly anything entered this part of the underworld. At least this meal would last it for a while. It pulled her closer and started to place her into its wide-open mouth.

Medri quickly took one of her daggers and hit hard into the inside of the creature's mouth. The dagger started to sap the creature's strength and give it back to her only to have her own strength be drained yet again. She struck hard again and again into its sensitive mouth until the stalagbeast threw her across the cavern. She landed with a thud and pain shot through her shoulder as she landed wrong. She had heard a snap, and at first she thought she had broken a bone and that the pain hadn't set in yet. But it was worse than she had suspected. Her last bone dagger was shattered.

She was enraged. She was tired of all of the plots; all of the assassination attempts, all of the fighting, the house wars, getting lost, and now this. All she wanted to do was rest. She wanted so badly to charge the stalagbeast and finish it off. She still had some spells left that could deal it damage. She would use the shattered dagger. She would use a nearby rock if she had to. She would use anything she needed to teach this insolent creature a lesson. She was a dark elf, the chosen species, and a female. Didn't it know better?

She closed her eyes for a brief second. She could try to kill this thing with spells and take her frustrations out on it, but she could die in the process. 'What was the point?' She thought. The stalagbeast was slow and it was obviously hungry. She smiled and knew that there was one thing she could do that would do the stalagbeast the most damage, and all she had to do was to quench her anger and use her wits. She sighed, turned, and left.

The stalagbeast screamed in frustration; she had landed beyond its reach. It had to catch her again if it wanted its meal. He tried to scurry itself along the cave floor, but she had turned and walked away. It tried harder to catch up, but her walking speed was faster than it could manage. Its prey would be lost and if it didn't find food soon, it would starve to death. The stalagbeast wished she would turn back and fight. At least it would have a fighting chance to survive, but being left like this it would die and there was nothing it could do to prevent it.

Medri heard the scream of the stalagbeast as she squeezed between two of the cavern walls to come into a wider tunnel. She smiled. Even if it did manage to make it this far, it wouldn't fit between the walls she had to flatten herself to get through.

The gap in the cavern wall had brought her to a cavern with two tunnels leading out and she chose the right passage. She still didn't know where she was going, but she was starting to be at peace and at ease with herself. Her encounter with the stalagbeast had taught her how to relax and how to think. She didn't have to be angry, she didn't need a plan and she didn't need all of the plots she had woven in her life. All she had to do was walk away.

After about a mile down the passage, Medri came to a cavern. She could see the far end of the cavern and she noticed that the passage continued. But there was something that prevented her from entering, acid slime. The entire cavern was covered with it. The slimy goop dripped from the ceiling, slid off the walls and pooled in the center. She knew the slime would eat through almost anything, and even if she found a way to cross the floor, she had to worry about the drips from the ceiling. She sighed. There was no way for her to move forward. She doubled back and took the left fork.

Chapter: Ensnarement

*M*edri had found another cavern to stay and rest before she moved on. Her muscles were sore from not able to rest properly and she hadn't hiked this much in her life. She was sure she had blisters on her feet, and if not, then she would soon. It would be nice to be back in the soft bed or at least the nice hot bath. She could almost feel the relaxing sensation it had put her in, like a gentle breeze. She stopped. It was a gentle breeze. It was subtle but it was definitely there. She continued down her passage and found the going to be easier than it had been in the past several days. The tunnel started to show signs of being worked on. Upon closer inspection she could see that there were chisel marks and the tunnel was flatter and broader. The signs were more evident the further she traveled. 'At least there's some sort of intelligent life, but the question is what,' she thought to herself.

After a short distance, her tunnel stopped but joined with a much larger one. This one was easily thirty feet wide and twenty feet tall. The walls were very smooth and the ground was level. This was a major tunnel. 'It could have been a lava tube, or a large worm tunnel, perhaps even a Watcher passage to begin with,' Medri reasoned to herself. She doubted either of those was true now. The tunnel was too well worked and too well rounded. This was the same size and shape as the tunnel exit from Malzebowan. For all she knew, she had gone in circles.

"Great, just great." She sighed then put her hands in motion and cast her spell. She closed her eyes and let the spell take over her senses. She was able to sense the presence of the living with this spell, but at the moment she couldn't detect any. It was just going to be one of those days. The wrong decision could lead her right back to Malzebowan. She closed her eyes again and sighed. Then she made her decision. She turned left and followed the tunnel.

After about a mile or so, she came to a smaller tunnel to her left. The air was still moving faster down the main corridor and she wanted to investigate the source of the cool fresh air, but to get to its source she would have to cross the intersection. Medri was still a dark elf and still paranoid. She figured she always would be. Perhaps it was paranoia or perhaps it was survival, either way she wasn't going to cross the intersection with the possibility of being seen. Her hands went into motion. She had a greater respect for this spell and was hoping she didn't have to use it so soon, but she had studied the length of the tunnel she had needed to cross and realized that the distance she needed to cover was close to twenty feet. The spell's needed duration would only be a short time this time. Her spell went off and she felt the cold sensation again, the sensation that life had just been sucked out of everything, and color and heat no longer existed. She again entered the shadow world.

She took her first tentative steps, being more careful this time, and kept more focus then she had in her previous attempt. She had crossed about half way through the intersection when she felt a strange sensation. It was as if her connection to the Weave had been pulled from her. Her steps faltered and she fell hard on the cavern floor. But this wasn't the shadow cavern floor; she was back on the solid world again. Something had cancelled her spell.

"Greetings dark one." A voice boomed from the intersecting corridor.

Medri looked up from the prone position she was in. Coming down from the darkness of the tunnel she could see a horror she had hoped she would never have to see up close. She had heard about them, learned about them, read about them, and saw them at a distance, but she never really wanted to meet one. It was a Watcher. If her memory served her correctly most Watchers or as most dark elf would call them, orb seers, were only about eight feet in diameter. This one, however, was easily twice that size and took up the majority of the twenty foot wide tunnel it had come down. It had its center eye fixed on her and Medri knew this was the source of the dispelling of her spell. Its eight eyestalks constantly whipped around, its several tentacles were in motion and its seemingly endless supply of smaller eyes continued to stare in all directions. She knew one of the stalks had the ability to disintegrate, but she didn't know which one. She only hoped that if it came to it that her natural ability to resist spells would hold long enough for her to get away, Medri had no intention of fighting this creature.

"I am Gau." Its voice boomed and seemed to fill as much space as its body.

Medri continued to stay lying prone; she didn't want to do anything that might seem aggressive. She didn't know if the orb seer was playing with her in an attempt to lower her defenses before it was going to try to kill her, or perhaps it was up to something even more sinister.

"It is customary to respond back with your name, dark one," it said when it didn't received a reply from Medri.

Medri thought for a second. There were spells that could take control of her if the individual spell caster knew her real name and there were rumors of some orb seers being spell casters. But she expected the orb seer would suspect her to lie. Perhaps she could get away with hiding the truth in the truth yet again.

"My name Medri." She rose to her feet and thought about making a run for it, but held her action for now. She would have to wait for the right moment.

"Good to meet you Medri. Yes, very good to meet you."

The orb seer looked her over in an attempt to take stock of her abilities, but continued to keep its anti-magic ray targeted upon her. It may have her at a disadvantage, but she was still a dark elf and this species was as unpredictable as they came.

"Where are you going, Medri?"

Medri thought for a moment. There was no point in telling a lie here. She shrugged and said, "I honestly don't know."

The orb seer laughed out loud at that reply. Medri could see its entire body shake with the laughter and didn't know if this was her opportunity to run. She could make a dash it, but upon further examination she could tell that the tunnel she was in was very straight and very wide, and there wasn't any place she could hide. She doubted she would get far. Her thoughts and hopes of running faded with that realization.

"That answer was truly unexpected", the orb seer bellowed. "Usually I receive some sarcastic remark, but yours was truly extraordinary. Because of your answer, I will tell you this: the tunnel you are on continues to the upper world, if you didn't already know. If you have never been there, then you are in for a time of your life. The tunnel behind me, however, is restricted, and will only bring certain and immediate death."

"Restricted? May I ask to the nature of the restriction?" Curiosity had overcome her fear. Medri knew that someday this might prove to be her downfall, but she was still a dark elf after all, and she would always have a thrill of living on the edge of danger.

The orb seer laughed again. Perhaps the day of her downfall was coming sooner than she had thought.

"I am a guardian Watcher. It is my job and my honor to stand guard over great artifacts. However, my latest mission seems to be more of façade than a real mission. One of your own species brought me here to this place and told me to guard the tunnel from the "ghost of the underworld". Usually I accept assignments without a grudge and for a considerable fee of course. This time one of you wizards had placed a spell on me and now I'm here against my own volition. Apparently this ghost has caused enough trouble for your species that I am to kill any dark elf who attempts to enter until the ghost is dealt with. I'm surprised you haven't heard all of this." The creature smiled a smile wide enough to swallow Medri whole. Then the orb seer's smile faded to a very serious expression, "This tunnel is off limits." Its voice was clear and concise.

Medri nodded. She understood the tone of its voice and understood perfectly where she stood with this creature. But that also meant that perhaps she would get out of this alive after all. "So, I'll just venture on this tunnel then." She said nodding down the main corridor. "And you are destined to stay here?"

Again the orb seer laughed. "For now, yes. But I will leave my post and soon. Good-bye dark one. We shall meet again." The orb seer floated its hovering body backwards and disappeared into the darkness beyond Medri's heat sensing view.

Medri was left with an odd feeling. Orb seers were as conniving and manipulative as dark elves. The sudden appearance and departure of any orb seer was to be questioned. To top it off, she was not only alive, but entirely unharmed. She had stumbled on yet another plot to ponder. Her head hurt from all of the plot twists she had been in recently and was eager to do as she had done with the stalagbeast, simply walk away. She tuned and continued her journey.

The further she walked down the tunnel the stronger the wind was. It was still a gentle breeze, but it carried a sweet scent on it, very intoxicating to her senses. She was used to the smells of her underground city, so this was something beyond her imagination. It was like a perfume in the air. She smiled. The underworld would be a lot more tolerable if it smelled like this instead of the dung, sweat, and other stale odors that were never circulated out into fresh air. The tunnel curved up ahead and she was sure she was close to the source, close to the upper world.

"Look what we have here." A voice came from in front of her. It was in the dark elf language and it was a male.

She had been careless. She should have been hiding as close to the sidewalls as possible, but she was out in the open and now she had been seen. Her heat vision picked up a male dark elf as he stepped out of the shadows up ahead of her. Although she couldn't see the full armament and armor of the male, she could guess from his demeanor that he was part of a dark elf raiding party. There would probably be a dozen of them, and from his attitude and the fact that he led the conversation, there would only be male. A female leading a raiding party wouldn't allow a male to take the lead in anything. She would have to deal with them the only way they knew how to be dealt with.

"Get out of my way and get back to your mission," she said in the most commanding voice she had.

She might have to resort to her spells but there were too many of them and if only one crossbow bolt could get through her defenses then she would be brought back to Malzebowan and she would have to start all over again.

"But we are done with our mission, Mistress." The voice had sarcastically drawn out the word "Mistress".

It was a disrespectful undertone and one that meant she was going to be their next mission. 'Perhaps', she thought, 'they knew about my leaving Malzebowan and were sent here to bring me back. Perhaps I was their mission all along.' She shook her head. Paranoia or not, she would have to defend herself one way or another. She went through her spells in her head. Her hands went into motion as she moved toward the figure that had stepped from the shadows and was now blocking her path.

As she tried to pass him, he shot a hand out and grabbed her by the upper arm, just above the elbow. She hadn't realized how sensitive that area really was, or perhaps he had spent enough time in his house dungeons to know how to apply pressure. Either way, it didn't matter. He had acted exactly as she had anticipated. Male dark elves were so predictable.

"Where do you think you are going, Mistress?" Again there was the sarcasm on the word "Mistress". She had to play this just right.

"Unhand me you worthless piece of Iblith! I am a female, I am your better and you should know that! You should bow to me in my presence. Release me. Now!"

"Don't give me that." He replied with a command of his own. "You don't have a snake whip, you don't have a house insignia, and we are far from anyone who will care about what happens to the likes of you." His grip tightened and he pulled her closer to him.

She could see more male dark elves slip out of the shadows from ahead of her and could hear more of them from behind her. She was surrounded. 'Good', she thought, 'I have them right where I want them.' She released the final word of the first spell.

The male dark elf yelped in pain as his hand began to shrivel. His fingers became useless, muscles weakened, and joints ached beyond enduring. It was as if his whole hand had aged. He could feel the process coursing through his system and his whole body stated to feel weak, tired, and arthritic.

Medri could have chosen a different spell that probably would have killed this arrogant individual, but she needed him alive, at least for now. She knew the others were already reaching for their crossbows. She was sure that these were poisoned to bring unconsciousness and not death. They still wanted her alive, at least for the time being, and that was a tactic she was going to exploit. She grabbed the aging male dark elf and pulled him close as she moved herself back to one of the cave walls. With him as a shield and the wall to protect her back, she had a better chance than out in the open. And with her shield being alive instead of dead, he could hold his own body weight and not be a dead weight. He would come around and pull his senses together in due time, but she was hoping that it would not be soon enough.

She heard the thuds of several crossbow bolts hitting the male dark elf and felt his body drop. Her living shield had served its purpose. She knew what spell had to be next before they reloaded. Again her hands went through their motions and a skeletal armor came over her body. It wasn't as effective as full plate armor, but it was the best she had. A few more thuds against the cavern wall and a couple off of her armor told her that she had chosen correctly, but now the next few spells would be tricky.

She started casting again. She figured the others would realize that their crossbows weren't going to be very effective unless they got very lucky. If she was correct then they were going to try to rush her. And her guess was correct. She could hear the running footsteps that confirmed her suspicions. Her hand reached into one of her pockets and produced a bone shard. All she had to do was to kill one of them and the easiest one was the one at her feet. He had served his purpose by being a shield for the crossbow darts and now he would serve another purpose, as the start of her undead army. She only needed enough time to kill him and then raise him as an undead before the rest of them reached her. The rest would be simple.

Her spell went off and the bone shard grew and elongated into a bone spear. She wished she still had her dagger. It would make things a lot easier and she would have one less spell to cast. She raised the spear up and started her downward thrust upon her unconscious victim when she was tackled. Her body hit hard against the cavern floor and her bone spear flew from her hand. The spell was ruined and the spear faded to nothing but bone dust.

She rolled on her back and punched straight out connecting with his jaw. Then she followed with a quick raise of her knee and caught him in the groin. The attacker rolled off of her in pain, but was quickly grabbed by two more.

"Hold her down," the first one said between gasps in his breathing. He wasn't sure if he had the ability to do what he wanted to do now, but he was definitely going to make her pay. With much pain he straightened up and advanced toward her prone body. He had noticed that she had started to finally grasp the situation she was in and also realized that there was no sense, no reason to put up a fight. Or perhaps she was just too scared. Either way, she had stopped squirming and struggling and now he was going to have his way with her.

Medri could identify arrogance when she saw it, but she needed him closer to her if she was going to show him the price of such arrogance. She went still. She knew the male species; all she had to do was struggle a little and then go limp. It was an easy enough strategy and he fell for it just as she suspected he might. Just as he came in range, she quickly brought her knee up to her chest and kick out as hard as she could. Her hard soled boots nailed her victim in the exact same spot she had nailed him before. He went down and started to tremble and shake in pain. He tried to scream, but the entire experience robbed him of his voice. He even found it difficult to catch a breath and he was on the verge of unconsciousness. It would be quite some time before he recovered. 'Two down, ten more to go', she thought.

Two more came and grabbed her by the ankles while another one approached. "Now you will truly receive what we all have in store for you."

"And you are the one to give it?" She asked coyly allowing her body to relax. She still needed some strength and there was no need to waste it struggling.

"Yes, in fact I am." Her new opponent had started to undo his belt.

But Medri only laughed.

"You think this is funny?"

"Have you ever heard of such a thing happening back at Malzebowan? Of course you haven't. You can't even understand the situation you are about to put yourself in. The glyphs on my corset hooks will end this quickly. Go ahead; let's see what you are made of. I intend to, as it splatters all over the cavern wall."

"You're lying. No one would ever trap their own clothing."

"Oh? Really? It prevents a body from being pillaged after it falls. Do you think we females would let you take just whatever you find off of a fallen female body? And I do say it has its advantages in preventing a situation like this."

"I don't believe you."

Medri only smiled and then shrugged to the best of her ability, as much as she could with two of the male holding her arms to the ground would allow.

The male dark elf smiled. "Well, I guess it doesn't matter. You will take the corset off for us, and we can have a little show in the meantime."

Medri's smile disappeared from lips.

"I see I have hit on something here. Get her up." The two that were holding her legs let go as the two that were holding her arms helped her up. "Now take it off. Take it off slowly, I want to enjoy this."

Medri gave a stare that would have killed. She yanked her arms away from the grip of the two had helped her up and they backed off, but only slightly. They may have had her surrounded, they may be stronger then she was, but none of them were going to totally relax their guard. Each one had moved their hands to their swords. They had seen her cast spells and it was possible that what she had said was accurate and they didn't want to be anywhere near a magical trap if it were to be set off. It was also possible that she was lying and only wanted to get her hands free so she could cast a spell. But they were too close and too many of them, they were sure she couldn't get a spell off fast enough.

Without taking her eyes off of the newest leader she started to undo her hooks on the front of her corset. The male watched closely. Was she moving her lips in a way to undo glyphs so they wouldn't explode, or do whatever they were supposed to do? Slowly, carefully, Medri continued to undo her hooks. She made her way down the front of her corset, one by one. She moved past her cleavage, down her chest, down her stomach and finally unhooked the last one. She smiled.

"It's about time I met someone who could better me." Medri spoke seductively, still keeping her eyes meeting his. Her mood had changed from angry Mistress dark elf to that of a seductress succubus. "I have no respect for a weak partner. But you … you let the others do your work for you. You let the others fall. And now you will be the first to receive the rewards."

She slowly opened her corset and let it fall from her shoulders to land on the floor. She wasn't ashamed, she wasn't shy; she was an elf and a dark elf at that. She let their gazes fall over her topless form, over her naked breasts. When she was sure that she had their attention, she slowly walked toward the one she had continued to watch. She didn't need to look around to know where all of the others where, she didn't even have to be a mind reader to know what state of minds they were in.

Once she got close enough to him, she reached out and slowly caressed his face. She could see the pleasure in his face; she could hear the rise in his breathing and could make out the increase of heat in his body. His eyes closed to take in the moment. She had remembered what she thought about the female in her society when they used their own sexuality to get their way. It was a compensation for those who had nothing else to use. And up to that point, she didn't have anything else to use. But it had worked. They had released her. And now … her hand dropped to his shoulder.

With a quick movement, Medri's hand sank deep into the male dark elf's shoulder, grabbed his shoulder bone through skin and muscle and pulled. The male screamed in agonizing pain and horror, as the last sight he saw was his own skeleton being pulled out from his body.

"Attack", she commanded the skeleton as she twisted her body around it to take cover. The skeleton turned and grabbed a sword from one of the other guards and quickly thrust it into his belly, impaling the guard and swiftly killing him.

The male raiders were taken off guard. There were now four of them down and the rest were demoralized. Where there was once a guard, a member of their own raiding party, there was now only a pile of muscles, skin and blood on the floor with his skeleton now in the midst of them attacking with full fury. Most were able to shake themselves from the horror and pull their weapons to defend themselves. Fortunately for the next male, he was one of those who were able to pull himself together and get his sword just up in time to block the skeleton's next blow, a blow that would have taken off his head.

Medri was sure that at least one would swing past the skeleton to attack her, but her mind had already gone through the series of events long before she had tricked them into letting her back up. Her hands went back into motion. As usual with most of her spells, the air grew colder, the light grew darker, and the very fiber of life seemed less evident. The darkness gathered and took shape and a fairly large size sphere came to rest in the center of the battle. She could see that her skeleton had been hit several times and was already on the verge of collapsing. But now, with the dark energy sphere in place, the skeleton started to heal and she could see what was remaining of the raiding party was starting to feel the negative effects on their life.

Before they could regroup, she sent her arms and hands into motion yet again. This one didn't give the same cold effect, this time her body simply faded from view. It was similar to a mage's invisibility spell, but it was one she didn't use often since it could easily be dispelled by most arcane or even divine spell casters. There weren't any casters here. She had thought about grabbing her corset before casting the spell, but that would mean walking through the battle. It was safer this way. She might be a creature of chaos, an individual drawn to danger, but she wasn't suicidal.

She watched as another guard fell as her skeleton ran its sword across his neck. Blood spewed and the poor guard could only gag and watch in terror as his life faded as quickly as his blood. But before his nearly decapitated body hit the floor, it straightened back up, turned, and attacked one of his former comrades.

Then Medri witnessed something to her amazement. A benefit from the black negative energy sphere she hadn't thought of before. The mass of the first kill, the body of muscle and tissue, began to twitch and move. It was becoming alive. Not really alive, more like an undead. It no longer had a skeletal frame to keep it upright, but it was still moving in its own way, it was crawling, kicking, and slithering its way into battle.

The mass reached out and grabbed hold on an ankle of a nearby guard. It wasn't painful, it wasn't powerful, but the horror it inflicted upon its victim with its mere presence was enough to stop the guard dead in his tracks. The guard's stomach churned and he felt nauseous just looking at the thing that was trying to drag him to the floor. He brought his sword high to slash down on it, but suddenly felt a jab. Something metal had pierced his ribcage. The zombie guard had brought its sword to bare, cut through his chest and burst his heart. The guard slid off the sword and the crawling mass of flesh let go as he too joined the ranks of the undead.

Medri was still weak from the spell she had cast when she pulled the skeleton out from its body. It wasn't a spell she took lightly. It took so long to cast and she had to make sure she touched the victim she wanted to affect. On top of that, it drained her. With the feel of the negative sphere she had cast, she could feel total exhaustion set in. She was away from the radius of its major effects, but even at this distance she could feel its cold, life draining energy. She pushed through; there was still a battle to fight.

One of the zombie guards fell. It had sustained more damage than the sphere could regenerate, if that was a word that could be used with undead. Unlike its skeletal counterpart, the zombie had more flesh and more muscle to hit. The skeleton had pockets of air between its bones. A sword would slip between its ribs or a cut would just miss under the rib cage where it would normally gut anything else. The skeleton was faring better than the zombies were.

But she was well aware of the situation before it had happened. She waited until the second zombie fell before she cast her spell. Dark energy again flowed through her, around her, and obeyed her command. The spell went off and darkness entered the zombies giving each one a reanimation at its fullest strength. Normally she could do that all day, but after that one horrific spell, she could only feel her own life draining. She could have waited for the sphere to fulfill its purpose, but that would take time. The cavern spun and for a moment she thought the floor had rushed to meet her. Then the sensation passed. She had to be careful; she knew that too much of the necromantic arts could consume her.

Another guard fell, and then another. The floor was slick with blood. Those that fell eventually became part of her ever-growing undead army. There were still four guards left when her negative sphere faded. Its duration was never long enough for her liking, but it always did its job. The undead that fell now would stay down until she summoned them up herself. It didn't matter, she doubted she would need to, and her suspicions were confirmed when the last of the guards fell.

With a sigh of relief, Medri waved her hand and dismissed her invisibility spell and became visible again. She decided the first thing to do was to retrieve her corset. It wasn't out of modesty; her corset was also her armor and her protection from the cold. As she approached it she sighed and shook her head. It was blood stained from a trail of blood that had pooled around it. She would have to wash it, but until then, she would have to wear it as it was.

Once she redressed she started to work, she still had some time, but not much. Medri knew that the smell of the dead would attract predators and scavengers. She placed two of the undead down one side of the tunnel and two more down the other; they would keep watch until she was done.

She summoned the skeleton she had raised. With a wave of her hand, the skeleton lost its animation and fell to the ground. Satisfied with the raw materials she needed, she set about taking inventory of the raiding party. The raiding party had the usual gear she had suspected they might have carried. Each had chain mail armor, a piwafwi, a long sword, dagger, hand crossbows with darts, and backpacks full of adventuring gear such as fire sticks, rope, grappling hooks, and dry rations. She even found adamantite coins from Malzebowan. What she didn't find, and what had surprised her the most, was the lack of house insignias. These were badges of honor and station, but not a single one of the corpses had a house insignia. Then either these were houseless rogues or they were told to keep their insignias at their house in fear of being caught. Without house insignias it would be difficult to trace back a failed raiding party.

She discarded her poorly constructed backpack and what was left of her old, stale rations. In their place she kept one of the newer backpacks and stuffed it with as much gear and food as she wished to carry. When she was pleased with her new set of gear, she took up one of the daggers and one of the thighbones of the skeleton and started carving.

It took her longer than she had expected to carve the bones into the daggers she had desired. She knew she had to wait until the next day when she could memorize the spells she needed and she definitely should get some rest between now and then. Medri thought about making camp where she was when she heard the unmistakable sounds of scurrying feet from down the tunnel she had come from. The scavengers had arrived sooner than expected. She sighed. With a move of her wrist, she instructed all of her undead down the passage to deal with whatever was heading her way. They would fall without her aid, she knew that, but she would be long gone before any scavenger arrived at her current location. Without a look back, Medri left and headed for the exit of the tunnel to the upper world for the first time.

Book: Land Above

Chapter: External

She had walked about a mile more or so, when the tunnel turned again. As soon as she turned the corner she found she couldn't help but to stop and stare in awe. Before her was a sight she couldn't even imagine in her wildest dreams.

The tunnel opened up to what seemed to be the largest cavern she had ever seen; only this one seemed to go on forever. But then, there weren't any connecting walls and there wasn't a ceiling. As Medri gazed up, she was overwhelmed with the enormity of the space and the tiny silver lights that dotted the dark sky. She was used to the ceiling being close, the tunnel walls being close. Now, there was nothing, nothing but space. And this space went on and on. She turned while she continued to look up, and tried to get a bigger and broader view. She tried to imagine the tiny lights that covered the dark sky as fires burning from cities in a distance, but that did nothing to bring the sky closer. She turned again and again, trying to get a barring under her new ceiling but only felt more and more lost. There was a sensation of falling into the great sky, of drifting into the sea of stars.

But it was her imagination. On the contrary, she wasn't falling up, but instead she fell down and her body crashed to the ground. The ground was soft, not hard like she was used to. For the first time that she could remember, she was scared, total terrified. The sensation of drifting away was so overpowering, so overwhelming that her body started to tremble and shake. She wanted to simply curl up where she was, in a fetal position, and protect herself from the non-existent ceiling. But that would leave her vulnerable.

Without looking up, she crawled her way back to the tunnel she had just exited from. Medri sat in the entrance of the tunnel with her back to the wall and her knees pulled up to her chest. She did her best to regulate her breathing back to a normal state since she knew she was hyperventilating and she could feel her heart racing against her chest. She was going to have to take this one small step at a time.

After about an hour of solitude, an hour of calming her body to a more normal state, she heard the scurry of little feet again down the tunnel. She needed to move. The tunnel was not the best place for her. Even if the carrion scavengers didn't find her, then the next dark elf raiding party probably would. This was definitely a well-used tunnel and it was for the better to leave it, as well as her underground life, behind her.

Medri got up, took a deep breath, steadied herself, and went back out of the tunnel once again. She kept her head looking forward; she did not want to go through the sensation of falling again. She had lived for hundreds of years in a closed-in set of caves, caverns, and tunnels and it would take some time to get used to no longer having a ceiling over her head. With short steady steps she continued forward.

The area that she had come into was a field. It was a small field, by most standards, but to her, it was amazing. The path from out of the tunnel, and for a little ways away from it, was dirt and rock. This she understood. But when the simple trail ended, she stopped. In front of her and all around her was a huge patch of green dotted with white and yellow. Beyond the green stood, what looked like, giant mushrooms. Only these were much taller, and different in appearance. She would investigate those later. Right now she wanted to cross the green patch and make her way to a set of boulders a short distance away. Perhaps she could find shelter there.

The patch of green reminded her of the acid slime in the tunnels she had encountered earlier. But it seemed to her that it was more like the ground had fur. Individual pieces, or strands, or even blades, moved and swayed to the gentle breeze. It was as if the ground was alive and as it breathed the green would move. She tentatively took a step. Her heart beat quickly and a cold sweat broke over her. She half expected the green to attack her in anger of her intrusion. She half expected the ground to rise up and prove that it was a huge animal after all. She half expected the green to burn through her boots like acid slime would. But none of these happened.

She bent down and felt the green blades. They were soft but unresponsive to her touch. She pulled a couple, and still there wasn't a response. When she brought the few blades of grass to her eyes for a closer look, she could tell that it was definitely some form of plant and told herself that her fears were unsubstantiated. But she still felt it never the less.

She continued her walk, still cautiously, toward the rocks. It would only be a dozen or so strides and she would feel more comfortable. Every step brought a new confidence and her stride was becoming like her regular gait. Her heart was no longer beating wildly. Once she had made her way to the clump of boulders, she was in more control of her own reactions. She slowly walked the perimeter of the boulders and found that there was a space between them that she could crawl through and use a make shift shelter. 'It's not Anarchia,' she thought but dared not speak aloud in fear of breaking the silence, 'but then, it's not Malzebowan either.'

Instead of immediately entering the crawl space, Medri sat upon the rocks. She still needed to magically imbue her daggers yet again, but that could wait until she had come to terms with more of her surroundings. She didn't want to be attacked while she was in the process of casting her spells.

Medri looked closer at the 'mushrooms'. She was closer to a few of them now that she had walked to the boulders. These plants were very tall, some taller than the tallest stalactite and stalagmite structures she was used to and was too high for her to contemplate without looking up into the dark sky. Their stems were thicker than any ogre was wide, and some were probably closer to three of their widths. They weren't really mushrooms after all, but they were definitely plants. Arms reached out from their trunks and each arm had smaller arms like fingers, and these fingers had foliage. Some had needle-like foliage while others had flat foliage that resembled her hand. She could make out some of the colors. Some were green, while others were red or yellow. Some of the other plants didn't have any foliage and resembled skeletons and looked naked and bare compared to the other species that surrounded them.

Then there were the smaller plants. They were round and most were only about knee level. There seemed to be more of these smaller plants than the larger ones, although the larger ones dominated the view. Some of them had small round pods of red or purple that reminded her of spores while others had blossoms of white. She wondered if any of these were harmful, if any of these were animated, or if any were poisonous. She also wondered if any of these were edible. She could use some form of food source, her palate could stand the taste of dried rations for only so long.

She shifted her attention to the smells around her. She could smell something like perfume, a sweet smell that might have come from the blossoms or even the round ponds. It wasn't like the cheap perfume that her kind, including herself, would buy and sell and use in the underworld. There was something more natural, something more pure, almost intoxicating, almost like a fine wine. She could even smell dampness in the air and the dampness in the soil. There wasn't any smell of bowch dung, of urine, of sulfur, of any of the foul disgusting humanoids that she had to deal with. This was fresh air and it filled her nose and her lungs.

Medri could breathe better as well. It was as if the air she had been breathing all of her life was stale and recycled. 'Perhaps it was', she thought. 'Yes, it must have been. This is what real air feels like.' She took another deep breath and filled her lungs. She could feel her head feel light and alive at the same time. She felt energetic. Her body needed this, it craved this, and she hadn't even known it had existed until now.

The exhilaration had given her confidence and she thought it was time to face the sky one more time. She braced herself and slowly turned her gaze skyward. She could make out the silvery diamonds against the black sky. They were beautiful in their own way. They were like gems in the underworld walls. But these were more alive. They not only shone more brilliantly but also seemed to twinkle and sparkle as if they had a power of their own. Some were larger than others, and on closer inspection, some were red and some were blue, but most were a silvery white. She wondered what they could possibly be and what function they could possibly have.

Then she saw them. Off on the horizon and just above the level of the largest plant life she saw two large white orbs. One was larger than the other. It seemed to her that these two orbs provided the light that allowed her to see through her normal vision instead of her heat vision. They looked like two eyes, looking straight at her, examining her very soul. She shuddered and wanted to scream. She had just run away from her society, a society that was based on a jealous goddess, one that threatened to follow anyone who dared to leave her. And here she was. That goddess had found her, here in the clearing, after all that had happened, she was found. And she was being judged. Those eyes saw right through her. Her blood ran cold and she waited for the judgment that would find her wanting.

But it didn't come. Neither the judgment nor the wrath of that horrible demon goddess had rained down upon her. She sat a moment longer, not daring to move. But hadn't these eyes seen her come out of the cave? Hadn't they been watching her all along? Surely, if these were the eyes of the spider queen then she would have been dead by now, her soul would have been condemned in the daemon webs. 'No', she thought. 'They had to be something else'. Then she remembered. There had been some talk of the upper world.

There were rumors of what to expect in the upper world. One of them was that a great ball of fire was ever present in the sky. It was larger than any fireball that any mage could cast and that it probably was a fireball cast by some god that had gone awry. This fire orb would cast its heat upon the whole surface and threaten to burn off the skin of its inhabitants. The mere presence would pass judgment on any who passed before it. And those that were foolish to look directly at it would have their eyes burned from their sockets. Even if one were to take all precaution, the light alone would blind any who traveled beyond the protection of the underworld.

Of course these were just rumors. Medri knew her species and the religion that ruled it well enough to know not to believe everything she heard. As a matter of fact, she rarely believed anything she heard. There were raiding parties that came to the surface world and they had come back well enough and fully intact. She also knew that most rumors and stories held some basis of truth, some seed from which the story sprang. She just didn't know what to truly believe. It was her disbelief in the rumors and stories that gave her the hope that the upper world could possibly hold some form of basis for her new life.

And it wasn't too bad so far. The sun hadn't scolded her, hadn't fried her and hadn't blinded her. The light she saw was tolerable and the air was cooler than she had expected. 'But weren't there supposed to be only one orb of fire?' She thought. 'And these two looked more like disks of silver than balls of fire'. She was confused. But then, all she had was incorrect information and propaganda to keep her in the underground and from traveling to the upper world. And it was this propaganda that kept her entangled in the web of the spider queen. She would have to continue to learn the truth on her own if she wanted to break away.

She continued to scan the sky and fought back the sensation of falling into the heavens and simply floating away. In one section of the sky, she could see puffs of what looked like steam clouds of smoke clouds. Only these were high in the sky and didn't seem to have a trail from their source. They also seemed more substantial than any cloud-like spell she had seen cast. They floated in the air and she wondered why they didn't just fly away when there wasn't a ceiling to hold them in or why they didn't fall like some of the spell effects that were known to her. Things were very strange for her here and she needed to get used to them if she wanted to survive.

She saw a movement out of the corner of her eye. At the edge of her field near the taller plant life she saw it. It seemed to be a rat, a normal cave rat. But this one was different. Its tail was thick and bushy and its movement was in quick spurts. She watched as the creature darted from one area to another. Its tiny claws dug at the dirt as if trying to find something, and then went on to go dig elsewhere. 'Or was it trying to bury something?' She asked herself. She noticed that its checks were full and wondered if it really had something in its mouth that it couldn't swallow or if the creature normally came that way. At one point the creature scurried toward her direction. When it came within arm's reach, Medri picked up her feet and curled them up on the rock she was sitting on to keep the creature from taking a bite through her boots. But the creature didn't make any aggressive behavior. Instead it stood on its hind legs and looked directly at her as if to study her ability to defend herself. It was similar to the behavior of the rat she had seen in her tub not too long ago. Or was this thing begging for food? She readied her grip on her daggers and steadied herself to bring them to bear if it was necessary. She didn't want to fight another were-rat. To her relief the creature dropped back to its four legs and scurried off in its own quick and unusual way. Perhaps it had seen that she was serious about defending herself and that she wasn't worth the effort. Perhaps it sensed she didn't have any food. Either way, it left her and she was glad to be rid of it.

Another movement caught her eyes. This was in the sky. There was a flock of bats that came across the horizon. Only these didn't fly in an unorganized massive swarm and they seemed to be much bigger that regular cave bats, but nowhere near the size of a riding bat. Their wings were long and straight, not as curved and short like a bat. Also they didn't have a furry skin or leathery wings. They seemed to be covered in a fluff,-like webbing or a cloud. But that wasn't right either. Then noise came from them. They seemed to be talking to each other and their voices carried throughout the otherwise quite scene she was in. But their language, if that's what it could be called, was beyond anything she had heard. Or were these creatures even intelligent at all? Was this just sound they made, like a bat would make as it flew by echo? Perhaps the sound helped guide their flight, or help them take flight. Or were they talking to her? She doubted that they had even noticed her.

And then more sounds. High-pitched whistles and chirps came from all around her. She hadn't noticed that the sounds had slowly been ever increasing, but now it was obvious that various animals were communicating. Were they just now waking up? Perhaps her presence had scared them to silence and they had finally gotten used to her. She saw movements in the various plants and saw that these were different species of the bat like creature she had just seen. These things were everywhere. They would chirp and whistle then fly off to another plant and do it again. One would start and another would answer. And then there were more of those rat-like creatures scurrying on the edge of the field. Life was starting to erupt all around her and she wondered if they were all part of an intelligent society that was ready to rush her at any moment or if this was normal for this area.

Medri continued to be distracted by the sounds and by the movement all around her that she didn't even notice the change in the light. When she finally did, she looked up toward the two silver disks and expected them to be further up in the sky, being the source of the light. But instead she had found that the two silver disks and descended. The silvery white diamonds in the sky were disappearing and the dark, black backdrop was turning a dark blue. She spun around curiously trying to find the source of the new light. From the other end of the horizon of where the silver disks had descended, the sky was turning, not only a dark blue, but also a light blue. And the puffs of smoke in the sky seemed to be on fire. They were red and orange and she was sure the whole sky would burst into flames.

Then, to her, it did. A great fireball burst forth from the horizon she was watching. She could see just the beginning of the top of the sphere, but it was definitely a great fireball. The two spheres she had seen earlier wasn't the sun, this was. She could feel the heat start to build and thought of how hot the great fireball would have to be if she could feel its warmth all the way here. Her eyes felt like they were on fire and started to water. She turned away shielding them, but thought she might be too late. She was sure they had been burned out of her sockets, and if not, then she would definitely be blind. But she would have to deal with that later. If she stayed then her skin would fry off of her body. She only gave a brief thought to the plant and animal life that she had seen and wondered how they would cope. Did they not know that they were going to fry as well, that they were going to burn to a crisp under the sun? She had to get away.

Quickly she slid off of the rock structure she had been sitting on. With her eyes still closed and shielded with one arm, she felt around until she found the opening she had seen earlier. Medri dropped to the ground and crawled her way in, squeezing herself through the small opening, until she was inside the small, cramped space she had chosen to be her refuge.

She could feel the heat in her tiny shelter start to build and she realized, as the sun start to light up the day that her small cave like structure wasn't totally enclosed. There were small sections where the light streamed through. Medri had to shut her eyes and keep her head down to try to keep out even the filtered light from blinding her sensitive eyes. Her eyes watered in pain. But that wasn't the only thing that was giving her discomfort. It was starting to heat up. She was used to the constant cool temperature of the underworld. But here the heat was building and in her stuffy hovel she had found, the heat was getting to her. She was sure the upper world would fry.

She took off her leather, blood stained corset and her leather boots to try to cool off. It was some help to sit there in as much shadow as possible without most of her leather outfit. But she was still hot and stuffy. Sweat started running down her face and down her half naked body. She had thought of also removing her pants, but she wanted something to protect her if the situation called for it. She already felt vulnerable as she was still paranoid about absent dangers at every corner, and now she was trapped in the small shelter and would have no way to defend herself. No, she would at least keep her leather pants, no matter how hot it got.

Sweat continued to pour in the stifling heat and she felt like the air was running thin. Hours passed and her body cramped. Still she sat trying to put herself in some sort of meditation to try to remove herself from the environment. If she still had a few of her spell she could perhaps travel to the shadow world, but her spells were gone. She was tired and hunger. With her head still between her curled knees, she fished around for her backpack and found some rations to eat. Her body was shaking from sitting in the same spot too long, her lungs felt like they were suffocating, she was tired from not having her regular meditation, and the dried rations didn't help improve her situation or her mood. She wanted to be angry, a part of her was scared, but she didn't have the strength to feel either. There was the sensation of going outside, just to let her body straighten out and then let the inevitable happen, her skin would fry and she would die. But she would hold out just a little longer.

She woke with a start. Somewhere during her time in her shelter she had passed out. Her body couldn't handle its predicament any more. Either it had decided to get the rest it needed or the heat and cramped muscles had overwhelmed her. She didn't know, and she didn't care. Her body was in more pain that she had imagined. Medri could feel her muscles spasm in protest. She would have to find a different form of shelter if she survived this day.

But then she noticed something. The shelter wasn't as hot as it had been. She could feel the cool air enter her protective cover and the air was not as stifling. She willed herself to crawl out of the rock, grouping for the opening and into the outside once again.

The air was definitely cooler and the bright fireball of a sun was almost completely beyond the horizon in the same trajectory the silver disks had taken. 'These objects were probably on a regular routine,' she thought to herself, 'coming up from one direction and going down in the other.' She did the best she could to watch the fire disappear on the horizon and saw the magnificent array of reds and yellows and oranges it displayed across the sky. When her eyes could no longer stand the strain of the bright light, she turned to face the opposite direction. There were purples, dark blues, and finally the start of the black sky again. She could see the first silvery diamond come forth from the dark sky. Despite what she had thought, despite what she had been told, the plant and animal life continued to live, if not entirely thrive under the presence of the sun.

A gently cool breeze caressed her skin. She closed her eyes. The breeze felt good on her half naked ebony form. She sighed. She was still tired and needed to rest before she could gain her spells back. Medri climbed the stone grouping to its top once again and sat as she had before. This time she folded her legs and went into meditation. She thought about retrieving her corset to cover her form, but the breeze was a pleasurable contrast to the heat she had just suffered.

After a few hours of meditation, Medri woke refreshed. She heard her stomach growl again in protest of hunger and the air had chilled to give her goose bumps, but she stayed in her meditative state for a little while longer. Her mind raced through the spells she wanted to cast, she had to make sure her daggers were imbued once again. When she was satisfied, she slid off the rocks and retrieved her corset and her boots and put them back on. 'This definitely feels better,' she thought. Medri felt more secure and a little warmer. Next she retrieved some of the rations and ate her fill.

With her body more at ease, her strength returned, and her spells memorized, she placed her two daggers on the stone boulders and began her enchantment. It was a comfortable feeling to feel the cold dark energies flow through her again. The air had cooled to chill her soul and what little bit of light that was being generated from the two silver disks darkened. Medri welcomed each sensation as a long lost lover; it was the only sensation she had left that brought her comfort of who she was, of whom she always had been. A necromancer

Chapter: Gorag

She had spent hours on her daggers and from what she could tell she still had several hours left before the silver disks disappeared and the bright fireball of a sun came back up. She was not looking forward to spending another day curled up under the rocks again; she had thought about going back to the tunnel that lead to the underworld, but that held its own problems. Perhaps it was best if she simply hiked through the foliage and took in her surroundings.

But before she could formalize some form of plan, she heard them. Most of the sounds she had been hearing all day and all night were alien but the sounds of footsteps was something she was familiar with. There were several of them, probably her size, and they weren't too far behind her. From the sound she could tell that they had probably just cleared the flora edge and entered the green patch. She twirled to meet them with her gaze, a dagger in each hand. What she saw made her grateful that she had finished her spells upon her daggers and that she had taken the time to finish dressing.

They were orcs and there were five of them. She could tell that one was a leader with two on each side flanking him. They each had short spears, studded leather armor and small shields. Each also had a morning star strapped to their hips. They were definitely coordinated, which was odd from all standards Medri had known orcs to be. Even the rags they had worn under their armor were less like rags and more like ordinary clothing that looked slightly used, and they were coordinated with matching black pants and a red tunic. Someone was training orcs, and this did not bode well. Medri knew in her underworld realm that the slaves always outnumbered the dark elves, and if they were ever educated to that point then the revolt would be unstoppable.

What also didn't bode well was the fact that she didn't study any offensive spells. She had a few defensive ones, but she needed the spells to imbue her daggers. If she had to come to yet another fight and her daggers broke again, she would just have to … what?

Scream in frustration? She shook her head. There was no need to act like the Matron Mothers she had left behind. But without her spells, she would have to outsmart them. Fortunately, that shouldn't be too difficult. She knew how to deal with orcs.

"You're late!" She glared right at the leader of the group. He was obviously bigger than she was, obviously stronger, but she had the sadistic history of her race behind her. Orcs usually were easily cowered.

Gorag nodded. It was like this every time he dealt with these dark elves. At least the dark ones would deal with him, the surface elves simply shot first with their bows and then shot again.

Gorag was the leader of the One Eye clan, a small band of orcs from across the river that ran not too far from here. It was almost a full moon ago that his shaman, Grog, had come to him.

"It is your destiny," Grog said once Gorag entered the shaman's canvas tent. Smoke and incense filled the tent and Gorag had suspected his shaman to be high on some narcotic. And even if he weren't, the lack of air would have induced hallucinations. Gorag didn't know what to do with him. He knew that the rest of the clan looked up to the shaman as their spiritual leader. But Gorag was the clan leader and he did not appreciate his shaman dictating what he could or could not do, even if it was the will of Orcneas. However, he did have to put up with him to keep the clan bonded, at least for now.

"Then tell me, oh great shaman of Orcneas," Gorag said sarcastically as he crossed his arms over his chest, "what is the will of deity this time."

Grog hadn't missed the sarcasm; he simply chose to ignore it. "You are to go across the river and meet up with the dark ones, right here." Grog pointed to a spot on a crudely made map. The area was south of a well-known elf town, one that was known to hunt orcs as sport.

"Let me understand. You want me to cross the river, enter into elf-controlled territory and meet up with dark elves? Where's the killing, pillaging, or more killing? You are trying to get rid of me so you can have the clan to yourself. If you said 'go attack that elf settlement here and Orcneas is with you', then I would believe you. But you are sending me to death without battle. How is that the will of Orcneas?"

Grog merely shrugged his shoulders. He did that quite often and Gorag was going to take his head if he did it again. Gorag found himself in a bind. If he didn't go, then he would lose faith from his clan and a new clan member would rise. And what if it really was the will of Orcneas? If he did go then he might lose the clan anyway to an upstart. But at least going could bring him into battle, and that was the will of Orcneas.

Gorag had taken four of his best and closest elite guards. Not only could he count on them in battle, but also they had the best opportunity to take over the clan once he was gone. A promise of battle and glory, a promise of killing elves, and the guards were more than willing to follow. They had crossed the river at night and slipped through elf-controlled territory undetected and he had found the cave where he would meet up with the dark elves.

And the dark elves were there. Gorag had thought that either this was a wild elf hunt or that he was being set up. But the dark elves did come, and contrary to his initial belief, they didn't open fire with their crossbows and spells. Instead they had a deal. There was an abandoned fortress nearby, long forgotten. All the orcs had to do was dig around the cemetery until they found a small box and bring the box to them. The payment would be adamantite coin. Of course the orcs never traded in coin, they never bought or sold, they only took what they wanted. But adamantite could be melted down, and that meant a weapon.

They had gone during the night and kept their profile low. The fortress was easy enough to find from their instructions and it was definitely abandoned. From the looks of things, it was abandoned a long time ago. The ceiling had collapsed, the walls had fallen and the remains barely looked like any form of structure. What little vegetation was around the fortress had died or was currently wilting. But it had fairly simple to find what remained of the cemetery, and only two days to dig each grave until they found the box they were looking for.

The box was about as wide as the orc's chest and equal distance all around. But it wasn't the finding of the box that has surprised Gorag; it was the condition it was in. The box was in excellent condition. It was black and smooth like obsidian with no seams or anyway to detect to get the box open. On top of the oddities, there wasn't even a scratch on the box. Gorag knew right away that this was the item in question. Curiosity almost got the better of him and he had thought of keeping it in hopes of someday finding out what was inside. But then the instinct of Orcneas kicked in. He needed the adamantite to make a weapon, a weapon that would kill.

And now he had returned to hand the box over to the dark elves. Only now there was a female and the rest weren't anywhere to be found. He had heard stories that the females were the ones to watch out for, but by the looks of this one, he doubted it.

"Where are others?" Gorag asked inquisitively. He knew dark elves couldn't be trusted as a whole, and if something had changed then he expected an ambush at any moment.

"They left." Medri suspected that this orc was referring to the raiding party she had killed the other day. This meant there was something about the meeting she didn't know about, anything she said now could be the wrong thing to say. She had led the conversation hoping the orc would excuse itself and would give her some information to go on, but this one was either too stupid or too smart. She waited a little longer and stared into its eyes hoping the orc would say something.

'She either doesn't know or we have been set up,' the orc thought. 'Either way we should just kill her and take any adamantite coins she may have.' He folded his arms across his chest. It didn't look like much, only a gesture, but it signaled to his troops to surround his victim.

His four were handpicked and weren't slow or stupid, at least by orc standards. They had kept an eye on him from the start and immediately went into action. The two outer flanking orcs went wide on either side of Medri and moved toward her back while the inner two flanking orcs took a stride forward to come up to her sides while Gorag stayed in the middle. They had her completely surrounded.

She shook her head and smiled. Orcs had to be some of the stupidest species of humanoids she could think of. She was pretty sure they were over confident with her being outnumbered and surrounded. Suddenly her smile disappeared and Gorag knew something was about to happen, but he could only stand and watch as the whole thing unfolded. She dropped to the ground and slapped her hand down and in doing so; she let loose her innate ability to create a sphere of darkness. She was gone from sight.

The two orcs from her back charged into the dark, black sphere and blindly thrust their spears where they had last seen her. But they hit nothing. From here they not only couldn't see their intended target, but they couldn't even see each other, or even the way out.

Medri didn't have to see the orcs to know where they were or even guess how they would attack. Not only did she have training in fighting orcs, but also she had training in fighting in the darkness. And, although this magical darkness also cut off her heat vision as well as her regular vision, she could hear the clumsy beasts. All she had to do was duck, and that is what she did. She bent her knees hard and dropped her chest to her knees. And it was just in time. She could feel the two short spears just pass above her body. Now it was time to go on the offensive.

Medri reached up and grabbed one of the spears and pulled toward her, hard. The spear acted like a direct link back to its owner and only confirmed the location of the orc. With the quick pull and the off balance attack, the orc had no leverage to retain a grip on his weapon and the short spear flew from its grip. Medri flipped the spear and thrust it back in the direction it had come from and wasn't surprised when she hit solid mass and a cry of pain erupted.

Gorag had given the order for the two to enter and finish the fight before it started. He wasn't going to take any chances with this one. It was only a heartbeat after he watched the two orcs enter the sphere of darkness did he witness one of his handpicked fighters stagger back out with his own spear sticking out of his belly. Perhaps the two had stuck each other. 'No, that couldn't be right', he thought, 'they came in at the wrong angles to hit each other.' He nodded to his two other guards and sent them into the sphere as well.

Medri had anticipated the on rush of feet well before she had heard them and she had returned to her starting position, crouched in front of one of the first orcs. She needed this position to take out these two and she knew she would probably meet her old friend, the one called "pain" one more time. But it wouldn't matter.

And she did feel pain. The remaining orc that was still behind her had landed a lucky blow and pierced her back and into her kidney. It was excruciating. She bit her lip to keep from crying out. She had to let the pain drive her focus. The orc would attempt to finish her, and when he did, that's when she would make her move. She felt the spear come out of her body and it was then that she knew the orc would raise it above its head and try to plunge deep and attempt to drive it through her heart. He plunged forward to where she was and found only nothing. She was gone again.

She sprinted forward as she pulled a dagger out in each hand. At the anticipated time she plunged both of them out, one to each side and caught the new orcs that had entered the fray. She felt some life drain from one of the orcs and enter her body and start to heal her wound. But she wasn't going to stop and let it finish. She took another step forward to go past the orcs to keep them guessing where she had gone. The wounds weren't deep and weren't going to kill them so she still had to be on her toes. Instead of staying behind them, though, she reversed her daggers and reversed her step. Both daggers struck true again, this time plunging deep into their backs. Again she felt some of the healing power from the life-draining blade. She still wasn't done. She took another step forward and was behind them again. Here, she spun in place, faced their back, reached out with both daggers and slit their throats. She was satisfied with her work only when she heard both bodies drop to the floor

Now there were two left. If she had to, she could always raise some of these as undead, but she hoped she didn't have to use what little spells she had available to her. She had to find the missing orc in the darkness then kill off the leader, and she knew exactly how to do just that. Medri reoriented herself with the lead orc and walked out of her dark sphere toward him.

If Gorag had been impressed from watching one of his guards come out of the sphere of darkness dying, then he was shocked to see the dark elf walk out on her own accord and totally unharmed. There was blood on her armor but he could tell that it wasn't hers, she had no apparent wounds. He knew one of his guards was dead, but didn't know about the others and he was starting to feel as if he really didn't want to take her on all by himself. He took a gamble. Perhaps there was at least one of his guards still alive.

"So you think you tough, walk in front of me, stand there? You're no tougher than me. I am Gorag, leader of the One Eye Clan." He hoped that if any of his guards were still alive that they would hear his voice and follow it like a beacon. With any luck, they would come up from behind her. She would regret coming out of the darkness as she had done, she would regret leaving her tunnels. And Gorag's hope and tactic had proven fruitful. One of his guards came through the dark sphere with his spear raised over his head, ready to finish the kill

Medri turned quickly and charged in. Her actions were too quick for the orc and she was inside his reach before he could do anything. And with his hands raised as they were, he couldn't even defend himself. She plunged both daggers into his neck and struck arteries. Blood gushed in spurts on both sides of the orc's neck and the poor creature died before it hit the ground.

As soon as Medri had turned, Gorag plowed in right after her. She might be able to get one of them, but not both. And if he timed his actions just right, he would be the survivor. This would work to his advantage. With all of his rivalries for clan leader killed off, his reign would last that much longer. But she spun back on him quicker than he had hoped or anticipated. She plugged both of her daggers at his neck. Gorag tried to duck, tried get out of the way. He did manage to not get hit in the neck. But he could only watch in horror as both daggers caught him in his left eye and plunged deep.

Both daggers' abilities enacted simultaneously. The first one exploded in a sphere of shards and discharged its bone fragments everywhere. At the same time, the second dagger's necromantic ability drained the life of the orc. The two powers weren't ever meant to interact. The draining dagger also exploded from being in too close proximity to the first. The force was incredible and knocked both combatants several feet from each other.

Medri had landed on her back and hit her head hard on a rock. She could feel blood running from the back of her skull and she did her best to keep consciousness from slipping away. But she didn't even come close to having the worst of the impact. The orc she had hit was still alive, very much alive. She could hear him screaming in full agony and from her barely conscious state; she could see him with his hands over his one bloodied eye running off into the foliage he had come from. Medri tried to sit up, but consciousness faded from her. Her eyes rolled up and darkness came over her.

Gorag ran and ran hard. He didn't know where he was running to, but he was trying to run from the pain. Perhaps his own adrenaline would dull the pain as he ran; perhaps he would find some surface elf to put him out of his misery. His mind was so focused on the pain that he didn't even notice the tower he had run past, a tower that wasn't there when he had first came this way a few minutes ago.

A humanoid figure stepped closer to the edge of the top of the tower. He needed to get a better view of the orc. Although he could sense him, and definitely hear him, he just wanted to get a better look. He knew that the orc still had the box, he could feel it, and he could sense it.

He was the one that had sent his dark elf to contact the orcs. He wasn't going to do this himself, there were always going to be fodder to toss out first, and both the dark elves and the orcs had played their purpose well. He needed the contents of the box, the contents that was sealed so long ago. Only he wasn't going to stoop to manual labor, he wasn't going to allow himself to be seen. He was in charge of the conspiracy and no one else had to know. The only thing his dark elf pawns needed to know was that he wanted the box.

But the box could only be opened with necromantic energy and sacrifice. He was an arcane user as well as a telepath, but he simply didn't have necromantic abilities. She did though, that one from the other city. The one he had "guided" through the shadow plane by creating another passage, a passage that put her in the right set of tunnels to bring her here. Yes, she had played her purpose as well. He was glad that she hadn't died on her way to Malzebowan. He was sure the necromantic explosion would be strong enough, and the sacrifices that had happened would be good enough, to open the box and he could simply take it from the orc.

He decided against it though. The power was strong enough that it could be followed and traced and he would have every creature after him in a short amount of time. They would find out what he was planning and do everything they could to stop him. 'No, that would not do at all', he thought to himself. The orc shaman was easy to kill off, and it was easier still to temporarily take its place. 'No,' he thought to himself yet again tossing his conspiracy around his mind. He would let the orc keep the contents of the box for now. Elves and other surface creatures would hunt the orc and he would know where to find the orc easy enough. The contents were in good hands for now.

Now, he had other matters to attend to. There was other fodder to set in motion, other items to find. He turned and went back down the hatch from his roof and entered his tower and moments later the whole tower vanished as if it had never been there to begin with.

Chapter: Repercussions

*M*edri had no idea how long she had been out. Her head still throbbed from where she had struck it on the rock she was still laying on. She reached her hand behind her to access the damage and when she brought her hand forward she saw blood. It wasn't much and it looked like it had stopped for the most part. She was still light headed, with a massive headache, and she felt nauseous. It would be better if she could find some water, perhaps a stream. She wasn't a medic by any means, but she did know enough about her own health that fresh water could at least clean out her wound.

She went to stand, or at least tried to. Dizziness overcame her and she had to catch herself and rest for a moment longer. When she was ready, she gently stood and cautiously stepped forward. She was going to enter the flora line. If the orcs could make it through, then she could as well. She took a few more strides, and then it dawned on her.

The light wasn't right. There was something different. She had expected the great fireball to start to come back up; she had expected the darkness to start to fade away. Perhaps she wasn't out as long. But still there was something wrong. She steadied herself and looked up.

The great puffs of smoke or mist, whatever they were, had gathered together and covered the sky. But instead of being white, as they had been, these were dark and black and ominous. They reminded her of thick smoke that was capable of blocking out light. There was something else as well. She could almost taste water in the air. It was similar to when she had been near an underground waterfall and she could have tasted the water there. But she didn't see a waterfall anywhere. She sighed and continued to walk. The upper world continuously held new surprises at every turn.

She passed by some of the taller mushrooms and made sure she stayed away from the smaller ones as much as was possible. There was somewhat of a trail left by the orcs and she had decided to follow it, but still the going was rough. Perhaps the orcs hadn't been so careful as to stay away from most of the flora; perhaps these plants were harmless like the regular fungi in the underworld. She stumbled over a root and brought her mind back to her task. A few more strides and the plants opened up again, this time they weren't separated by a field, but by a road.

This was an actual road. It didn't have to be in the underworld for her to recognize the purpose. She could even see wheel marks. That meant civilization, which also meant trouble. She knew the upper world knew about the reputation of dark elves. Even if she hadn't participated in raids, even if she hadn't tortured any creature, which she hadn't done either one; she still would be held accountable for her own race. Her species gave no mercy and none was given back.

But where there was civilization, there would be water. That was given. All she had to do was follow the road, stay away from patrols, keep clear of the civilization, and find the source. 'Easy enough', she thought to herself sarcastically. But then, she had crossed the underworld twice and survived a house war, not to mention all of the adversaries she had recently faced. She nodded to herself. If she could survive all of that, then she could take on this task.

Medri stayed on her side of the road, but still in the plant life hoping that it would give her cover if anything or anyone came down these roads. She could probably take care of herself, but she didn't want to draw attention to herself. If this was similar to the underworld then news would travel fast and being noticed was the last thing she wanted. The best thing she could do right now was to stay inconspicuous.

About an hour later she had come to another field just ahead of her. She stopped. The field held a wide walled city and she was just in the outer perimeter of the clearing, still hidden by the foliage. It was only about a hundred yards between her and the wall of the city, but she could see the guards that were just on the outside of the city and a few of them that were standing on guard on top of the wall. It was very well defended and any potential enemy could be spotted well ahead of time.

She could also see some of its inhabitants just outside one of the gates. There were a couple of elves, a dwarf and a human all gathered together in a circle. And from the looks of things, they were studying the sky. 'So,' she thought, 'this phenomenon is rare, perhaps even unique.' The elves wore very fine gold colored chain mail. The armor could have passed as dark elf armor if it weren't the fact that it was gold in color. They also wore black leather boots, dark brown pants, and a dark green tonic was worn over the chain shirt. The dwarf had full plate mail. She couldn't tell what color clothing he had under the slightly rusted and highly dented armor. She could see, however, that the dwarf had grown a flaming red beard that was in such stark contrast of his armor, that she doubted anyone could miss it even at twice her distance. The human was dressed like a wizard. He had on a wizards robe in dark blue with white mystic icons on it. As if to complete the quintessential and prototypical appearance, he wore a long white beard that fell almost the full length of his chest. Medri giggled to herself. She thought the beard appearances between the dwarf and the wizard were too similar to be coincidental, but she doubted either the dwarf or the human would see any such similarity.

But despite the humor she had found, she came to the conclusion that this meeting was far more than just a few citizens who came together to talk about the weather. She believed that if the great fireball of a sun were to be out, then there would be more citizens out enjoying it or working in it. She had come to realize that the surface dwellers might be slightly fire proof and used to the bright light. But now that it was dark, when it should have been light, there was no one around except for this small gathering.

The elves seem to represent the general populace of the city and probably members of some high counsel. The dwarf was probably a cleric or priest of some deity that the upper world worshipped in the hope of clearing the sky and returning it to normal. And the wizard, well that was far more obvious. These then represented the power of the city.

But this was their problem, not hers. As a matter of fact, if it weren't for the unprecedented darkness, she wouldn't be able to move about as she had. What she was looking for was beyond the city, further down the road, and in sight. It was a river. This city had been built not too far from its banks and from the size of the river; there would probably be enough water traffic to generate significant coin for this settlement. Her problem was getting from here to there.

She looked down the direction of the road she had come from. Nothing. She glanced back at the small group in the field and then at the guards. They seemed to be occupied. She nodded. She pulled her hood over her head and drew her piwafwi close around her. Then, when she was ready, she made a quick dash to the other side of the road. The sprint was very short, but it felt like forever. She sat at the other side in the shadows of the vegetation and waited. Then she made a quick look back down the road and again toward the city. She hadn't been spotted. Her heart was racing, but she had made it this far.

Medri turned herself into the foliage to angle away from the city while still going toward the river. She would eventually reach her goal, but it would take her longer than if she had gone straight ahead, though this would keep her unnoticed. She hoped she would find a spot where she could stay hidden and enjoy the water that she had realized that she had been craving for quite some time.

After some hard walking through the vegetation, Medri finally came into view of her goal, the river. It was wider than she had thought and definitely wider than any river she had seen in the underworld. It was also traveling faster than she had expected, but the water wasn't very fast near the bank. As she drew closer to it, she realized how thirsty she had been. She had thought she just wanted to wash her wounds, but she was now certain that she had been driven here out of absolute thirst. She knelt at the riverbank while still protected by the shadows of the foliage and drank. It was cool and refreshing. Again and again she cupped her hands and drank. Then she cupped her hands one more time and washed the back of her head. There was still some blood and her head still hurt, but she was sure the wound would be cleaner.

Once she was refreshed, she placed her back by one of the tallest and widest plants; one that towered far above her and one that would hide her from most anyone. She crossed her legs, closed her eyes, took a big sigh, and let herself slip into her meditation. There were spells she wanted to study and she wanted to take a short swim before moving on. Both of these were best done in the privacy of the darkness and since she had no idea how long this unscheduled blocking of the sun would last, she would make the best of it by resting now and moving again once it got darker.

After several hours of meditation, Medri woke. She felt the cool air once again and knew the sun had gone down and that this was the dark half of the day. She looked up and saw that the great puffs were still overhead and from what she could tell, still very black.

She couldn't see the white diamonds or the silvery spheres in the sky.

Her body still ached from all of the hiking, was still exhausted from the prior day she had spent under the rocks, and she just wanted some time to try to unwind before she started hiking off to who knows where. She undid her corset and let it drop to the ground. She paused there and let the gentle breeze play over her. It was a wonderful feeling. She put her arms straight up, arched her back, and stretched. Next she unzipped her boots and then her pants. Again she raised her hands and arched her back. It felt good to stretch the sore muscles. She then turned and slowly entered the water.

The water was cold and immediately sent a shiver down her body. She was used to the warmer waters that had run near the lava vents and had cooled off enough to be enjoyed. But she didn't mind. She was still trying to get used to the heat, even during the coolest and darkest part of the day. She continued to move into the river and let her feet slowly feel along the smooth silt on the rivers' bottom. With a quick push off, she glided her body into deeper end, making sure she stayed away from the faster flowing middle.

After a few minutes of just soaking and getting used to the temperature, she stood. Slowly she scooped up the river water and let it wash over her face. A second scoop and her hair was soaked. Medri did her best to wash out the small wound at the back of her head, there were be a good sized bump back there for a couple of days.

When she was satisfied with washing herself, she came back to shore, but didn't come all the way out. From her position she reached up and took hold of her leather outfit. It was filthy and her corset was blood stained. It took some time, washing piece by piece, to clean as much as she could. If she could find a good leather restorer who could clean it better and even repair a few cuts then her outfit would look far better than she can hope to achieve on her own. Then again, anyone dealing in that trade would mean civilization, and that meant getting caught.

Medri climbed out of the river and found a spot of moss she could lay on. She laid down on her back and let the cool breeze caress over her naked ebony body. Her eyes scanned upward wondering if she could see some of the diamonds in the sky, but the tall foliage blocked her view and she actually was relieved. The coverage felt like home. She took a deep breath and exhaled. She was at peace and was totally relaxed. For the first time that she could remember, she was totally relaxed.

She didn't know how long she had lain there, but eventually her sense of reasoning got the better of her. She was alone and naked in the middle of nowhere, with no weapons and her spells weren't memorized. And yet she still felt relaxed. She would move on, but she wasn't in a hurry. Slowly she rose and put back on her outfit. First she donned her pants, then her boots. She would have put her corset on before her boots but she always found it more difficult to put the boots on while wearing her top. Her goblin slave would have helped her to put them on. She did miss him. Next she put back on her corset and cinched it up. She definitely felt better and she was sure she looked better.

She reached for her backpack to see what ingredients she had left. This would dictate what spells she would memorize. But as she reached for it, she noticed it was missing. She quickly moved her head around searching the area. Still she found nothing. She got up and started a more thorough search of the area. Perhaps she had moved it without realizing what she had done. Her search still yielded nothing. There was nowhere for her pack to hide. Then she stopped, and froze. Medri realized to her horror that someone had taken it.

Gorag had run screaming into the night. He had run into several trees from being blind in one eye and totally blind in pain. He was sure the elves in the area had heard him. Had they simply let him run in pain rather than putting him out of his misery?

When he could run no more, he found a place to sit. From what he could tell of the area, there were briars all around. He found a place between them for shelter and took stock of his situation. With a careful feel of his hands, he ran his fingers across his eye. It was gone. It was shattered and destroyed. Only a bloody empty socket remained. Gorag let out a furious blood-curling scream of primal rage.

He finally took control of himself. He had to survive. He was hurt and it could prove to be fatal if he didn't act. He would have to cross back over the river and find his tribe; perhaps his shaman could heal him. Until then, he was going to see what it was that had caused all of his troubles. He was going to see why he had lost some of his best fighters, why he had lost an eye.

Gorag unceremoniously dumped out his backpack and let its contents spill all over the forest floor. There, among his gear, was the box. There was the cursed black box that had been the root of all his recent trouble. He picked it up and examined it and found that one of the edges was slightly opened. He remembered that the box was completely closed before. Now it was more out of curiosity than pride that had urged him on to open the box. He tossed it open and saw the contents. It was a skull.

It was definitely humanoid, similar to his but not like an elf. Perhaps it might even be human, but he couldn't tell, he was never concerned what a skull looked like after he bashed one in. He took it out and examined it, letting the box fall to the ground. The skull still had an eye in one of its sockets, its right eye. Like him, its left eye was missing.

There was a rumble off in the distance. It sounded like thunder; a storm was closing in fast.

Gorag remembered. His own god had lost an eye. Orcneas, his orc deity has lost his left eye in battle against an elf. Gorag had lost his left eye in a battle against an elf. And now he was holding a skull, roughly his size and shape that had also lost its left eye. Perhaps his shaman was correct after all, perhaps this was his destiny. Gorag seized the skull in a mighty grip and held it aloft laughing with power.

Lightning flashed overhead and lit up the whole sky as thunder boomed simultaneously. The storm had arrived. The rain fell thick, soaking everything it touched instantly. The gods had spoken. Gorag thrust the skull into the air again, and again lightning crashed and sky exploded with a fury of light and sound.

Chapter: Joshua

*N*ot too far off, in yet another briar infested area of the woods, there was another who had felt the power that had been unleashed.

The briar patch here was all gnarled, twisted, and contorted in a mass of brown hard thorns. It was only about ten feet in diameter and easily missed by all the other brush around. And nothing else grew here. Not a tree, not a bush, not a blade of grass, not even a weed would give root to this unhallowed area. Only the half dead thorns would have anything to do with the area, and then just barely at that. The ground on which the patch had taken hold of was black. It wasn't like black enriched soil, but black like a cancer that had spread its evil hatred on the land. If the world did have a cancer, then this was it. Not only was most plant life edged away from this spot, but so too were the animal life. Every bird would fly around it and every squirrel would keep its distance.

Suddenly, from the ground, between briars, the earth erupted as a hand shot up from the ground. It reached up as if feeling life for the first time, as if breaching its burial mound brought it more life with each passing second. Then a second hand erupted from the earth. The two reached up and the arms attached to them started to come out of the shallow grave. After what seemed like an unearthly stretch of joint and muscle, the hands worked in tandem to dig out the life that they were attached to.

The man tore at the loose earth and discarded it in handfuls. First he cleared his face away, and then went to work on his chest and stomach. When he was satisfied that enough of the rotted dirt was cleared, he placed both of his hands on the ground and pushed. With his strength returning with every passing second he could feel the rest of the earth give way and in a short time, he was free. His burial mound held him no longer.

He wore black leather boots, dark brown leather pants and a dark blue tunic. He had always worn dark blue; it was part of his uniform, and a favored color of his god. But that was part of his former life before his transformation. His new god never cared what he wore, so now the dark blue tunic was more out of habit. It had reminded him of how much he had fallen and that anger had always given him focus to do what he needed to do. To complete his ensemble, the man wore a gold color breastplate and gold color gauntlets.

His name was Joshua and he used to be a follower of some long forgotten god. At least it was long forgotten to him. Now his new god had taken him over. It wasn't by choice, at least not initially. But as the time went on, and his missions for his new god had been more and more perverse; the following had become easier and easier.

Joshua stood fully upright, ignoring the brittle thorns all around him. He stretched his body and revealed in how good it felt after all the years being buried. He hadn't remembered being buried or why he might even have to come to that. Had he died? If so, did his master bring him back to life? He didn't know. The only thing he did know was that his god would tell him in due course what his new mission would be.

Joshua looked down into the grave he had just dug himself out of. His cloak and mace still lie where he had been. He bent and retrieved them both. This cloak was a light blue and his mace was as wicked as they came. It still had bloodstains from when he last used it. He smiled with that thought as he ran his hands over it.

He looked around to take stock of his surroundings. Besides the briar patch, he knew he was in a forest. No, not just any forest, but the forest that was not too far from Grandfolk, where he had done his last mission. He looked up. It was nighttime. He knew that, without even knowing how he knew it, and yet he did. But he didn't see the twinkling of the stars or the shimmering of the twin moons. All he could see were those foreboding clouds, big, black, and angry looking clouds. He could even smell the rain it threatened to bring and the ozone in the air. This was no ordinary storm that had blown in. That much he was certain. He had seen plenty of storms in his life, and had even conjured a few, but this one with beyond his comprehension. He also knew that his god didn't create it. There was another force at work here, something just as evil as his god. Joshua nodded. This was the first sign of his new mission and he would enjoy it as he always had and always will.

Joshua went to take a stride forward and found that thorny briar patch stood in his way. He was so caught up in everything else that he had forgotten about such a trivial object. And yet wasn't that always the case with him? He threw back his head and laughed aloud and let his flaming red hair fall about him like a mad man.

But just as quickly as the momentary fit of madness had overcome him, so too did it pass and a look of solemn seriousness surmounted him. His green eyes surveyed the area ahead. He took off one of the gauntlets and passed his hand over the briars. The light brown, brittle wood rotted before his eyes. It shriveled and twisted even more beyond its already perverted shape. Then it turned a dark brown, and then black before the whole briar patch dissolved into a pile of rotting mulch.

He saw the brilliant flare of a lightning flash and knew he wasn't far from one of his goals. And yet he also knew that this particular goal would be the last piece. There were others and he had to get to them first. And even as he understood this, he didn't understand where the thought had come from or what it all meant. But he did know that he needed some help on this mission and he would go into Grandfolk to get it.

Although Grandfolk was an elf city, it was also on the fringe between known civilization and the wild lands of orcs and goblins. This was the city that any adventurer would stop last before moving on into glory or death. The lands to the north were crawling with humanoid monsters, and even some monsters less humanoid and more grotesque. 'Yes', he thought. Grandfolk was the exact place he needed to be to find the help he was looking for. And he knew he would recognize them when he saw them.

But that would have to wait. This storm would be noticed and the gates of Grandfolk would be closed tonight. He would have to wait until morning and then he would be able to move about more freely. Until then, he would head to the river and bathe. It wasn't that he was conscience of his personal hygiene, but he knew that the civilians of Grandfolk would be. It would be a necessity.

Then it started to rain and rain hard. The downpour was torrential. His visibility was cut to about half and immediately he was soaked to the bone. He threw back his head and laughed again. This was one of his many faults he simply could not prevent. It didn't matter if he did get soaked; he would still make the trip to the river. The rains only made the dirt that had clung to him turn to mud.

He found his way easy enough to the river and knew he was only about a mile or so downstream from Grandfolk. The brush and small trees, and even animal life that got too close to him, would simple die and wither away at his mere presence. When he found a bank on the river he found that it would be the perfect spot.

He started to undress before he made his way into the river to wash away the remains of his burial mound from himself and his clothing, when he saw a fireball go off not too far away. His first reaction was to go investigate and then when his curiosity was sated, he would kill the mage that had cast it just for sport. But he had to focus. Getting distracted to pursue his own pleasure in further spreading chaos was another one of his many flaws. Perhaps that was why his new god liked him so much. He was always unpredictable. But he thought better of it. A dead body would raise suspicions. There would be guards, wizards, priests, and who knew what else. All of this would be a complication to his goal, and although he wouldn't mind a complication, he knew he still had a mission to do and he had to focus.

He let the idea drift away from his consciousness. Then he stripped off his gear, stripped off his clothing, and slid into the river. Tonight he would spend in the forest and tomorrow he would gather his newly recruited conspirators.

Chapter: Maldev

*L*ightning flashed overhead and Medri ducked, rolled into a forward summersault, and positioned herself behind one of the thickest vegetation she could find. She had dealt with lightning bolts enough times to know better than to give any wizard an opportunity to continue to target her. She did have her spell resistance, but that didn't always hold up against very powerful mages. And this one must be powerful to pull lighting strong enough to light up the whole sky like it did.

She looked from behind her cover. She couldn't see anyone, but that didn't always matter. There was a spell that allowed a caster to remain invisible even after attacking. No doubt a wizard of this magnitude would have access to such a spell. She only wished that she had access to a few of her spells. She didn't have time, or at least, didn't make time. One of her spells would give her the ability to find anyone living in her area. But now she would have to do it the hard way. She had to be observant.

She concentrated all of her senses. She could hear the river and the wind starting to pick up. She could hear the rustling of the branches from the foliage. She strained even further.

Something caught her attention to her right. She jumped and scanned the ground. One of the rat-like creatures she had seen the other day scampered out of one of the lower vegetation. It didn't even take notice of her. She let out a sigh of relief. She knew she was getting paranoid, but paranoia had always kept her alive.

Then she felt it. Icy cold, pouring rain fell down from the sky. It sounded like frying sausages from a street vender. It also seemed like a waterfall from the underworld, one she would stand under to take in a full shower. But this water was falling from the sky and covered the whole area as far as she could see. Her heart raced and pounded. Perhaps this was yet another spell from the great mage; perhaps he had opened a portal to the elemental plane of water to drown her.

Minutes passed and it continued to rain. Medri tried to find some cover under the branches of the taller foliage, but it was to no avail. The water down pour was unrelenting. She started to shake in the cold, as water dripped down her hair, down her face. She was soaked and felt miserable and didn't know what to do. She sat down with her back to one of the tallest foliage, curled her legs to her chest and waited.

Minutes passed and more lightning flashed in the sky. She wished whoever was doing this would come in close so she could at least have a fighting chance, but no one came.

After what seemed like forever, the water stopped. She noticed that the river didn't even increase in size, that the ground, although very wet and muddy, wasn't washed away, and that the plants were still intact. 'This was another upper world experience', she thought to herself. It would take some getting used to if she wanted to live up here. She would have to find some shelter. Then her stomach growled and she added to her mental list that she would also have to find some food. She tried to stand. She was hungry, tired, soaking wet, freezing cold, her body ached and she miserable.

A fireball went off right on top of her. The light momentarily blinded her and the heat, although might have been a welcome feeling from the freezing cold she had felt, was too hot. Medri threw her piwafwi on top of herself and dropped into a roll. She let the resistance of her piwafwi and her own natural spell resistances shake off the effects as she went into motion. The lightning and water downpour earlier might have been a natural occurrence, but she knew a fireball when one hit her.

She ran through the vegetation, turned, and then turned again. She was hoping she could put some of this foliage between herself and the mage that was definitely out there. Suddenly she stopped and listened. This time she heard footsteps, running footsteps. She ran on again, turned behind another plant, stopped and hid.

The footsteps stopped running, but Medri could still hear them walking toward her. She looked around and saw some good sized rocks in her area. She wasn't going down without a fight. She listened, got a good idea where the mage was and nodded. With cat like reflexes, Medri sprang from her hiding place and let loose a fist sized rock. Only a lucky shot would have hit, but that wasn't her intention. If the mage wanted to remain invisible then she was going to level the battlefield. As she released her projectile, she let loose her innate ability to create darkness upon the rock, and at the same time, she charged the area she knew it would hit.

The rock landed and a small area around it enveloped in pitch black. Medri sprinted and enter the sphere of darkness. She ducked in anticipation of an attack, although she had no idea if one was close or not, it was just out of habit. From her crouching position she did a leg sweep and connected. It wasn't a hard kick, but it was enough to locate her foe. Immediately she struck out with her hand and hit, but again not hard. She believed she caught a thigh muscle and she was aware that her blow didn't do much damage; it was yet another exploratory movement. Quickly she came up and brought her knee with her, nailing her opponent in the upper thigh. She was hoping for a more painful and direct hit, but she would take anything at this moment. Then she struck out hard, straight, hoping to hit center mass. She hit chain mail.

'What?' She asked herself in surprise. Mages didn't wear chain mail, or at least very few of them did. Metal armor interfered with magic, restricted the movements of the mage and made it difficult to cast spells. Unless the spell caster knew what he was doing, there was a great possibility that any spell could go awry.

A blow hit her hard, a backhand across the face. Not only had she found her opponent, he had found her. All of her strikes had given away her position. The force of the blow made her knees buckle and she fell to the ground. Her jaw stung hard and Medri was surprised by the precision of the attack. It was clear to her now that the mage was trained to fight in darkness as well as she was.

Suddenly the sphere of darkness winked away and the mage dropped his invisibility. There, before her, stood a male dark elf. He was about as tall as she was which was considerable since male dark elves were typically smaller than female. He had shoulder length white hair that was a mess. His red eyes were wide and wild. There was a look of hatred and anger about him that made her shudder to her core. He had on a black adamantite chain shirt and a deep purple piwafwi with red lining. She did notice that he didn't have a house insignia, which meant he was a houseless rogue. He had black leather pants and black leather boots to complete his outfit. He carried a battle-axe in his right hand. She knew he was probably a paid houseless rouge, one that was promised a position in a house if he would track her down and bring her back dead or alive. This wasn't an upper world surface elf or even a human she could try to reason with, this one was going to kill her.

Medri rolled with hit, got to her knees, and sprinted off. She twisted between the vegetation, and continued to sprint. She had played her Senet piece, and found that she was no match. She couldn't fight this dark elf and she couldn't reason with him. She was running out of options fast and had to put some distance between herself and him as quickly as possible.

She didn't hear his footsteps behind her. Curiously, she glanced over her shoulder and saw that he hadn't left the spot where she had left him. If he wasn't going to chase her, then maybe she could get away. She was just about to turn around and sprint harder, when she saw his hands gesturing creating the movements needed for a spell. She hoped her resistances would kick in or perhaps she could run beyond his range. But before she could have a chance, she saw the spell discharge. A bright blue ring appeared over the mage and he was gone. Her heart sank since she realized what had just happened.

She tried to stop, she tried to hold up, but she was already running too fast. She could only watch as her head turned back to look in front of her. Another light blue oval was already disappearing and the male dark elf mage had already stepped through. He was right in front of her and she couldn't stop. He took one step toward her as his fist came forward. His blow caught her right under her rib cage and knocked the wind out of her. Medri fell to the ground.

Medri lay on the ground and tried to catch her breath. Her body still ached, she was incredibly tired and she was still soaking wet from the downpour. She was dizzy from the lack of air and the pain she was in. She wanted her body to get up and move, but she had lost all of her strength.

"Who are you?" She asked between gasps of breath. She was going to try to talk to him, reason with him, and if needed, plead with him.

"My name is Maldev, and I am going to kill you." His voice was steady but filled anger and hate. No, she thought, he wasn't a hired houseless rogue after all. The tone of this voice was personal and his actions were a private vendetta.

All she could do was lay there and watch as the houseless dark elf mage straddled her fallen body. He then grabbed her by her hair and pulled her head back exposing her neck. She didn't even have the strength to resist. Then in horror, he lifted his axe and let it fall toward her neck.

… To be continued in the Orbbelgguren Series: Istobarra Rising

Special thanks to these web sites:

http://www.grey-company.org/Maerdyn/resources/translator/

http://www.eilistraee.com/chosen/language.php

http://www.angelfire.com/rpg2/vortexshadow/dark_elfnames.html

More books by this author:

Orbbelgguren Offshoots

Eclavarda Rising
Emilia
The Quick and the Blade
The Tempest
Sai Katan
Quithxell

Star Wars

The Hunt for Quintano Roo
The Hunt for Holocron Theta
The Hunt for Planet Xarus

Horror/Suspense

Lost Souls
Buried Souls
Restless Souls
Monsters

Sci-Fi

Apocalypse book 1: Harbinger
Apocalypse book 2: Armageddon

Military Modern Thriller

The Eden Protocol

Remember, if you liked any of these books, please be kind and leave a review. Reviews will inspire others to share your experience. Thank you.